PRAISE FOR

ALIAS EMMA

"A thrilling read . . . I could not have loved it more."
—LISA JEWELL

"Emma Makepeace is a worthy heir to the Ja⌐ ⌐ond
mantle."   —JA⌐   'ON

"Turbo-charged pacin⌐
gettable characters
                                                ⌐MAN

"Totally addictive . . . Al⌐   ⌐s that perfect combination of exciting new character, explosive action
scenes, and a thrilling cat-and-mouse chase through
the streets of London. Once you start reading, you
won't stop."   —LISA GARDNER

"There are fast reads, and then there are reads that
throw you right out of your chair. *Alias Emma* is in the
latter category."   —LINWOOD BARCLAY

"Pure candy for those of us who love a good spy story—
this is a novel you'll struggle to put down."
                                —*Business Insider*

By Ava Glass

ALIAS EMMA

THE TRAITOR

THE
TRAITOR

THE
TRAITOR

A NOVEL

AVA
GLASS

BANTAM
NEW YORK

A Bantam Books Trade Paperback Original

Copyright © 2023 by Moonflower Books Ltd.

Published in the United States by Bantam Books, an imprint of Random House, a division of Penguin Random House LLC, New York.

BANTAM & B colophon is a registered trademark of Penguin Random House LLC.

Published in the United Kingdom by Penguin, an imprint of Penguin Random House UK, London.

LIBRARY OF CONGRESS CATALOGING-IN-PUBLICATION DATA
Names: Glass, Ava, author.
Title: The traitor : a novel / Ava Glass.
Description: New York : Bantam, 2023
Identifiers: LCCN 2023013934 (print) | LCCN 2023013935 (ebook) |
ISBN 9780593496848 (Trade paperback) | ISBN 9780593725511
(Library Hardcover) | ISBN 9780593496831 (Ebook)
Subjects: LCGFT: Spy fiction. | Thrillers (Fiction) | Novels.
Classification: LCC PS3604.A883 T73 2023 (print) |
LCC PS3604.A883 (ebook) | DDC 813/.6—dc23/eng/20230407
LC record available at https://lccn.loc.gov/2023013934
LC ebook record available at https://lccn.loc.gov/2023013935

Printed in the United States of America on acid-free paper

randomhousebooks.com

2 4 6 8 9 7 5 3 1

Book design by Jo Anne Metsch

To Jack. Always.

Courage is a capital sum, reduced by expenditure.

—IAN FLEMING, *Dr. No*

THE
TRAITOR

PART ONE

LONDON

He was exhausted. He wanted to keep working but the numbers had begun to swim across the lighted screen, refusing to line up in neat, military rows so he could find the pattern he knew must be hidden among them somewhere.

It was just that he was *so close*. If he could only stay awake he was certain he'd find what he needed. But it was after two in the morning, and when he closed his eyes and rubbed his knuckles against his forehead he still saw the numbers, burned on his retinas.

He would sleep for a few hours and then start again.

His hands went through the nightly rituals. Turning off the laptop. Flipping it over to remove the battery. Unplugging the Wi-Fi box and router, wrapping each cable neatly behind every device.

It seemed pointless. To be hacked you had to be discovered, and being discovered would mean . . .

He stood abruptly, pushing the chair back so hard it squawked a protest against the wooden floor, and walked away from the things that frightened him. When he crossed the living room, he didn't have to make a single turn—the apartment held almost no furniture. A sofa, a bed, a chair—that was all he needed. More would be superfluous.

He checked the three locks on the front door and punched the eight-digit code into the alarm. Then he flipped the light switch and the room plunged into darkness. Instantly, he wanted to turn the lights back on again. It took effort to stay in the dark.

The work was making him paranoid. Everywhere he went, he saw shadows following him. All day long he'd felt watched. Now the sensation that he was not alone was almost overwhelming.

As he walked the straight line to the bedroom, he reminded himself that nobody could possibly know who he was or where he lived. He'd been careful. By the time he climbed into bed, he almost believed it. When he closed his eyes, he saw the numbers again, floating behind his eyelids like tropical fish.

He had to finish this work before it finished him.

"Tomorrow. It ends tomorrow." He murmured the word aloud, like a promise.

He could not have been asleep long when a sound shook him awake, and he sat up with a start. In the pitch black, he strained his ears, but all he could hear was his own panicked breathing, quick and harsh.

He thought perhaps he'd dreamed the sound. But then it came again. A soft breath—like a sigh.

The lights came on, blinding him. He flung up a hand to shield his eyes.

There were two of them. One stood by the door next to a large black suitcase. The other leaned over the bed, grinning.

That was when he knew he'd been wrong about everything.

They did know who he was. And what he'd been doing.

And they had come to make him stop.

1

"Target approaching."

From her position inside the imposing marble-clad bank lobby, Emma Makepeace cast a glance through the bulletproof glass of the front window to the traffic beyond.

The tiny electronic receiver tucked inside her right ear had been crackling with updates for the last fifteen minutes as a young man made his way through the streets of London, unaware that his every movement was being observed.

She pretended to peruse a page on the computer screen in front of her as a gleaming scarlet Bugatti prowled into view, stopping abruptly on the double yellow line in front of the private bank. As the bus behind it—its own red shading drab by comparison to the ruby glow of the sports car—adjusted to this unexpected obstruction, the car door swung open and a tall young man with a shock of dark hair jumped out, a leather duffel bag in his hand.

Sergei Gorodin was twenty-two, smooth-faced, and dressed entirely in Gucci. He didn't glance at the bus as he strode from the car toward the bank with all the confidence of a billionaire's son. The liveried doorman hurried forward to welcome him.

"Little Bear is on site," Emma murmured, angling her chin down toward the microphone built into the lapel of her dark blazer as Gorodin stepped inside.

She kept her eyes on the door as a thin man in a navy-blue bespoke suit approached her and asked quietly, "Is there anything I can help you with, Miss Davies?"

Craig Reece was one of the bank's investment managers. Everyone who worked with him described him as unfailingly polite, with a natural ability for turning money into more money. He was incredibly popular with the bank's many Russian clients. What none of them knew, of course, was that he also worked for MI5.

Reece had brought Emma in today to gather evidence against Sergei Gorodin and his father, a property investor whose wealth had proved very hard to trace. The other bank workers believed she was a consultant specializing in international currency exchange, helping Reece with a complex transaction.

"I'm almost finished," she said, her quick nod indicating she had already spotted Gorodin.

"Excellent." Reece stepped back. "If you need anything . . ."

Emma kept her focus on the young Russian man, who walked past her desk without a sideways glance, heading straight to a glass-walled office at the back.

"I just need to look one thing up." She stood, and gave Reece an easy smile. "Two seconds."

Her heels clicked against the marble floor as she hurried after Gorodin, who opened the office door without knocking. Inside, the bank manager stood to greet him.

Emma watched as the two shook hands, and then the bank manager reached over to close the slatted blinds, screening the glass room from outside view.

Casually, Emma paused at the row of filing cabinets next to the office, opened a drawer and pulled out a file.

The blinds didn't quite meet the edge of the wall, and from this angle she had a clear view as the manager opened a safe behind his desk and began pulling out thick stacks of cash, setting them on the desk.

Taking a pen from her pocket, Emma pointed the tip at the window and clicked the tiny button on the side.

"Cash is changing hands," she whispered.

"Copy that. Pursuit is in place," said Adam's voice in her earpiece.

In the glass office, the bank manager handed Gorodin a sheet of paper, which he signed with a careless scrawl. Then he gathered the thick stacks of money and shoved them into the bag. Emma clicked the pen again.

Gorodin didn't stick around for long goodbyes. As soon as the money was in place, he snapped the bag shut and swung toward the door.

Hastily, Emma closed the filing cabinet and headed back toward her desk.

"Get ready," she warned the microphone on her lapel. "Little Bear is on the move."

Reece stood up as she approached, a question in his eyes. Emma inclined her head in response. "I'm all done here," she said, angling her body so she could see Gorodin crossing the lobby with long strides.

"Of course. Thanks for your help on this project," Reece replied smoothly as the Russian passed his desk.

Emma smiled. "It's been a pleasure. I'll be in touch."

She followed Gorodin past the doorman and out onto the Strand.

After the heavy quiet of the bank the noise and bustle of the street was jarring; the squeak of brakes, the shrill complaint of horns, the rattle of trains from nearby Charing Cross Station: all seemed louder now. Gorodin appeared not to notice any of it as he headed straight for the red sports car and tossed the leather duffel casually onto the passenger seat.

Emma had to admire the way he treated half a million pounds in cash like a bag full of gym clothes.

The Bugatti started with a throaty, predatory roar and shot out into traffic.

"Target is on the move," she said.

"I have eyes on," Adam said in her earpiece.

A black BMW rolled by, and Emma caught a glimpse of Adam's low forehead and wiry dark hair before both cars melted into the blur of city traffic and disappeared.

He would tail Gorodin across the city, although they already knew where he was heading. For the last three weeks he'd come to the bank every Wednesday with an empty bag, and walked out with it looking much heavier, before driving straight to his father's office. Now they had proof of what was in the bag. The next step would be finding out where that money ended up.

Emma's phone rang, interrupting her thoughts. The number on the screen was the Agency's emergency line.

She answered quickly. "Makepeace."

"I have a message from R. Are you in a safe place?" It was a woman's voice—as emotionless as a machine.

Frowning, Emma stepped out of the flow of pedestrians. "Yes. Continue."

"This is the message: 'You're off the Gorodin case. I need you elsewhere. An address will be sent. Go to it immediately.'" The woman's flat monotone paused. "The message ends. Do you need me to repeat?"

"No. I've got it," Emma said.

The line went dead and a text appeared on her secure screen: *75 Thames Mansions, Flat 652, W6.*

Emma's heart began to race. The Gorodin project was just

getting underway. If the Agency wanted her off it already, something big must have happened.

Dropping the phone into her pocket, she began to run.

Emma was part of a small intelligence unit so secret it didn't have a name. The Agency didn't appear on any government lists. It wasn't in any phone book. Only a handful of very senior officials even knew it existed. The reason for the secrecy was obvious, once you understood that the Agency's work focused on identifying and stopping Russian spies working inside Britain.

Lately, that work had been constant. Tensions between London and Moscow were the worst anyone could remember. Everything felt dangerous—as if the world had become flammable and each nation clutched a lit match.

In that febrile atmosphere, the Agency's work was silent. Invisible. And absolutely necessary.

At twenty-eight, Emma was the youngest intelligence officer on the team. She'd only been with the organization three years, but after an undercover operation last autumn in which she'd single-handedly fought off a Russian assassination unit, her star was in the ascendant. She was being trusted with bigger operations. And as she parked in front of a glass-and-steel apartment building so close to the River Thames the blue-gray water reflected in its windows, she had a feeling this was going to be one of them.

There were no police cars on the street. No ambulances. Just one lone guard stood by the door and she recognized the unmarked black van used by MI5's forensics team parked near the corner.

Other than that, there was no evidence of any activity.

Whatever had happened here, the Agency didn't want anyone to know about it yet.

It was June, but the damp air had a chill to it, and Emma buttoned her jacket as she walked to the front door. England was never ready to accept summer until July arrived. It had to be dragged into the warmth against its will.

The Special Branch officer outside the front door gave her a doubtful look as she approached.

"Emma Makepeace," she told him. "I'm expected."

He scanned her fingerprint on a glossy black device and glanced at the readout before reaching into a bag at his feet and handing her a respirator mask.

"Put this on before you go in," he said. "The lifts are safe to use."

Emma stared at the mask, her nerves tightening as she absorbed its significance.

"Can you tell me what happened here?"

The officer shook his head. "They'll explain when you get up there."

Going inside suddenly seemed like a terrible idea. All the same, Emma pulled the mask over her head, tightened the straps, and walked through the door.

As she stepped cautiously across the empty lobby, her breathing rasped heavy and loud through the protective webbing. The room had high ceilings, stone floors, and modern leather chairs, all of it artfully designed in muted shades. It looked expensive.

By the time she reached the elevator, her heart was racing but her hand was steady as she pushed the call button.

On the sixth floor, she found more subtle décor and absolute silence. Her footsteps echoed as she walked to number 652. She hesitated for a moment, bracing herself, before opening the door and stepping inside.

The apartment was small and filled with soft, gray daylight that streamed through tall windows. The walls were white and completely bare of art. The living room was empty, aside from a sofa. There was a faint, unpleasant smell she could just make out through the protective filter. Something sweet and sickly.

"Ah, excellent. You've arrived." Charles Ripley appeared from a hallway on the far side of the living area and removed his mask.

Tall, with graying hair, in his navy-blue suit and forgettable tie, he might have been mistaken for an estate agent. That was intentional. Looking ordinary is the best thing a spy can hope for.

Nobody knew as much about Russian spies as Ripley, and there was no one Emma trusted more. Right now, though, his craggy, angular features gave her few clues as to why she was here.

"We've got a bit of a delicate situation," he said. "As you can probably tell."

As he spoke, three forensic investigators in white moon suits emerged from a room behind him carrying equipment bags. They shuffled toward the living room, their progress blocked by Ripley.

The one in front spoke first.

"Excuse me," the woman said, her Essex accent muffled through her mask.

"Oh, I do beg your pardon." Ripley stepped aside.

"No worries." In the living room, the woman paused to pull off her protective visor and hood. Beneath it, she was perspiring, strands of fair hair clinging to her red cheeks.

Emma knew her as Caroline Wakefield, a scientist who worked under the Home Office. Her specialty was chemical weapons.

"We're finished. It should be safe now but I'd wear your gear in there just in case." Glancing at Emma, she added enigmatically, "Weirdest bloody thing I've seen in a while. I wish you both luck getting to the bottom of it."

With that, the forensic team lumbered to the door with a rattle of equipment cases and a swish of white fabric.

When they'd gone, Emma gave her boss a quizzical look over the top of her mask. "Well, are you going to tell me what's going on?"

"I'll do better than tell you," he said, stepping back. "I'll show you."

Motioning for her to follow, he pulled his mask back on and headed down the hallway to a large bedroom. The décor here was as minimal as the living area—there was nothing but a chair, a dresser, and a double bed where the sheets were thrown back, as if someone had just leaped out of it.

The windows were wide open but the sickly-sweet smell she'd noticed in the living room was more noticeable.

Smudges of fingerprint dust stained the doors and windows. The low five-drawer dresser had been shifted away from the wall, and it was clear some drawers had been opened. The few things on top of it—a bottle of cologne, a leather tray—had been dusted for prints.

Otherwise, the room looked perfect. Nothing was broken. Nothing was damaged or knocked around. Everything appeared almost unnaturally tidy.

The only odd thing was the suitcase on the floor. It was dark and very large—the sort you'd take on a long trip. Or a journey you weren't planning to come home from.

The top of the case was open, and what Emma saw inside was so unexpected it took a second for her brain to grasp what she was looking at.

It was a man, naked, kneeling and bent forward. His hands lay open helplessly at his sides. His skin was as white as paper.

Ripley gestured at the corpse. "This is Stephen Garrick. He worked for the Neighbors."

Emma drew in a sharp breath. "The Neighbors" was Ripley's term for MI6.

"What the hell happened?" she asked.

"That is the question we need to answer." Ripley's tone was flat.

Emma's mind spun through the possibilities. Chemical

weapons were suspected or Caroline wouldn't have been there and the masks wouldn't be necessary.

She walked carefully closer to the suitcase and circled it to get a better look. "Who found him like this?"

Ripley pulled a black antique cigarette case from his pocket, but didn't open it. "A cleaner came in early this morning on her regular visit. Garrick wasn't here, as far as she could tell. The suitcase was locked and sitting right where it is now. When she tried to move it out of the way, she couldn't lift it. She phoned Stephen Garrick, but his phone was switched off. This was unusual enough that she contacted Garrick's father. He owns the flat." He paused, looking at the cold, pale shoulders that tilted up out of the suitcase. "When the father arrived, he tried to open the suitcase, but it was locked with a padlock. In the end, he was the one who called the police. Eventually, at his insistence, they cut the lock. And found this."

"Jesus." Emma bent over to get a better look at Garrick.

"Don't get too close," Ripley cautioned, his voice sharp.

Instantly, Emma straightened and stepped back. But in that second she'd had time to see that Garrick's face was contorted and bloated, his tongue protruding grotesquely. His arms and shoulders were as smooth and unmarked as a child's, but his face told a different story. One of pain and fear.

She looked at her boss. "What did they use on him?"

"We believe it was a nerve agent, but we haven't identified it."

Emma shuddered. She didn't want to be in this room, this apartment, or this building. The use of nerve agents by Russian spies was infamous, and she knew if it was novichok that had killed Stephen Garrick, even minute traces could be enough to cause permanent damage to anyone who encountered it.

Sweat beaded her brow as she forced herself to stand still and look again at the sparsely furnished room, focusing on the details. The process steadied her breathing.

"This all feels wrong," she said, slowly. "It's almost theatrical. Why the suitcase? What's the message?"

"My thoughts precisely." Ripley pointed through the open door, down the hallway to the living room. "There's no evidence of a break-in. The front door is the only access to the flat, and it was triple-locked."

Emma walked to the open window and looked down, breathing in the outside air deeply. There was no balcony. The glass-and-steel wall outside was smooth and unscalable.

"I don't think they got in this way," she said, turning back around to survey the smudges of fingerprint dust. "Did forensics find anything?"

"No fingerprints. No DNA," Ripley told her. "Only minute traces left of the chemical they used."

A targeted assassination, then. Well planned and perfectly executed. But why? This sort of murder was usually saved for those the Russians believed had betrayed them. And to betray, you must first be part of something.

You have to be on the same side.

"What did Garrick do at Six?" she asked.

"He was a numbers analyst."

Emma's eyebrows rose. Numbers analysts were low-profile civil servants—basically accountants.

"Why would the Russians want to kill a numbers analyst?" she asked, bewildered.

"I think it's obvious. Either he was taking Russian money and not giving them what he promised, or he stumbled onto something he wasn't supposed to find." Ripley cast a dark glance at the suitcase on the floor and the pale body folded forward, as if in prayer. "There's one thing I can say for certain. If the Russians are willing to murder a British intelligence officer in his home, then none of us is safe. Who knows what secrets he might have revealed before he died?" He met her gaze. "We have to catch the people who did this. And we have to make them pay."

2

Emma Makepeace was born to be a spy. It was in her blood. In the chaotic years after the fall of the Soviet Union, her father had been a spy for Britain, sharing information he believed might prevent a nuclear war. But he'd been found out, and Russia had no patience for traitors.

Emma had still been in the womb when her mother fled Russia, forced to leave her husband behind in order to save herself and her unborn child.

Emma had been only months old when two British intelligence officers came to their house in the south of England to tell her mother that her father had been summarily executed before he could get out of Russia.

Russia never forgives or forgets. And neither did Emma.

Her mother, in mourning and desperate for her young daughter to know her father as she had known him, taught her.

In soft, velvety Russian, she told Emma of her father's bravery. And how much he had longed to meet her. "He will watch you always, whatever you do," she promised.

As a child, Emma hadn't believed it was possible for her father to see her fail at algebra or do well in history, but she did believe in revenge. And she devoted her life to making the Russian government pay for breaking her mother's heart.

She rushed through university before enlisting in the army, where she joined a military intelligence unit. There, her fluency in Russian, Polish, and German marked her out as someone with promise.

That was when Ripley had identified her as a potential agent. On the day she left the army, he offered her a job.

Over the years, her concept of revenge changed. She no longer believed the best revenge was to find the person who pulled the trigger, or even the one who had turned her father in. Instead, she took vengeance one case at a time. By making it much, much harder for Russian spies to operate in her adopted homeland.

When she left Stephen Garrick's flat that morning, Emma drove across London to a small, secure car park a short walk from the Houses of Parliament. A shorter walk in the opposite direction took her to a long, crescent-shaped road lined with red-brick Victorian buildings. This was deep in the political heart of the city, and most of the houses were occupied by think tanks, lobbyists, and businesses connected with government. Simple door signs in brass or wood held enigmatic names that betrayed little about what might actually go on inside. One of the signs read "The Vernon Institute." Emma opened the unassuming door beneath it and went inside.

The small entrance hall held nothing except a second set of doors. These were modern, and made of thick, bulletproof black glass. Emma stepped forward and stared directly into the small, electronic device mounted on the wall. After a second, a light blinked green and the doors unlocked with a *clunk*.

A low hum of activity greeted her as she walked into the main office.

The room was long and narrow, leading into a corridor holding a number of smaller offices. On her left, a straight staircase with an oak banister led up to more offices.

Emma paused to drop the car keys into a box by the door where a handwritten sign pleaded: "Please clean vehicles before returning."

Spotting her, Esther, who handled the Agency's communications, pulled off her headphones. "Ripley says to go straight up," she said. Her voice was the steady monotone from the phone that morning.

"Thanks," Emma said. But instead of heading up the steep stairs, she bypassed them, and turned in to a small, windowless room where the walls were lined with metal shelves holding rows of electronic equipment. The air smelled strongly of fresh espresso.

"Hi, Zach," she said, holding out the pen camera from the bank job that morning. "Got something for you."

A skinny twenty-something with an unruly mop of dark curls glanced up from the four computer monitors arranged in front of him like a shield wall. He wore a Metallica T-shirt under his suit coat, and bright blue Converse trainers.

"Awesome. How'd it go?" he asked, taking the pen. The word "PEACE" was tattooed across the backs of his fingers.

The surveillance operation from the bank already seemed a long time ago, but Emma said only, "It worked like a dream."

"It's a tidy little piece of kit." Zach unscrewed the end of the pen, extracting a microchip scarcely larger than a piece of glitter, which he dropped into a device on his desk. "A bit old school, but it gets the job done. Can't ask for more than that."

He turned the screen so she could watch as a dozen images materialized of the young Russian, stuffing cash into the leather holdall.

"Nice," Zach said, scrolling through the pictures. "Very clear. Who should I send these to?"

"Send them to Adam. I'm off that operation now."

"Oh, so they moved you to the MI6 agent?" Zach gave her an interested look. "Caro from Forensics dropped off some images earlier of that suitcase setup. That was messed up."

Remembering the pale shoulders jutting out of the suitcase, Emma suppressed a shudder.

"Here's the thing I don't understand," Zach continued. "How the hell did the killers find out he worked at Six? Those spooks are dead serious about hiding their identities."

"Give me a little time." Emma turned to the door. "And I'll tell you exactly what happened."

Ripley's oak-paneled office held only a large desk and two leather chairs. The room held the faintly sweet haze of smoke from his Dunhill cigarettes. There was nothing on his empty desk to indicate whose office it was, or what took place there and yet, somehow, his personality was indelibly etched in every inch of it.

When Emma walked in, her boss was on the phone, and he waved her to a chair.

"Yes," he was saying as she sat down. "Send him straight up as soon as he gets here."

An arched window behind the imposing oak desk offered a view of tilted red Westminster rooftops and the gray-blue English sky.

As he listened to the other person on the phone, Ripley slid a file across his desk to her. The word "CONFIDENTIAL" was stamped across the top.

The first page held a picture of a slim, fair-haired man with wide blue eyes who bore only a faint resemblance to the pale, tormented body she'd seen that morning. In this image, his skin was flushed with health. Straight hair the color of straw tumbled across his smooth forehead, and a slight smile curved the corners of his lips.

Ripley put the phone down, pulled a cigarette from the slim black case he always carried, and lit it.

He'd once told Emma where the case came from. He'd worked for MI6 in Russia in the dying days of the Cold War. Back then, many bitter ex-KGB agents had used him for revenge against their own government, giving him valuable secrets they'd protected for years.

One man in particular had surprised him by coming forward. For years, the man had been assigned to follow Ripley and find evidence that he was a spy, rather than, as his cover would have had it, a junior diplomat. Ripley had enjoyed losing him in Moscow's notorious traffic, or dodging into dark alleyways and then emerging in the light. But on multiple occasions, he admitted, the man had outsmarted him. On one memorable day he turned up at the address where Ripley was headed to, arriving before Ripley got there, and giving him a jaunty wave when he walked up.

Ripley believed him to be a brilliant spy on the wrong side of history. It turned out the man, whom he'd never identified, agreed. One day he slipped Ripley a stack of documents, which could have cost him his life. They explained precisely how his department worked. Who ran which office, where they lived, what he thought of them. It was a gold mine.

When Ripley asked him why he'd done it, the man handed him his cigarette case.

"You've taken my country and my beliefs, you might as well have everything," he'd said with a bitter laugh.

When Ripley later opened the black case, he'd found, in addition to five Russian cigarettes, a razor blade. He still kept it there, behind his Dunhill blues.

"Always have a weapon you can easily reach," he'd said, when he first showed Emma the hidden blade. "Someplace they're unlikely to search."

And as she sat in the high-backed chair, flipping through Stephen Garrick's file, Emma could feel the short-bladed knife tucked inside her right boot. She'd only ever had to use it once, and on that night it had saved her life.

There were no more than twenty pages in the file—very thin for a background brief on an MI6 officer—but Garrick had only been with the department two years, and his role was minor. Emma flipped through the pages quickly.

"His salary was modest," she noted. "But that was quite a posh flat. Can't be cheap."

"His parents own it," Ripley reminded her, reaching for his lighter. "His father is a very wealthy man. And, unfortunately for us, he has vast political connections."

Her brow creasing, Emma flipped back to the front page of the file again. "Garrick . . . Wait. His father is *Lord* Garrick?"

Ripley's nod was tense. "This case is going to get far more attention than we'd like."

Emma couldn't argue. John Edward Garrick was a famous investor and property owner. He didn't just invest in corporations, though, he also invested in politicians. He paid a lot to all the political parties, and in return his views were listened to.

This case was going to end up in the press, and it was going to catch *fire*.

Before she could say as much aloud though, someone knocked on the office door.

"Enter," Ripley called in a cloud of smoke.

A portly man with thinning hair and a round, likable face stepped inside.

"Andrew." Ripley motioned him in. "I'm just briefing Emma on the Garrick case."

"Oh, excellent." Setting the bag down, Andrew took the chair next to Emma and ran a hand across his thinning hair with a sigh. "I've got to say I'm glad to have you on this operation, Emma. It's an ugly one. We need our best."

In a neat gray suit, with a laptop case slung over one shoulder, Andrew Field could have been any London office worker midway through a particularly busy day, but there was nothing ordinary about him. He was a highly trained Russia specialist at MI6, with an encyclopedic knowledge of that country's secret service.

"Any news from forensics?" Ripley enquired.

"I've asked Caroline to brief us," Field told him. "She should be here shortly."

"Do you have any idea who was behind this?" Emma asked.

"Not yet," Field said. "We're examining CCTV footage around the house now, but I don't think we'll find anything. If it was the GRU, they're too professional to be caught out that way."

Ripley exhaled a stream of smoke. "You haven't found anything useful in Garrick's emails?"

"Stephen was a back-room investigator. As far we can tell, he never knowingly met a Russian agent. His entire team has been taken to secure locations until we get some information." Field paused, his eyes meeting Ripley's. "I've had C on the phone already asking me what the hell happened, and I haven't got an answer."

"C" was the head of MI6.

"Dammit, this is just what I was afraid of." Ripley's face darkened. "They'll all be in here before long. MPs. The Home Secretary. We'll have to bar the door." He blew out a distracted stream of smoke. "Your people have checked the obvious things, I assume? New girlfriend from Russia? New mate who was terribly interested in everything in his past?"

"We've been working through Stephen's contacts all afternoon," Field told him. "He had vanishingly few close friends. No new love interests. His last relationship ended eight months ago, apparently amicably. Since then there seems to have been no one."

"I suppose we have to consider the possibility that he hid political beliefs from us," Ripley suggested. "He was a very bright young man. He would have been capable of deceiving our background check when he was hired."

"We have no doubts about his loyalty." Field's demeanor didn't change but a new edge entered his voice. "He was extremely well vetted. If he was a closet Russia sympathizer we'd have known."

Ripley's brow lowered. "That is not necessarily the case, Andrew."

The air in the room seemed to cool by a few degrees. They all knew how much was at stake. If Andrew was wrong, and Garrick was a double agent, then Andrew's job was on the line.

Emma was almost glad when someone knocked at the door.

"Enter." Ripley's voice was as sharp as a gunshot.

The door swung open and Caroline Wakefield stepped inside. The forensic scientist's expression was studiously blank but Emma thought she saw a warning in the depths of her blue eyes as she closed the door behind her.

"The results are back on the chemical used to kill Stephen Garrick," she said. "It's a bit unusual, so we ran it through twice. We're certain it was VX."

"VX?" Ripley looked stunned.

Emma's mouth went dry.

VX. Full name: Venomous Agent X. She'd studied it during her time in Army Intelligence. It was a twentieth-century chemical weapon, developed at Porton Down during the Cold War. Absorbed through the skin or inhaled in even the tiniest quantities, it disrupted the nervous system, paralyzing the muscles so the victim couldn't so much as draw a breath. Death by asphyxiation was the inevitable, excruciating result.

It was banned by the United Nations, but that never made much difference to things as far as Emma could tell.

Ripley turned to Andrew. "Did we know they had stockpiles of VX?"

"I think," Field said, "at this point, we should assume they have stockpiles of everything."

"There would be something elegant about using a weapon we invented, I suppose," Ripley observed.

"The personal touch," Field agreed.

Emma barely noticed their dark humor. She kept thinking of Stephen Garrick's face, contorted with pain until it was unrecognizable. There had been nothing elegant about it.

Field turned his attention back to Wakefield. "Was there anything else in the flat? Any other substances?"

"We're still running final tests but so far we've found nothing," Wakefield told him. "It looks like a clean kill."

"If you find anything at all, let me know immediately," Ripley ordered. "And make sure the apartment building is safe before the residents return. What have they been told, by the way?"

"Gas leak," Wakefield said. "The usual story. So far it's staying out of the press."

Ripley nodded. "Good work, Caroline."

When the forensic scientist had gone, Ripley and Field exchanged a glance. "It's not the GRU, then," Field said. "VX is too old-fashioned for them."

The GRU was the Russian military intelligence branch—the one responsible for most assassinations carried out abroad in the name of that country's government.

Ripley didn't look convinced. "They could have used it for deniability."

"Why the suitcase, then?" Beneath his thinning hair, Field's high forehead furrowed. "That was designed to draw attention."

Emma picked up Garrick's file again. "Maybe we can figure out who if we understand *why*. The answer has to be in his work."

"Yes, that's my thinking as well." Field turned his small piercing eyes to her. "The problem we have is that Stephen's skills were quite . . . unique. It's hard to explain, but I'm not sure anyone in my office truly understands his reports."

"His file contains the word 'genius' several times," Emma said.

"It's not an exaggeration, I assure you." Field pulled his laptop out of the case and opened it, typing quickly. "This is from a report he wrote two months ago on an operative who was funneling Russian government money from Dubai into London." He turned the device so Emma and Ripley could see. The page was covered in long, intricate formulas that took up every inch of space. "The Home Office was absolutely baffled when they saw it. Stephen had to sit down with them to explain it, but once they got it, they banned the target from the UK for life and handed the file to Interpol."

Ripley gestured at the screen with his cigarette. "Who was it? Could he have found out about Garrick and taken revenge?"

"Only if one of my people told them, and that's impossible." The crisp tension returned to Field's voice. Emma had never seen him this unsettled. He was rarely rattled.

Ripley must have noticed, too, because he quickly moved on. "What other cases was Garrick working on?"

"What about this one?" Emma held a page from Garrick's file. "He was investigating the daughter of a Russian government official who was supposed to be in London working for an international charity, but Garrick traced money from her charity directly to Russian Intelligence. She was banned, too."

Ripley made a dismissive sound. "We do five cases just like it every year. What else?"

"There's only one other," Emma said, turning to the last page of Garrick's file. "An investigation into two Russian oligarchs. Nothing seems to have come from it. It looks like the whole thing was canceled before it finished."

Field grimaced. "It was a bit of a bastard, that one. The investigation ran for months and found nothing concrete. Then we had budget cutbacks, and it wasn't considered a good use of funds to keep going." He glanced at Ripley. "You know how these things go."

"All too well," Ripley agreed morosely.

Emma flipped back to the start of the file. "Nothing Garrick worked on seems likely to cause the Russians to take this kind of action. They're obviously making a statement. But why?"

"That's the question we want you to answer," Ripley said. "Find out what we're missing. Retrace Stephen Garrick's last days. Did he meet someone we don't know about? Make promises he couldn't keep?" He gestured at Field. "We'll work with you on this. But we don't have much time. The heat is going to come down from above, and it's going to come down hard. Before that happens, we need to know who killed him and why. Most of all, we need to make bloody sure nobody else ends up dead."

3

Emma spent the rest of the day immersed in Stephen Garrick's life. Andrew Field sent her a link with secure files on every case the dead man had ever worked on. In all that paperwork, she could find no evidence of where Garrick had gone wrong. He'd been meticulous. Even obsessive. She didn't see a traitor or a fool in those pages: she saw a man in love with the truth.

By the time she finished going through the files, daylight had faded to black outside the window.

Picking up the phone on the desk she'd commandeered, she dialed three numbers.

"Hey, it's Emma," she said. "I need a favor. I want to look at the CCTV footage on the Garrick case. Can you find it for me?"

"Sure, come down," Zach replied. "I'll hook you up."

Ten minutes later, she was in his small office, watching as he typed with dizzying speed, only glancing up at the screen occasionally.

"I want to look outside his house first," Emma instructed, dragging a chair closer to his. "Start with the day before he died."

He glanced at her. "You're tracing all his movements?"

She nodded. "I've got to understand what he was up to. Nothing in his file gives me any indication what was really going on."

Zach frowned at something on the black screen in front of him, muttering under his breath as he typed a machine-gun volley of clicks.

While she waited, Emma looked around the room. She'd rarely spent much time in here. Zach hadn't been with the Agency long, and the previous tech specialist hadn't been particularly friendly. The walls were covered in metal shelves, holding stacks of unidentifiable equipment. A short black safe squatting in one corner was where Zach kept the technology nobody knew they had.

Emma liked him. He was only a year older than her, having been recruited by MI6 while still hacking his professor's computers from his halls at Cambridge. He'd confided to Emma once that he hadn't been sure he wanted to work for the government at all because he didn't like the political party in power. But then his recruiter had described in blunt terms three recent deadly terrorism attacks prevented in London by intelligence work, and he'd changed his mind.

Zach was a caffeine addict, and even at this hour the room held the rich scent of coffee. Emma, who had been up since six that morning, felt her mouth water.

"It smells so good in here I could drink the air," she said.

"You want coffee?" Zach gestured at a sleek black-and-silver pod coffee machine on the shelf to her left. "Help yourself. Be careful, though. The purple pods will blow the top of your head off."

By the time Emma had filled a cup and sat down again, Zach's thirty-inch monitor showed a clear image of the street in front of Stephen Garrick's building, and he was scrolling quickly back through time. On the screen, people walked jerkily backward, cars drove in reverse, and birds flew by tail first.

Emma lowered herself back into her chair and wheeled it closer to get a better view.

"This is yesterday morning," Zach told her.

Emma took a sip of coffee, watching people going in and out of the apartment building—a woman and a man, a man alone, three men, a man in a suit, a woman in jeans, all moving quickly as the footage scrolled forward in time.

"Actually, I'm going to make myself a coffee. Take over." He slid the mouse to her. As he got up he added, "I think I'm in the mood for purple. I can sleep when I die."

As the coffee machine whirred back into life, Emma barely noticed. She was watching day become night, and the street in front of the Edwardian building in Hammersmith going still. There were lights on in some of the windows, and she counted up to Garrick's sixth-floor flat. The lights went off at two in the morning. And then, thirty minutes later, switched on again.

"Interesting." Zach sat down next to her, his eyes on the screen. "That's his flat, isn't it?"

Emma nodded, staring at that glowing window. Behind the curtains, someone was torturing Stephen Garrick. Spraying a nerve agent in his face, and watching him die in agony. Then stuffing his body into a suitcase, and deep cleaning the room. But *why*?

They scrolled back and forth in time. Just after four in the morning the lights in the flat were switched off again. Job done.

Nobody went in or out through the building's front door at any point during those hours.

"Creepy," was Zach's assessment. He glanced at Emma. "You want to keep going?"

"Yes, let's go back a few days. Maybe we'll catch someone running surveillance or breaking in."

He set the film to scroll back. Night became bright afternoon and then pale morning.

Ordinary-looking people walked in and out of the Garrick's

building. Cars drove by. Delivery vans made U-turns and sped away. Taxis idled and then drove off. Boats roared by on the blue strip of the Thames on the left side of the screen.

Emma blinked hard to keep her focus, opening her eyes just as a blue Prius rolled by. The sight of it triggered something in her memory.

"Stop!" she ordered.

Zach paused the recording with just a corner of the car still on the screen.

"That car." Emma tapped the screen. "I need to see the registration number."

He scrolled back until the full number plate was visible. "You got something?" he asked.

"I'm not sure . . ." Emma flipped Garrick's file open and rifled through it until she found the description of his car. The plates matched.

"That's Garrick's car," she told him. "When did this happen?"

Zach checked the timestamp. "This is two days ago. About eighteen hundred hours." He leaned forward, studying the car. "He's just pulling in? Where's he going to park?"

"There's a small car park behind the building," Emma said, looking up from the file. "He'll probably go in through the back door. Is there a camera there?"

"Let me check." Moving his coffee aside, Zach opened a second window on the monitor and quickly typed something Emma couldn't see. A series of numbers came up on the screen, and he grimaced as he read them. "No camera behind the building."

"That must be how his killers got in." Emma thought for a moment, and then pointed at the car. "He's coming back from somewhere. I want to know where he's been."

"Not a problem," Zach said. "I can track the car. It'll take a little while, though."

"If you're sure you've got the time?" Emma said, already knowing what his answer would be.

"Hey, it's either this or sitting at home playing Grand Theft Auto," he told her. "Personally, I'd rather find a killer."

For Emma, watching him work the footage, expertly tracking Garrick across London, brought back memories of the night nine months earlier when the Russians had hacked that same CCTV system and used the cameras to hunt her down. On that occasion, the city's famed Ring of Steel surveillance system had been her enemy. Tonight, it was her friend again.

The work was going to take time, so Emma ordered pizzas (vegan for Zach), and went out to buy two cans of Pressure Drop beer from the shop down the road. When the food arrived, Zach ate quickly, holding a slice of pizza delicately in his left hand and typing with his right.

"The ANPR system is good," he told her between bites, "but it needs a bit of massaging. You've got to tell it exactly where to look or a search can take days. I don't want it searching Scotland."

ANPR was Automatic Number Plate Recognition—it could search any CCTV in the country for a particular license plate and link up a journey from start to finish through hundreds of cameras.

"I'm limiting the search to London." Zach typed a code into the system, and then hit enter with a decisive thump. "Now let's see what we've won."

The dark screen churned. Slowly, images began to appear, each showing a tiny square of street at a different time of day.

"Here we go." Zach dropped the pizza box into the bin, wiped his fingers on a napkin, and leaned forward, typing hard. Immediately, the images rearranged themselves on the screen—some bright with daylight, others gray with rain, and a few dark and glittering with headlights.

Tapping the top image he said, "This is about five hours before you spotted his car."

"Let's see it." Emma moved her chair closer to his and rested her elbows on the desk as he hit play.

The screen lit up, showing a street in Kensington. It was bright daylight, just before noon. Cars, taxis, and buses jousted for space in eerie silence, and then stopped as a traffic light turned red.

"There." On the screen, Zach tapped his finger against Stephen Garrick's blue Prius, which moved slowly in heavy traffic.

"I'm going to speed this up," Zach said, and typed a brief staccato command. The car jerked forward, speeding across the metropolis until, abruptly, it stopped, and the Prius was parked on a street, surrounded on both sides by modern buildings that towered over it, casting it in shadow.

"Where is this?" Emma asked.

Zach pointed at the data to the right of the screen. "St. Edward's Street, in Pimlico."

Emma pointed at the CCTV image. "Can you zoom this? Is he still in the car?"

Zach typed quickly, and the computer zoomed in on the blue car. Even with the shadow and reflections off the windshield they could both see Garrick in the driver's seat, his blond hair glinting. As they watched, he raised a black object to his eyes and directed it up so that, startlingly, he appeared to be looking directly at them.

"What's that in his hand?" Emma asked.

Zach's brow creased. "Binoculars, I think."

"What the hell?" Emma breathed. "Is he running surveillance on someone?"

"That's what it looks like." Zach watched the dead man with interest as he raised the binoculars again. "I think he's watching someone in that building." He pointed at a brick structure on the right side of the screen.

Picking up her phone, Emma typed a secure message to Ripley.

Who was Garrick surveilling in Pimlico? He was following someone there the day before he died.

She turned her attention back to the screen. "Can we speed this up? Let's see how long he stayed there."

Zach sped the footage forward until the Prius angled out of the parking place and shot away.

"Look at that." Zach pointed at the timestamp on the camera. "He was there more than four hours."

Emma stared at the blue car. "What the hell was he doing? Numbers analysts don't run surveillance. They're office guys."

Her phone buzzed and she picked it up to see Ripley's reply:

Garrick wasn't following anyone. He was on extended leave for two weeks before he died.

"Check this out." Zach tapped her arm. He'd already opened another of the CCTV files and was following Garrick's car down a different London street. He'd sped up the footage, which was rushing forward on a rainy day.

"When was this filmed?" Emma watched the blue Prius dart around a stopped bus.

"Two days before the clip we just watched." Zach pointed at the screen. "He's at Trafalgar Square. Who drives to Trafalgar Square?"

"Spies." Emma kept her eyes on the car, which was turning at high speed into an underground car park. But the footage ended there. "Shit. We'll lose him."

"Oh, ye of little faith." Zach opened a second window and typed something quickly. A moment later, another window opened. "Here we go. This is the same camera. We should see him when he comes out."

"There!" Emma pointed at Garrick's distinctive blond hair as he emerged from the pedestrian exit of the garage, walking quickly, his face tilted down.

As they watched, he headed down the Strand, near the private bank where Emma had been only that morning, threading through the crowd, just as she'd done, visible and yet invisible, unnoticed until he reached the distinctive recessed entrance to the Savoy Hotel. A few doors away, he stopped in front of a shop, leaning back against a wall, pretending to look at his phone. He stayed there, trying to blend into the scenery, as the minutes ticked by.

Emma, who had done the same thing many times, albeit with much more skill, was baffled.

"He's definitely conducting surveillance. But that wasn't his job. Something else was going on." She stood up. "I need to talk to Ripley."

4

Emma waited impatiently by Ripley's desk as he and Andrew Field watched the footage Zach had sent up to them. Ripley's expression remained impassive but Field watched for only a few seconds before turning away and typing something on his laptop, a cigar clenched between his teeth, his expression dark.

"Does anyone know what he was doing?" Emma asked. "Who could he have been following?"

"What did you say the street is called?" Ripley asked.

"St. Edward's Street," Emma replied. "In Pimlico."

"I can have someone check on it." Ripley reached for the phone but Field's voice stopped him.

"I think I know what he was doing there." Field turned his laptop around so they could see the image on-screen of a dark-haired man. He was tall and heavily built, wearing a designer suit, his striped shirt unbuttoned at the throat, revealing a thicket of chest hair. He had pale skin and a prominent mole on his right cheek. His eyes were hidden behind sunglasses.

"Andrei Volkov owns Riverside House on St. Edward's Street, in Pimlico. He uses the penthouse flat as a bolthole when he's in London." A new tension lay under Field's steady voice. "Until last month, Garrick led a team investigating him."

Emma leaned over to study the image more closely. "I remember that case from Garrick's files. Wasn't Volkov suspected of selling chemical weapons?"

"We were trying to prove that Volkov and Oleg Federov were acting as black-market arms dealers for the Russian government, and using the UK as a base." Field's voice was measured. "We believed they were selling chemical weapons to a number of unsavory governments. Afghanistan, Iran, Syria—a real rogues' gallery. An interested party warned us that they were encouraging those governments to use the weapons against us." He glanced at Ripley. "Revenge, apparently, against NATO."

"This is the investigation that was shut down before it finished?" Ripley was watching Field closely.

"Yes. Budget cuts meant we couldn't keep spending money with nothing to show for it," Field said. "We simply ran out of time."

"But these images were captured a few days ago," Emma pointed out. "The operation was over by then, wasn't it?"

"The operation has been over for *weeks.*" Field's voice rose. "Stephen should have had nothing more to do with Volkov after that. Where else did he conduct surveillance? Did you say the Savoy Hotel?"

"Yes," Emma said. "On the ninth. At one in the afternoon."

Field glanced at Ripley, something unreadable in his expression. "Volkov often has meetings at the Savoy."

"Right." Ripley picked up his phone and dialed. Despite the hour, it was answered almost immediately. "Sam! I hope I haven't woken you. This is Ripley. I need a favor. Can you find out if a man named Andrei Volkov was at the Savoy on the ninth of this month?" He listened briefly, and then said, "Yes, the

ninth. It's a bit tricky—he may have just been at the bar or restaurant." He paused. "Of course. I can wait."

Emma's phone buzzed and she glanced down at the screen.
It was a message from Zach.

*I've gone back through the last two weeks. Garrick was on that
street in Pimlico nearly every day.*

When she showed it to Field, his expression tightened visibly.
But before he could respond, Ripley ended his call and looked
across his desk at them.

"Andrei Volkov and Oleg Federov had lunch together at the
Savoy the day Garrick stood outside." There was a pause and
then he added, "I suppose that's it, then."

"You think they killed him?" Emma shifted her gaze from
him to Field. "Volkov and Federov?"

Neither man responded right away. Field stared at his cigar,
which appeared to have gone out. Ripley looked past her at the
wall over her shoulder. Both seemed lost in thought.

"I don't understand. Why would he follow them?" Emma
pressed. "The investigation was closed."

Field spoke first. "Andrei Volkov and Oleg Federov have a
massive organization together. Their finances are incredibly
complex; dozens of shell corporations funneling money all over
the world to hide what they're really doing. Only Stephen could
begin to understand it. It was the biggest thing he'd ever worked
on. He didn't sleep. He didn't eat. He became obsessed. He believed there were actually three people in this organization. Andrei Volkov, Oleg Federov, and someone else—someone he
couldn't identify. Someone British, with connections. Possibly
inside this government. But he could never find proof. And then
the operation was shut down. He took it very badly." He paused.
"A week later, he announced he was taking a temporary leave
from work."

"When was that?" Ripley asked. "Remind me?"

"Two weeks ago," Field said. "His supervisor thought Stephen was suffering from stress. He was glad he was taking time off. But it appears he couldn't let go."

Emma could see it all in her mind. She'd read the files. Andrei Volkov and Oleg Federov were both tightly connected to the Russian government. Federov, in particular, was notorious. He was ex-FSB, and known to be a thug. Either man might easily have noticed Garrick the first time he staked out the Pimlico building. He was so obvious. The whole time he was following them, *they* must have been watching him. When they figured out he worked for MI6, they must have assumed the entire British spy agency was responsible. Killing him with a nerve agent in the middle of London, leaving the body hidden in plain sight . . . Suddenly, it all made more sense.

"The suitcase was a distraction," she said, piecing it together. "They *wanted* us to think it was the Russian government doing the killing, so they made it look like a GRU assassination."

"That poor fool." Field threw his cigar savagely into the ashtray. "That stupid, stupid fool. Why wouldn't he just let it *go*?"

Ripley alone seemed unaffected by the situation. "I must say, I'm astonished Volkov and Federov would take the risk of killing someone who worked for Six," he said thoughtfully.

Field met his gaze. "What are you thinking?"

"I'm thinking if those men took that sort of a risk, then Garrick must have been right about them."

There was a pause. The air in the room seemed to shift, charging with sudden electricity.

"If those men really are dealing chemical weapons from the middle of London . . ." Field began.

"This case should never have been shut down. It needed time to run." Ripley picked up his cigarette case and turned it slowly in his hands. "We have to do what Stephen Garrick couldn't. He went after the money. We should go after the *men*. His death gives us that opportunity."

"We must assume they interrogated Garrick before they killed him," Field reminded him. "He will have told them at least some of the truth. They'll expect us to come for them."

Ripley didn't blink. "So, we'll have to be careful."

Something unspoken passed between them. The two men had worked together for thirty years—their relationship was closer than some marriages Emma had known.

Field broke the silence first. "In order to arrest them, we have to prove Volkov and Federov are personally involved in selling weapons. Stephen couldn't prove it and he was a genius."

"Stephen Garrick wasn't *us*." Ripley's voice held a note of finality. "We have other ways of getting what we need."

His words hung in the air, swirling like smoke.

Finally, Field pulled a box of matches from his pocket and struck one, sending a faint scent of sulfur into the air. Holding it steady, he relit his cigar, drawing hard until it smoldered.

Turning to Emma, he said, "I guess you'd better get ready. Looks like we're about to attempt the impossible."

5

Over the next twenty-four hours, they considered multiple ways to get close to the two Russian men. Andrei Volkov was part-owner of a five-star hotel near Waterloo Bridge called Mine, which charged eight hundred pounds a night for the cheapest room overlooking the traffic-clogged streets. But Ripley dismissed the idea of placing anyone from the Agency there with a terse, "It won't get us to him."

They toyed with the idea of placing someone inside one of the Russians' houses as a cleaner or personal assistant. But each man owned multiple properties and stayed on the move, traveling from one country to the next by private jet or yacht, protected by guards who served as a private army. They were never in any house for long. Their money made them as untouchable as gods.

In the end, it was Emma who came up with the idea. It was the day after Stephen Garrick's body had been discovered, and she'd been rereading Andrei Volkov's file, searching for a crack in his life she could step into. Finally, she'd thrown the document down, and said, "It seems to me he lives on his yacht more than in any of his houses."

There was a long pause as her words sank through the smoke that filled Ripley's oak-paneled office.

Ripley glanced at Field. "Could be an option."

Field, who'd been slumped in a chair, red-eyed with exhaustion, straightened. "Not could be. *Is.* I know someone who could make it happen. But we'd need the right person. Young. Good-looking."

In tandem, he and Ripley turned to Emma and studied her speculatively. They were like a pair of old druids. They didn't even have to speak aloud.

"We'd have to train her up," Field said, thinking aloud. "And it would have to be quick because they'll know we're coming for them. They're going to run. But she can handle it, can't she?"

Emma opened her mouth to agree but before she could speak, Ripley held up a cautioning hand. "Hang on. This is one hell of a risky operation. She'd be completely cut off. Isolated."

"But think of the *access*." Field said it almost reverently. "The crew on those yachts live alongside the owners. There's nowhere for them to hide. It's perfect."

"There'll be nowhere for Emma to hide, either." Ripley's voice rose. "If we're right, these men have already used a chemical weapon on one British agent and there's nothing to stop them from doing it again."

"But—" Field tried to interrupt but Ripley spoke over him, suddenly furious.

"I don't give a damn about access. Emma would be too exposed out there."

Field's forehead furrowed.

Ripley turned to Emma and said abruptly, "You should get some rest. Go home. I'll call you when we know more."

Emma wanted to refuse but she knew there was nothing to

gain from arguing. Ripley knew what she was capable of. And he must be able to see how much she wanted this.

And yet, when she stood up, her feet dragged. With her hand on the door, she turned back. "For what it's worth, I want to do it. I know it's got risks, but I can handle it." Ripley's face closed, but she kept going. "We can't let them get away with this. If I'm the right person for this operation, send me."

Emma used the Agency's car service to take her home. In the backseat, she tried to understand Ripley's sudden resistance.

She knew how dangerous it would be to go undercover on a boat that might well hold the man who killed Stephen Garrick. In the wrong hands, it was a suicide mission. She was one of the youngest people at the Agency, but in the last year she'd proven herself more than once.

As the car crossed Westminster Bridge, she looked down at the water glittering blue and gold in the late-afternoon sun, and remembered a frantic speedboat chase on the river nine months ago. That was the last time she'd had an assignment that put her life on the line. Since then, she'd been given soft jobs—light surveillance, easy targets. Ripley hadn't said anything about it, but she got the impression he had been giving her time to heal, physically and mentally. That was what she hoped, anyway. The worry, of course, was that he'd lost faith in her for some reason, after the job that nearly killed her.

Reaching up, she touched the smooth skin of the scar on her left shoulder, where the Russian bullet had hit her. And for the first time in a while, she thought about Michael Primalov's hands, gentle but firm on her skin as he dressed the bullet wound in her shoulder. He'd been bewildered by the ruthlessness of her world, as she'd fought to keep him safe from the spies intent upon killing him.

The two of them had formed a bond that night. A bond only survivors can understand. And yet, although she'd thought about him many times since then, she'd never once tried to find him. He and his parents had been given new identities, new lives. Tracking him down could put his life in danger again.

But now and then, when she was very tired, Emma allowed herself to wonder what might have been, if absolutely everything had been different.

Nothing, she told herself, firmly, as the car pulled up in front of a white Victorian building in the Crystal Palace neighborhood of south London. *Nothing would have happened.*

Their lives were too different. Even if everything had been fine and he hadn't needed to go into hiding, it wouldn't have mattered. They couldn't be together. She could never have told him the truth about her work. And he would have hated being deceived.

As she climbed the steps to her flat, she put Michael out of her mind. She'd worked thirty-six hours straight, and every part of her longed for sleep.

The small apartment, with its polished wood floors, simple furniture, and pale walls, had an anonymous feel. The furniture was from a mainstream chain; the framed print above the sofa of Piccadilly Circus on a rain-soaked night was a mass-produced image.

When she'd moved in two years ago, she'd loved the built-in bookshelves on either side of the fireplace but she'd never had time to fill them. They were as bare and glaring as an accusation.

Emma had never much minded the fact that she had no time for reading. No time for hobbies. But looking at her home now, she didn't like how much it resembled Stephen Garrick's starkly empty flat.

The apartment was rented in the name "Emily James." Emily worked as a civil servant for the Foreign Office, or so the landlord believed. But he didn't really care, since the rent came through right on time every month. That had little to do with Emma, of course.

When she'd first begun working for the Agency, she'd had a meeting with someone from MI6 who helped her set up a bank account in a false name, through which all her bills had been paid ever since. A portion of her income went to that account each month, ensuring that nothing was ever overdue.

Debt was a door temptation could walk right through, and intelligence officers weren't allowed to have any of it. Even their credit card statements were monitored.

In a strange way, Emma thought money was beginning to lose its meaning to her. When she needed it on a case, Ripley gave it to her, stuffed in envelopes. In her own life, she had no desire for more of it, and no time to spend what little she had left after her bills were paid.

She was too tired to keep thinking. Wearily she turned off the lights and crossed the room, stripping off her clothes as she walked, falling into the cool sheets with a sigh of relief.

Her last thought was that Ripley had to let her do this job. If he didn't, there was no point in staying with the Agency. She hadn't become a spy to watch Russian children carry money around London.

Seven hours later, when the phone woke her up, she couldn't remember dreaming at all.

"Makepeace," she said thickly, raising herself onto one elbow.

"I need you to come into the office." It was Ripley's voice, tireless and crisp. "You're going to France. You may be there several weeks. Best if you throw away the milk."

6

When Emma arrived at the Vernon Institute at noon, she could sense the hum of energy the second she walked in, like the buzz from a high-voltage wire. The same excitement raced through her veins like a drug.

She headed straight to the oak staircase leading up to Ripley's office. There was no time to lose. Everything needed to happen quickly.

As soon as she reached the landing, though, she heard voices from his office. The door had been left slightly ajar, and an unfamiliar male voice said, "My phone is ringing off the hook, Charles. I just want to know what your plans are. I don't want to get in the way. I want to make sure you have everything you need to handle this. I want to help you."

There was a pause before Ripley replied. "Our plans are still developing."

Emma recognized his bland, noncommittal tone, the one he always used when talking to government ministers who'd shown up to meddle.

"We appreciate how critical it is to get to the bottom of this horrible crime," he continued soothingly. "And we are focusing all our energies on it."

The other man didn't back down. "Forgive me, but I can't go back to the Security Council with 'focused energies,' Charles."

The contempt in his voice made Emma wince, but Ripley must have expected this sort of reaction once the press got its hands on the case. The tabloid headlines she'd spotted on the way to the office had screamed: "SUITCASE MAN IS SON OF LORD." Someone—probably the police officers who'd been first to arrive at Garrick's flat—had described the scene in surprisingly accurate detail. Eventually, the press would find out the dead man was a spy and then all hell really would break loose.

The operation hadn't even begun and the pressure was already on.

If the man was on the National Security Council he was most likely an MP—probably a cabinet minister. They were the only ones brave enough to stand up to Ripley like that.

When Ripley replied, his tone was even. "Of course I understand your position. I can tell you we have suspects identified, both Russian nationals, but we have no evidence to pin the crime on either of them."

"I need their names," the man said.

Ripley said politely, "I wish I could tell you more. It's simply too early in the investigation."

The man's voice grew cold. "If you don't tell me more about these men now, you can expect to be called before Parliament within the week to explain it all in great detail. I'm not leaving without . . ."

"Emma. What are you doing out here?" Ed Masterson demanded, making her jump.

She spun around to find Ripley's deputy standing at the top of the stairs, watching her with disapproval.

"I'm waiting to speak to Ripley," she said, instantly defensive.

"You should have come to me when you realized he was busy," he told her, lowering his voice to a hiss as he spotted the half-open door. "Are you eavesdropping?"

His accusing tone made her shoulders tense.

"I'm *waiting*."

"Well, stop waiting," he snapped. "Go see Martha and get your legend in place."

Masterson was tall and slim, with straight, fair hair. He might have been attractive, but there was something about his bone structure that gave him a pinched look.

Emma disliked him immensely.

"I haven't been briefed yet," she said stubbornly. "Ripley told me to come straight up."

"Listen, I don't want to argue with you with the minister right there," he whispered, jutting his thumb at the door. "Can't you just do what you're told for once?"

It took effort to smooth the fury from her face, but Emma managed it.

"Of course," she said coolly. "Right away."

As she walked down two flights of stairs to the basement she imagined killing him in five different ways, each more satisfying than the last.

She and Ed Masterson had had a tense relationship ever since the operation in which she'd rescued Michael Primalov. Masterson had been in charge that night, and refused to send anyone to help her. She blamed him for the bullet wound, and the months of soft jobs that had followed.

Most of all, she despised Masterson's ambition. After that night, he'd twisted the facts, accusing Ripley of abandoning his post. It had been a naked attempt to take the top job inside the Agency. An internal investigation had been launched that lasted seven weeks and ultimately cleared Ripley of wrongdoing. Unfortunately, it also found no evidence that Masterson had broken any rules.

A low thunder of percussion and a blast of trumpet greeted her at the bottom of the steps—she always heard Martha's office before she reached it.

"Hello?" Emma called, as she stepped into a long room filled with clothes, her voice drowned in the music.

Disguise specialist Martha Davies had been given virtually the entirety of the basement for her work, and the tools of her trade spread out in all directions—racks of sober suits and rails of ties, and beyond that, colorful dresses for all occasions, from a BAFTA award ceremony down to the perfect skirt and blazer for an estate agent. A makeup station stood at the center, surrounded by baskets of glasses, silicon noses, and dental prostheses that could change the shape of someone's face enough to render them unrecognizable. It was an Aladdin's cave of disguises.

As Emma walked through the racks, a tall woman dressed in a yellow and orange 1960s caftan that swirled dramatically around her figure emerged from a back room with her arms full of fabric, singing along with the jazz pouring from the speakers.

"Hey," Emma said.

Martha squeaked, nearly dropping the clothes.

"Jesus, Emma, you scared the bollocks off me. I didn't hear you come in. Give a girl some warning, won't you?"

"Sorry," Emma said. "That prat Masterson said you were ready for me."

Martha was the one person at the Agency who despised Masterson more than Emma did.

"Well, Masterson is a duplicitous, cowardly toad, but he's right on this occasion. I am actually ready for you." Setting the clothes on a chair in front of a tall mirror, Martha bustled over to the stereo and turned the volume down. "Ripley says you're going on a superyacht, you jammy bastard. I've got about a thousand things you could wear, but you'll only need a few."

Martha spoke rapidly, barely pausing to breathe, in a broad

Manchester accent. As she talked, her hands separated the clothes with swift, sure movements, arranging and rearranging dark shorts with clean, white tops, narrow trousers with crisp blouses.

"You'll have a uniform apparently, but you need these to look legitimate. You can't show up without a suitcase." Martha held up a flowing blue dress to Emma, eyeing her critically, before nodding and adding it to the pile. "Oligarchs love a uniform. It makes them feel important. It's pathetic. Now, try these." Handing her a stack of clothes, Martha directed her to the mirror.

Emma pulled off her top, throwing it carelessly on the floor before yanking the sundress over her head. "Can you give me the basics of the brief?" she asked as she dressed. "Ripley was in a meeting when I got here. I haven't had a chance to talk to him." She studied herself in the mirror, wrinkling her nose at the sight of her pale shoulders. "I don't even know whose yacht I'm going to be on."

"You'll be on Andrei Volkov's modest little boat," Martha told her. "It's only a hundred meters long and it has just two swimming pools. It's currently anchored in the south of France. We think it will be heading out soon, and we don't know where it's going next, which is why everything is in such a sodding rush." Martha eyed the dress. "That'll do. Put it in the good pile and try this next." She handed her a pair of short black trousers and a loose jacket.

Emma held the jacket up in front of her. "Do you know who I am?"

"You're Jessica Marshall," Martha revealed. "A posh girl from Surrey. You've been working in a boring job and you're looking for excitement. You've applied at an agency that supplies staff to the mega-rich. I don't know exactly what you'll be doing, aside from serving cocktails. You'll get a full brief in France from the MI6 team there."

Emma stepped into the trousers. "Do you know who's running the operation? Is it Ripley?"

"I don't think so. Try this." Martha gave her a white blouse. "It's all blowing up here. That minister in Ripley's office is Martin Dowell. He showed up without warning, demanding to know what we were doing about the murder." Lowering her voice confidentially, she said, "Apparently, the Prime Minister is involved. Everyone wants answers. Ripley's got to stay here and fend off the wolves. He says if the MPs start meddling the whole thing will fall apart."

Emma pushed her arms into the jacket and studied herself in the mirror. "Shouldn't Masterson be handling that? It's the only point of him."

"The ministers want the boss on something this big. Dowell coming in here today like a one-man army is just the start." Martha nodded approvingly at the combination of trousers and jacket. "That's a keeper. Bloody hell, I'm good." As Emma removed the blouse and kicked off the trousers, Martha held out another dress for her to try.

Before Emma could pull it on, a voice floated across the room. "Hey, is Emma down here?" Zach stepped out from the stairwell. Spotting Emma standing in her underwear, he grinned. "Nice outfit."

"No boys!" Martha announced. "We're naked."

Emma pulled the dress over her head.

"What's up?" she asked, straightening it into place.

"You're going to need this." He tossed her a phone.

Emma caught it in mid-air and turned it over interestedly. It looked like an ordinary smartphone with the usual clutter of apps on the screen.

"What does it do?"

Zach stepped closer to point at the icons on the screen. "All the contacts ring through to us. If you get into trouble, dial any number; we'll monitor the line twenty-four hours a day. I'll have the apps all working before you get to France. Jessica is very active on Instagram, so you'll be able to post as her. Also, there's a tracker hidden so deep in this baby nobody will ever find it. We'll always know where you are."

Her brow furrowing, Emma ran her thumb across the smooth glass. "You're sure they won't find the tracker? They'll be looking for something like that."

"I'm telling you, the guy who *invented* that tracker couldn't find it where I've hidden it," he said smugly. "Just don't lose it. It's our only connection to you."

"I'll guard it with my life," she promised.

"Cool." He headed back to the stairs, pausing to glance back at her. "Hey, good luck out there. Keep your shirt on."

"God, he's so adorable," Martha sighed when he was gone. "I love them young. Now, come with me. I've got to do something about your hair. You don't look *yacht* enough. I need to glam you up."

PART TWO

THE *EDEN*

7

Five hours later, Emma rolled a small black suitcase out from the baggage department into the airy bustle of Nice Airport. June in London was cool and damp but in the south of France it was already summer and the air was warm silk against her skin as she paused to survey the waiting crowd.

Someone from MI6 was supposed to meet her, but as she stood looking around the wide corridor packed with chauffeurs holding signs, hopeful families, and impatient cab drivers she could see no familiar faces.

With all the chaos at the Agency, her briefing from Ripley had lasted only ten minutes. The lines on his face had seemed carved deeper than usual when he handed her an envelope. "Here's your passport and tickets."

As usual the passport was perfect. Emma's photo was on the photo page, but the name listed was Jessica Anne Marshall, age twenty-four.

The ticket was two-way—the return flight scheduled in two weeks. This wasn't, she knew, because they expected her to come back on that day, but because one-way flights attract attention.

As she slipped the documents into her shoulder bag, Ripley had told her seriously, "I'm not going to flannel you. I've had my misgivings about this assignment. It's going to be tough. There may be chemical weapons on that yacht. You saw Stephen Garrick's body; you know what VX does. I wouldn't blame you if you backed out. Nobody would."

Emma shook her head. "I want to do this, Ripley. I'm ready."

He studied her face for a moment, and then said, "As you wish. Did Zach give you the phone?"

"I've got it."

"Good. You'll get everything else you need in France and—"

Someone knocked on the door, and Ripley cut himself off with weary impatience.

"What?" he asked, raising his voice.

The door cracked open, and Masterson peered in at them. "Sorry to disturb you, Rip. I've got Cabinet Office on the line."

Ripley swore viciously.

Emma glanced at him with surprise. It wasn't like him to get this rattled.

"I'll be done in a minute," he told Masterson, his tone curt.

The door closed silently and his deputy disappeared.

"Is everything OK?" Emma asked tentatively.

"Not in the slightest. But that's nothing new." Ripley turned his wrist to glance at the Omega watch with a black leather strap. "You'd better get moving. A car is waiting to take you to the airport. Someone from MI6 will meet you in Nice. Don't worry about finding them, they'll find you." He paused, his face shadowed. "Keep your wits about you out there, Emma."

She could sense his nerves, but there'd been no time for more. She'd collected the suitcase and walked out to find the car in the street, the engine purring.

From the backseat, she'd made one phone call using her personal phone. Her mother answered on the second ring.

"Alexandra!" The velvety Russian accent she'd never lost held both pleasure and suspicion. "Why do you call on a working day? Is everything wrong?"

Alexandra was Emma's real name, but her mother was almost the only person who knew that. She'd assumed the name "Emma Makepeace" when she joined the Agency, and it was the only name by which her colleagues knew her. Within Intelligence, everyone's true identities were stringently protected. She had no idea what Zach's and Martha's real names were.

"You mean 'something,' Mama," Emma corrected her mother automatically. "Is *something* wrong."

She could almost hear her mother frown. "Yes, of course. Do not distract. Is there trouble?"

"There's no trouble." Emma glanced out of the window at London's familiar green trees and red double-decker buses. "I just wanted to let you know I'm going to France for work. I'll be away at least a week."

Her mother believed she worked for the Foreign Office, which helpfully explained Emma's absences and frequent travel. But she was suspicious of all governments, and worried constantly that Emma would get into some sort of trouble.

"France? Where in France?" her mother asked.

"Don't be jealous," Emma said. "I'm going to Nice. But I will be working, not sunbathing. I promise."

"You should sunbathe," her mother announced unexpectedly. "You do not do anything for fun. It is a shame."

"I do some things for fun," Emma objected, stung.

She glanced at the driver, but he was trained by MI6 and it was his job to hear nothing from the backseat. His eyes were fixed on the road ahead.

"You do not," her mother said flatly. "You work too much.

You worry too much. You need joy in your life." None of this was presented as a question or an introduction to an argument, but simply as fact.

Emma gave a sigh. "Fine. I have no life. But right now I'm taking my complete lack of a life to France and I'll be in meetings all day, and I've got work dinners every night. I'm just letting you know so you don't worry if you don't hear from me."

"See?" Her mother sounded triumphant. "No life. Only work."

"*Mama.*" Emma suppressed a sigh. "I'm doing my best."

There was a pause. "I know that, my darling." Her mother's voice softened. "It is for me to worry about you, and for you to do what you must. Do good work in France. I will not worry. Call when you get back."

Suddenly, Emma wanted nothing more than to sit in her mother's sunny kitchen in Surrey, drinking the fragrant black tea she loved, and listening to her gossip.

"I love you," she said.

When the call ended, Emma stared out of the window.

Her mother had good reason for not trusting governments. One government had murdered her husband. Another government had failed to protect him.

And Emma had carried the weight of his death on her shoulders all her life.

"Jessica! There you are." The Scottish-accented voice shook her from her reverie, and she spun around to see a lanky man hurrying across Nice Airport toward her, the sun through the windows turning his fair hair gold. Before she could stop him, he swept her into a bear hug, practically lifting her off the terrazzo floor. "God, it's good to see you. So sorry I'm late. Parking is a nightmare. I had no idea it would be this busy."

He grinned at her, dark blue eyes alive with energy.

Emma knew him as Jon Frazer, an MI6 agent based in

France. They'd worked together the previous year tracking down a Russian spymaster in Paris. The last time she'd seen him, he'd had auburn hair and a casual appearance. Now his hair was lighter, and he wore a well-cut suit, the jacket swinging loose over his long torso. His crisp white shirt was open at the neck, revealing a strip of smooth, tanned skin.

"You look good," Emma told him. "I like the hair."

His smile widened. "It was time for a change. Here, let me take your bag," he said, reaching for her case. "The car's this way."

He navigated her across the arrivals terminal to glass double doors leading out into the French sunshine.

"How have you been?" she asked. "It's been a while since Paris."

"Oh, you know, getting by. Staying out of trouble." He shot her a sideways smile. "Although that's about to change, I reckon."

In the car park, he stopped beside a black sports car and popped the trunk open, sweeping the suitcase into it in one easy movement. He was long and lean, with an almost casual physicality. Watching him, Emma had a flash memory of the way his body had felt against hers when they'd pretended to be lovers in a Paris hotel on the mission last year.

Unaware of her scrutiny, he closed the trunk and motioned at the passenger door. "Hop in."

It was just after six o'clock but the sun was still high and the leather seats were pleasantly warm. Emma leaned back and let the heat soak in as Jon started the engine and steered the car toward the exit.

"Ripley didn't tell me you were involved on this operation," she said when they were on the road.

"I'm not just involved. I'm running it," he said.

Emma blinked at him. "You're *running it*?" She didn't know why this surprised her. When they'd worked last year, he'd proven himself smart, quick, and capable, and it had been clear that Field trusted and relied on him.

"What? Are you suggesting I can't handle it?" He shot her an impish grin as the car pulled to a stop at a red light.

"Of course not. I'm just surprised," she said quickly.

The light turned green and the powerful car leaped forward onto a slip road leading up to a narrow curve of motorway.

"Well, you shouldn't be. I'm the one who requested you for this," he said, his eyes on the road. "I liked working with you, and I thought you'd be ideal. Turns out Andrew already had you in mind."

Emma's expression didn't change, but a new warmth spread through her. This must have been what had finally convinced Ripley to assign her to this case.

"I'm taking you to meet the person who's going to get you on the yacht," Jon continued. "We'll fill you in on all the details."

"I'd love to know how you got a place for me on Volkov's yacht so quickly," Emma said. "We only came up with this idea yesterday."

"For that you can thank the lady you're about to meet," Jon said, slowing as traffic merged. "She runs an employment service of sorts that places workers on yachts. Basically, she provides beautiful young men and women to mix cocktails on yachts and serve them to very wealthy people without asking any pesky questions. She convinced one of the hostesses on the *Eden* that her mother was ill, and she needed to go back to England for a few weeks, creating a last-minute opening."

The *Eden*. Emma remembered the image of Andrei Volkov's yacht from his MI6 file—a creamy wedding cake of a boat.

Ahead, the Mediterranean sun illuminated the city's cream and terra-cotta apartment towers, glinting off the wrought-iron balconies. The city's buildings were crowded tightly together, and she could catch only brief glimpses of the cerulean ocean beyond, until Jon turned off the elevated motorway and suddenly the sea was right in front of them — its waves catching the afternoon sun and sparkling like facets of a perfectly cut diamond.

Jon didn't seem to notice the extraordinary view as he steered down narrow, winding streets with the confidence of a local.

"Once you're on board, you'll be looking for whatever you can find about the chemical weapons deals," he said. "Mostly, we want to know who Volkov's working with. You should keep note of anyone who comes on the yacht and the conversations they have with Volkov, especially if Oleg Federov shows up." He shot her a look from behind his sunglasses. "But be careful. Volkov and Federov are going to be paranoid. And that makes them dangerous."

Emma nodded. "How will I reach you when I'm out there?"

"You won't," he said bluntly. "Not unless it's an emergency. We'll arrange to debrief you whenever the boat comes into port."

Jon slowed the car and signaled before turning in to a short driveway between open metal gates. He parked next to a fountain in front of a three-story, lemon-yellow building, with filigreed wrought-iron balconies overflowing with vermilion flowers.

"This is us," he said.

Whatever Emma had been expecting, it wasn't this. But she followed him through air scented with roses and sea salt to the front door. He rang the bell, turning to glance at her. "You'll like Annabel. She's worked with us for years."

The door opened and a small, stylishly dressed woman with piercing blue eyes looked out at them.

"Oh good. You're here." Annabel had a cut-glass accent and a no-nonsense manner. Her blond hair was frosted with silver and brushed the tops of her slim shoulders as she stepped back to let them in. "You must be Emma. Welcome."

Their steps echoed off cool marble floors as they followed her down the wide hallway to an elegantly decorated dining room where jugs of iced lemon water had been set out on the polished top of an antique walnut table.

Clearly, Emma thought, taking in the high ceilings, tall windows, and expensive furniture, spying paid more in France.

"Normally we spend two weeks training new hostesses, so we can't waste time," Annabel explained, handing a narrow crystal glass to Emma. "I'm sure Jon has explained, but I was with MI6 until twenty years ago, when I went off the books. That was when the clever Russians became suddenly very interested in yachts. I keep an eye on our floating oligarch friends from here." Annabel studied Emma critically. "Have you ever been on a yacht?"

"No," Emma said, barely restraining herself from adding "ma'am" to that. Annabel was one of those Englishwomen with an innate ability to appear formidable while barely saying anything. She had a rich, throaty voice that spoke of a private education, thousands of French cigarettes, and many glasses of wine.

"Never mind," Annabel said. "Everyone throws up the first time they're on board so they won't be surprised if you do. We've made it clear this is your first job at sea. They'll expect you to need a lot of training. I'll give you the basics, but I've read your file." Her lips curved up slightly. "I think you'll be fine." She glanced at Jon. "Does this operation have a name yet?"

"We're calling it Gold Dust," he told her.

She gave a crisp nod. "Good. Let's get you ready. Come over here."

Annabel crossed to a long antique table with chairs for twelve. There was nothing on it except a series of photographs, which had been set in a long row. She pointed at an image of a sleek vessel.

Emma recognized it even before Annabel spoke. "This is the *Eden*. Over ninety meters long. Volkov had her custom made in Sweden, at a cost of eighty million dollars. She's high-tech and surprisingly fast. She has two swimming pools, a helipad, a spa with a sauna, and a glass elevator. Basically, she's an oligarch's wet dream."

Jon stepped forward. "We've got the blueprints of the *Eden*, and we'll go over them later until you know that boat better than your own house."

"First, though," Annabel said, "you need to meet the team."

Next to the image of the yacht were photos of two men in naval-style uniforms, smiling seriously. "This is the captain and first mate." Annabel tapped on each image in turn. "You'll rarely encounter them. They keep their distance from Volkov's people. They're hired to get the *Eden* from one place to another and that is all they do. They're the first ones off when it comes into port."

She moved to the pictures of several attractive young men and women in navy blue pullovers bearing the words "THE EDEN" in white.

"The *Eden* has a very small crew. Normally a vessel this size would have at least a dozen crew, if not twice that. The Eden has eight. It's a skeleton crew."

"Why so few?" Emma asked.

Jon answered, "Because Andrei Volkov is paranoid and cheap. He doesn't want anyone on his boat at all, but he also wants to be waited on constantly. A small crew is the compromise."

Annabel pointed to a photo. "This is Amy, the hostess you're replacing." Emma studied the image of a girl with tawny skin and a bright smile. "You may be asked about her. Just tell everyone her mother is very ill. All our thoughts are with her."

"Is her mother really sick?" Emma asked.

"She has a few minor problems but she's generally fine." Annabel gestured at the image of a young woman with auburn curls and a scattering of freckles across her heart-shaped face. "This is Sara Ellis. You'll both be doing the same work—cleaning cabins, serving food and drinks. Sara works the morning shift, and you'll handle afternoons and evenings. She's a gossip, so she should be useful. Either way, she should be easy enough for you to handle—she's quite innocent. She's been on the *Eden* for six months. I placed her through my agency, so I'll vouch for you if she gets in touch and asks any questions."

Next, she tapped on an image of two men—one, round-faced and older, with a likable smile. Next to him was a much younger man, with a long face and a head of dark hair. "The *Eden's* cook, Conor Monroe, and his assistant, Lawrence Baker. Both have good potential to be allies to you on board, I think. They despise Volkov."

"Why are they still working for him?" Emma asked.

"Money." Jon shrugged. "Volkov pays well."

Annabel pointed to the image of a tanned man with sun-bronzed hair. He looked to be in his late twenties with even features and a wide smile. "That's the chief steward, Jason Donnelly. Call him the 'stew'; everyone does. He'll be your immediate supervisor. You'll need to keep an eye on him. We suspect he may be part of Volkov's organization but we're not certain."

Emma studied the picture with interest. "What do we know about him?"

"He's an Australian national; no criminal record," Jon told her. "He's thirty-three years old, and he's been working on yachts for over a decade. He's been on the *Eden* for two years. I'll give you his full file to read before you go."

Emma glanced at Annabel. "What exactly does a chief stew do?"

"They keep things running on a yacht—they make sure the staff are all doing their jobs, and that the owners are happy," the older woman explained. "On the *Eden*, Jason does more than most stews; he acts as a sort of ship's manager. He keeps an eye on food and drink supplies—makes sure everything is well stocked. He also helps out with serving when things get busy." She paused. "Amy says he's quite friendly with Volkov and his girlfriend, so I'd consider him a risk."

"Understood," Emma said.

Next was a picture of Volkov, standing on the deck of the *Eden*. The shot was grainy, as if it had been taken with a long-range lens. Emma studied it with curiosity. He wasn't unattractive. Stocky and muscular, he had a broad face and sharp blue eyes. He was forty-eight years old, but still had a head of thick, dark hair.

"And here's your man," Jon said.

"What's he like?" Emma asked.

"He's whatever he needs to be on the day," Jon said. "Impetuous, charming, dangerous, funny." He paused. "I suppose he's interesting because he's not your typical oligarch. He lucked into his money when he got into a business deal with Federov that paid off hugely. He doesn't strike me as smart, but he's canny. And that can be just as dangerous."

"I think it's fair to say," Annabel interjected, "we don't really know enough about Volkov. He's always flown under the radar. And we would very much like to know more. That's where you come in."

"I'll get everything I can while I'm out there," Emma promised. "What do I call him, by the way?"

"Call him 'sir' unless he tells you otherwise," Annabel advised.

"What about his wife?" Emma asked.

Jon, who had taken a seat on a chair, gave a sardonic laugh. "You'll never meet Olga. She stays in Monaco with the kids. It's the mistress you need to worry about."

On cue, Annabel handed Emma a picture of a leggy blonde, modeling a bikini. It was a professional shot, clearly taken for an ad campaign.

"This is the mistress?" Emma guessed.

Annabel nodded. "Madison Clary. Twenty-four years old, from northern California."

"She's a model?"

"They're *all* models, darling." Annabel's tone was dismissive. "She's done catwalk work in London and Paris, and ads for a major cosmetics company. That sort of thing."

In the picture, Madison's back was arched, emphasizing her lean figure, her long arms outstretched. She was striking but the prettiest thing about her was her eyes. She had wide, bright blue eyes that lit up her face.

"How did she end up with Volkov?" Emma asked.

"They met at a party in Paris," Jon told her. "The beautiful young American woman met all that gorgeous Russian money, and true love was born."

Emma gave a brief laugh. "What's she like?"

Annabel thought for a moment. "I'd say she's naive. She plays the sophisticated world traveler, but there's a dangerous innocence to her."

Jon nodded. "Be careful of her when she's been drinking. She could get you into trouble."

"I can handle that," Emma said, without hesitating. "Is there anyone else I'm likely to meet?"

"We've saved the best for last. And by best, I mean worst." Reaching up, Jon tapped an image of a scowling, dark-haired man smoking a cigarette, peering suspiciously at something in the distance. It looked like a surveillance shot, probably taken quickly. But even in that poor-quality photo his eyes appeared flat and empty.

"This is the guy you really need to look out for on the *Eden*." Jon's voice was serious. "Volkov's bodyguard, Cal Grogan. Ex–Special Forces turned mercenary. Well trained. Well prepared. Utterly ruthless."

Annabel's lips curled. "Every one of the girls I've put on that yacht has been harassed by him. He's a thug."

Emma picked up the photo to look at it more closely.

"He's a thug, yes, but he's not stupid," Jon cautioned. "He was trained by the best, and he can spot danger a thousand miles away. He's the only one I think might be smart enough to figure out who you are." He met Emma's gaze. "Be ready for him. He won't like having you there. You're an unknown factor, and to him, every unknown thing is dangerous. Expect to be searched and questioned, maybe even threatened. But whatever happens, we need you to *stay on that boat*. It's the only place where we can get the information we need to bring these bastards down."

8

By the time she left Annabel's house four hours later, Emma felt dazed. When she closed her eyes, she saw the blueprint of the yacht, spear-shaped and the size of a small hotel. Jon and Annabel had talked through every facet of the work she'd be doing, from how to walk on the deck when the boat was at sea, to how to serve a cosmopolitan from a tray. Along with that there'd been background research for everyone working on the *Eden*, and now she needed to sleep and give her mind a chance to process it all.

Jon, on the other hand, seemed wired. His fingers tapped on the wheel as he pulled out of Annabel's cobbled driveway into Nice traffic.

"It's nearly ten o'clock: you must be starving. I know a place that serves oysters so fresh they jump off the plate. You up for it?" He glanced at her, crinkles deepening around his narrow blue eyes.

Emma's vision of a soft hotel bed and a few hours of complete isolation evaporated. But Jon was running this operation. She wouldn't let him think she couldn't keep up.

"Sounds good," she said.

"You'll love this place," he promised as he navigated the dark, tangled streets with practiced ease, steering between four-story buildings made of pale stone.

Emma cracked her car window and let the fresh air clear her head. Outside, the night was fragrant with the scent of ocean air and night flowers, and the streets were alive with lights and activity.

She watched elegantly dressed couples strolling beneath palm trees toward the waterfront with a mixture of curiosity and envy. The women in silk dresses and men in sharply tailored suits couldn't be further away from the life she lived, chasing after Russian spies and oligarchs, hunting killers and chemical weapons.

They turned away from the city center, and as they left the tourist area behind, gradually the streets grew quieter.

"You OK over there?" Jon asked when she hadn't spoken in a while.

"I'm fine." Emma sat up straighter and closed the window. "You seem to know Nice pretty well."

He took a sharp right turn before replying. "Yeah, I've spent a lot of time down here. Nice and Saint-Tropez are my primary territory at the moment," he said. "It's Moscow on the Med."

Emma gave him a curious look. "Does your work focus mostly on Russians?"

"It does now. I used to spend all my time hunting terrorists and organized criminals but they moved me to Russians full time last year."

It made sense. The Russian government had been very active throughout Europe in recent years, and their operatives moved seamlessly from country to country. France and the UK had a longstanding mutual protection agreement that meant their spies often worked together on international operations.

The road had begun winding up a steep hill, and soon the streetlights grew more infrequent.

Jon pulled into a parking space and cut the engine but didn't immediately get out of the car. "You sure you're not too tired for this? It's been a long day."

His eyes searched her face, surely seeing the exhaustion there.

"I'm completely fine. Ravenous, in fact," Emma insisted. And it was true; her stomach growled as she reached for the door handle.

They'd parked in a quiet, residential neighborhood. Outside, the air was cooler by several degrees than it had been in the city center, and the breeze held tantalizing scents of butter and something indefinable but delicious.

She followed Jon to an ordinary-looking building she would have walked right past on any other night. Inside, it held ten small tables scattered around a neat dining room.

"*Bonsoir*, Nick." A man in a black suit called out to Jon. He walked over and shook his hand.

Emma didn't raise an eyebrow at the name change. The more names, the more identities, the safer you were in this business. A moving target is harder to hit.

The two men spoke in rapid French, and then Jon turned to her and said in English, "This is Marco. He runs the place. Marco, this is my friend Jess. She's just arrived from London and she needs some real food."

Marco motioned for them to follow him to a quiet corner. "You chose a good night. We got in a shipment of gorgeous oysters," he said, in lightly accented English. Glancing at Jon, he said, "Shall I bring your usual?"

Jon glanced at Emma. "Is white wine OK?"

She nodded. "White wine is perfect."

The room was bright, and jazz played from hidden speakers. Despite the late hour, all the other tables were full, and she wondered how they'd been lucky enough to get a table without reserving. Then she wondered if maybe that wasn't a coincidence, and Jon had always planned on bringing her here. It wouldn't surprise her.

That's the thing about spies—manipulation is easier than explanation. Deception becomes habit.

She and Jon made casual conversation until Marco returned with a bottle of wine and a large silver bowl filled with ice and topped with twelve pearlescent oysters—all as perfectly placed as the numbers on a clock. He filled their glasses and then left them alone.

"Cheers." Jon held up his glass, and she clinked hers against it. His dark blue eyes held hers, and Emma could see the intelligence in their depths.

The wine was crisp and cold, and tasted faintly of pears. Emma knew she'd have to be careful not to drink too much of it.

"So when exactly do you think I'll join the yacht?" she asked, reaching out to pick up an oyster.

"Tomorrow," he said. "They're sending a launch for you."

Emma froze. "And you're just telling me this *now*?"

She'd known they would be moving fast, but not this fast.

"I wanted you to focus on preparation," he said calmly. "I didn't want you distracted with worry."

Emma's appetite abandoned her.

"This is *insane*," she whispered heatedly. "I expected to have at least two or three days to get ready for this operation. This is happening too fast. We're going to miss something."

"I disagree," he said. "Jessica Marshall has never been on a yacht before. If we prepare you too much you'll seem too polished. Andrei Volkov would notice that. If we put you on while you're still a bit rough you'll be more believable. Plus, we think he might decide to sail at any point. We need you on board before that happens."

Emma could see the logic but a faint flutter of panic still stirred in her throat.

Going deep undercover is hugely complex and filled with danger. One slight misstep, especially in the isolation of a boat at sea, could lead to her death. Even if she used Zach's phone and called for help, it was unlikely backup would come in time.

She'd known this from the start, but now that it was right in front of her, she was afraid.

Still, she could hardly admit that. And it didn't matter anyway; scared or not, she was going to do her job.

Christ, she hated boats. Nothing good ever happened on a bloody boat.

Jon was watching her with those steady eyes that always seemed to be squinting into the sun.

"Fine, then." She picked the oyster back up and sipped it from the shell. It was as fresh as Marco had promised, and tasted of lemon and brine. She set the shell down on the plate and glanced up at Jon. "Tomorrow it is."

He gave her a look of approval that reminded her, unexpectedly, of Ripley.

"I never doubted it," he said.

For two hours they sat in the quiet corner, talking and eating Marco's remarkable food. After the oysters came steaming bowls of rich bouillabaisse, and then plates of creamy gnocchi in butter. By the time they were served thin biscuits and petit fours, Emma held up her hands in surrender.

They'd drunk through the first bottle of wine she'd pledged to be careful with and were now working on another. But the cold dread had gone, and Emma was filled with a new confidence she knew she should be wary of but which, right now, she was willing to accept.

It was midnight, and the dining room had emptied out; they were the only customers left. Waiters were clearing the other tables.

"Should we get coffee?" Emma suggested.

"Actually, I better get you to your hotel." Jon motioned for Marco to bring the bill. "You need to rest."

Contrarily, Emma felt wide awake as they got into the car. All her nerves seemed alive, and she saw the French city with clear focus as they headed back down the hill.

She was almost disappointed when they pulled up in front of a grand building with a curved drive lined by palm trees.

"This is where we get out," Jon told her.

He retrieved her suitcase from the trunk and handed the car keys to the valet who'd run toward them. Bypassing the front desk, he headed across the quiet lobby, straight to the elevators.

"Let's meet in the restaurant at ten," he told her as the elevator rose. "We can have breakfast and go over any last-minute questions you have."

On the seventh floor, the doors opened to reveal a quiet, dimly lit corridor. Emma's feet sank in the soft gray carpet as she followed Jon to room 721. He swiped a key card against the lock and held it out to her.

"There you go," he said.

Their fingers brushed as she took the card. His skin was warm against hers; his fingers were long and steady. When she didn't immediately pull back, his eyes flashed up to meet hers. She drew in a breath, and his gaze swept down to her lips and back up again. Warmth spread through Emma's body.

I could invite him in for a drink and see what happens, she thought irrationally.

Immediately she suppressed that idea, mortified it had ever entered her mind. He was her boss on this operation. Now wasn't the time for any of this.

She recognized that, with dinner over, she was looking for another distraction to keep her from thinking. From being afraid. But Jon was the wrong distraction to choose.

"Well, thanks for everything," she said quickly. "See you to-morrow?"

His expression didn't change, but she had the discomfiting impression that he knew everything she'd been thinking, and that he was thinking the same.

But all he said was, "Sleep well."

Then he turned and walked away.

9

At noon the following day, Emma stood on a pier in the blazing sunshine looking out at the vast blue sea. Behind her, Nice glowed yellow, apricot, and cream. The air was heavy with the scent of salt water and seaweed and, all around, snow-white yachts and sailing boats bobbed, their hulls and rigging thudding and jangling with every wave, creating a soothing concert.

She hadn't slept much. After Jon had left her in the hallway, she'd paced the room going over and over the day's events, convinced she wasn't ready. Certain she'd fail. Wondering why she'd even considered inviting Jon in.

It was nerves. She hardly knew him. They'd worked together once before. He'd been funny, charming, observant. His soft Scottish accent was a pleasure to listen to. But that was it.

At two in the morning, to quiet her mind, she'd raided the minibar of its tiny bottles of whisky. The alcohol had done its work and, at last, she'd slept.

Now, her body thrummed with nervous anticipation. She

wore the outfit Martha had chosen for Jessica Marshall's first day—short black trousers with a fitted white blouse, and a pair of deck shoes. She'd pulled her hair back into a ponytail low on her neck. Wearing little makeup, she knew she looked believably twenty-four.

Everything that made her Emma Makepeace was gone. Jon had taken her phone and all of her belongings with him. They'd be stored until the end of the mission. From here on, she was Jessica Marshall.

In the distance, a distinctive blue powerboat with clean white trim sped toward her. It was long and lean, moving fast, skimming the surface like a bird. She couldn't see from here, but Emma knew it would have the words "THE EDEN" on the back in white.

She shadowed her eyes against the glare of the midday sun.

There were two people on board. A burly man hunched over the steering wheel—Volkov's bodyguard Cal Grogan, she assumed. The other man was taller and less bulky, and stood behind the front passenger seat, barely shifting as the boat bounced across the wake of a passing ship. Jason Donnelly. The chief stew.

Grogan steered the vessel in a swoop toward her, and Jason lifted one hand and gave a salute.

Hesitantly, she raised her hand in reply.

Somewhere behind her, Jon would be watching. It was the last time anyone would have her back for a while. After this, she'd be on her own.

As it neared the end of the pier, the boat slowed, its engine dropping from a powerful roar to a purr.

"Here we go," she whispered to herself. But she wasn't nervous. She was excited.

Picking up her suitcase, she walked to the end of the long pier, fixing a bright smile on her face.

Jason jumped from the boat and strode rapidly toward her, thrusting out a hand. "You must be Jessica."

Emma shifted her suitcase to shake his hand, and gave an awkward laugh. "Yes. I'm Jess Marshall. Are you Jason? It's such a pleasure to meet you."

She made her voice a little higher than usual, and filled it with girlish enthusiasm.

"Sorry we're running a little late." Jason motioned for her to follow him back to the boat.

"I completely understand. There must be so much to do on a yacht the size of the *Eden*," she said.

"This is your first job on the water, isn't it?" he asked.

Emma nodded so hard her ponytail bounced. "I'm *super* excited to get started. This job—it's a dream come true for me. I'm so grateful for this opportunity."

"I love your enthusiasm." Jason grinned, a wolfish flash of white teeth against tanned skin. "I'm sure you'll do fine. We were sorry to lose Amy, but Annabel always sends us the best."

His light Australian accent indicated either good schooling or family money. Emma, who had read his file the day before, knew it was the latter.

"Prepping for sail is an adrenaline rush every time," he continued. "Provisions have to be ferried out and loaded up, cabins need to be cleaned and readied for the owner and whoever he's bringing along. You'll be very involved in all of that." With a sideways glance he added, "The boss is particular about everything, as you'll learn."

"Sounds a bit intimidating," she said, with a nervous giggle.

Jason didn't disagree. "You get used to him. It's mostly bluster. As long as you keep the champagne chilled and the caviar stocked, Andrei's happy."

Cal Grogan stayed behind the steering wheel, observing the two of them with an unreadable expression. He had dark hair cut short, and a deep scar above his right eye that gave him a sinister look.

Jason leaped on board easily, and then turned back, holding out a hand for Emma's bag. She clutched the edge of the vessel as she clambered on, but lost her balance when the boat swayed beneath her, and she grabbed a seat back for support.

Grogan snorted a contemptuous laugh, and even Jason suppressed a smile.

"Don't worry, you'll get your sea legs," he promised, before jumping off again to undo the bow line tying the boat to the pier, leaping back on with lithe balance.

The second the lines were cast off, Grogan gunned the engine and the launch shot away from the dock.

Caught off guard, Emma felt herself flying backward. A hand caught her wrist.

"Hold on," Jason shouted above the engine, guiding her into one of the white leather seats. Turning his head, he snapped, "Jesus Christ, Cal. She could have fallen off."

Grogan said something in reply that Emma couldn't make out above the roar of the motor and the wind.

Jason resumed his post behind the passenger seat as Emma watched Nice's apricot-and-cream skyline slip slowly away.

They'd been on the water no more than ten minutes when she sensed Grogan easing up on the throttle. She leaned forward to see an enormous yacht anchored at the edge of the harbor. She'd seen dozens of photos, but none of them did the *Eden* justice. It was as vast as a small cruise ship, with a white hull and navy-blue trim that lent it a jaunty air.

Grogan cut the motor. The silence that followed shocked Emma's ears. Ropes shifted and metal fixings clanged as Jason tied the launch up to fittings on the large flat deck at the stern of the yacht.

Grogan jumped off the powerboat with ease. But Emma

stepped unsteadily to the edge; the boat seemed to shift and bob with every step.

Jason lifted her suitcase to the deck and then turned back, pointing to a leather-covered step. "Just put your foot there and step off," he advised Emma. "Don't try to jump it."

Emma handled the transition better this time, stepping carefully onto the superyacht's steady deck.

"Thanks," she said, allowing herself to flush. "We did some of this in training, but not enough."

"No worries." Jason stepped back, gesturing at the double glass doors ahead of them. "Welcome to the *Eden*. I'll show you to your cabin and get you started."

Grogan shook his head. "Boss wants to see her first."

"Oh, great. Someone could have told me that sooner." Jason's tone was mild but Emma could hear the irritation beneath it. "We've got a lot to do today."

Grogan's only response was a disinterested shrug.

"Right, then." Jason sighed. "This way, Jess."

Turning on his heel, he strode through the doors. Emma followed, dragging her suitcase.

Inside, the *Eden* looked for all the world like a boutique hotel—the corridor was decorated in neutral shades of taupe and cream. Wall sconces emitted a subtle glow. Smooth carpet cushioned the sound of the suitcase wheels. Air conditioning kept the temperature comfortable and dry. Try as she might, Emma couldn't detect the movement of the ocean beneath them. It was disconcerting how land-like it all seemed.

She made herself see past the glamour of it, focusing on the elements she'd studied the day before, when Jon had spread a blueprint of the yacht on Annabel's long table.

"The *Eden* has six floors connected by staircases here and here." Jon had pointed at markings on the document. "It has a lift here, but it's rarely used by staff. The living and entertaining areas are on the top two levels. Volkov's office is on the floor below the bar. Residential suites are below that. Staff on the next floor down. The lowest level is where you find the aft deck and storage." He tapped a point at the back of the blueprint. "The aft deck is the only way on or off the *Eden*."

They'd decided it would be too dangerous for Emma to bring listening devices on board. The odds were her belongings would be searched and the devices would be found, in which case her life could be at risk. Even if she managed to place a microphone somewhere, the *Eden* stayed too far offshore for easy monitoring.

Instead, she was going to have to do this the hard way. And now that she was here, it all looked even more daunting than she'd expected. The city was too far away, and Cal Grogan was far too close.

Halfway down the corridor, Jason stopped abruptly and pressed a button hidden in the wall design. The walls parted silently and an elevator appeared. Emma followed the steward inside. Grogan crowded in after them, and they stood in silence as the elevator rose smoothly.

After a second, Jason cleared his throat. "The, uh, crew doesn't use the lifts for day-to-day work," he informed her. "The stairs are faster."

As he spoke, Jason's gaze twitched from her to Grogan, as if the bodyguard's presence unnerved him. The muscular, thick-necked guard ignored the two of them, staring at the door.

The elevator floated to a stop and the door slid open to reveal a short, elegant corridor. At one end, glass doors led out into an open deck, where Emma could see the vivid blue of a swimming pool glinting in the sun. In the other direction, the hallway was truncated by a pair of polished double doors.

Jason glanced at Grogan, who made an elaborate "after you" gesture that only seemed to make the steward more irritable. His face set, he strode to the doors, knocking briskly before opening them.

The room on the other side was enormous. Spanning the entire width of the vessel, it was decorated with clean-lined sofas in dark gray arranged around a glass coffee table. The only art was a huge painting of a little girl holding a machine gun on a string like a balloon. Emma thought it might be an original Banksy. Otherwise, the room was dominated by vast windows offering panoramic views of the blue ocean and the city of Nice glowing golden in the distance.

At the far end of the office, Andrei Volkov sat behind a desk the size of a dining-room table.

Feigning nervousness, Emma let go of the suitcase, leaving it by the door, and stepped forward hesitantly, followed by the other two men.

Volkov watched her every move, waiting until she stopped. Then he stood and leaned forward, placing his hands on the desk. His eyes fixed on her face.

"Tell me one thing," he growled in a thick Russian accent. "Who the hell are you working for and why are you on my boat?"

10

Emma froze. "I . . . I'm sorry? I don't understand."

Volkov regarded her without sympathy. "We know you're not who you say you are. Tell us the truth. Are you CIA? MI6? Police?"

Barely six feet tall, Andrei Volkov did not exactly tower in this room but he had, Emma thought, real presence. His voice was as deep as a grave, and the way he looked at her promised pain and oblivion.

She had expected all of this, but Jessica Marshall would be terrified.

"I don't understand what's happening." She made her voice quiver, and glanced pleadingly back at Jason. "You've seen my passport. You have all my paperwork. I'm Jessica Marshall. That's just . . ." She let her voice falter. "That's just who I am."

"Is it really?" Volkov's voice dripped with doubt.

"Y-yes," Emma stammered.

"I think it is very convenient that you apply for your first job

on a yacht right when the other girl . . . What was her name?"
He gestured impatiently at Jason.

"Amy," Jason supplied quickly. He looked nervous now, his
cocky attitude completely gone.

"Yes. So you show up right when *Amy* has a sudden emergency." Volkov's tone made it sound as if Amy, too, might have
been lying about her name. "It is convenient, yes? I think too
convenient."

"I came because Annabel asked me to come here," Emma
reminded him. "I'm signed to her agency."

Volkov turned to Grogan. "Search her."

Instantly Grogan turned to her and began patting her down.
Affecting shock, Emma held out her arms as his hands skimmed
her body roughly, touching her far more intimately than necessary.

When he finished, Grogan glanced at Volkov. "She's clean,"
he said, stepping back.

Volkov wasn't satisfied. "So you say you are Jessica. Let's do a
test." He motioned at Grogan. "Take her phone."

Stepping closer to Emma, Grogan thrust out his hand. When
she didn't move, he made a quick gesture with his thick fingers.
Emma noticed that the tip of his left ring finger had been amputated just above the knuckle. The skin at the end of it was rough
and jagged. "You heard the man. Your phone."

Emma dug in her bag and pulled out the phone Zach built
for her. Her hand trembled as she held it out. In her mind, she
heard Zach's voice: "*I'm telling you, the guy who invented that
tracker couldn't find it where I've hidden it.*"

She sent up a quick prayer that he was right.

Grogan gestured at the phone without touching it. "Unlock
it."

Emma typed in the code. As soon as she finished, he snatched
it from her hand.

Gulping in air, Emma pretended to force the tears back as the two men bent over the device, opening apps, checking the contacts list, talking in low voices.

It bothered her how smart they were. They knew if she was an MI6 plant her phone would be a weak spot.

Above the sound of her own tense breathing, Emma heard Grogan concede quietly, "It looks legit. But you should test it. Make her call someone."

"Good idea." Volkov motioned for Emma to come closer. "You. Call your mother, please."

She reached for the phone but he held the device back, out of reach. "I will dial. You talk. We watch."

He tapped a button and put the phone on speaker. They all listened as somewhere in England, a phone rang.

Emma swallowed hard. The Agency had better be ready for this.

The phone rang again and again and no one answered. Grogan and Volkov exchanged looks. Abruptly the ringing stopped. A female voice spoke through the speaker. "Jess? Honey, is everything OK? I thought you were starting your new job today."

The voice was familiar, but it took Emma a moment to realize it was Martha.

"I . . . I'm fine," she said, holding Volkov's gaze anxiously. "I just wanted to say goodbye and t-tell you I'll . . . I'll miss you."

"That's so sweet of you." Martha's voice exuded warmth. "You know we'll miss you, too. We've both been thinking about you all day. Your dad's right here. Do you want to speak with him?"

Emma's eyebrows rose infinitesimally, but all she said was, "Sure. Put him on."

"Jess?" It was Ripley. "We're very proud of you taking this job on. We know you're going to do brilliant work and have a wonderful time. But if you need anything at all, you just call. And if you change your mind, you can always come home. All you have to do is say the word."

"Thanks so much . . . Dad."

"Darling, I tucked a new pair of shoes into your suitcase," Martha interjected, clearly getting into the role. "I thought they would be good on a boat."

Emma had no idea what she was talking about.

"Thanks, Mum," she said.

"Enough." Volkov ended the call abruptly and turned to Grogan, who held up his hands.

"I didn't hear anything that worried me," Grogan said. "But just to be safe, I think we keep the phone."

For the first time, real anxiety gripped Emma's heart.

"No!" she said, before she could stop herself.

Both men turned to look at her.

"I need to be in touch with my family. I'm supposed to call my mother every night," she explained hastily. "We're very close."

Grogan made a dismissive gesture. "There's no signal most of the time when we're sailing, so you couldn't call your mummy anyway. We'll return it to you when we anchor."

"But my whole life is on that phone," Emma tried again, desperately. "My friends. Everything."

"We'll take good care of it." Volkov barely glanced at her as he walked around the desk and opened a cabinet. Behind the door stood a large black safe. The keypad lit up when he touched it. Angling his shoulder so she couldn't see the screen, he typed quickly. Emma counted six digits before the door unlatched with an audible click and Volkov threw the phone inside. The safe was open for mere seconds—Emma had a fleeting glimpse at the stacks of papers inside before he slammed it shut again.

Volkov turned back to her. "If you are who you say, we will have no problems," he told her. "If you lie, you will suffer."

He motioned to Jason, who headed for the door.

As she and Jason walked out of the office, Emma silently seethed. The one thing she'd wanted to do was hang on to that phone. Without it she was unable to file any information with the Agency, or tell a soul if she needed help. She doubted they could monitor the tracker through the safe's thick walls.

She'd only just arrived and she was already cut off.

Emma thought Jessica would be too upset to speak after what had just happened, so she said nothing as she walked. Occasionally she sniffed, and swiped the back of her hand across her cheek.

Jason hummed to himself as he strode straight ahead, hands shoved deep in his pockets.

What else has he seen out here and pretended not to notice? Emma wondered.

This time, he didn't summon the elevator, but headed to a utilitarian stairwell. Lugging her suitcase, she followed him down steep flights that were more ladders than stairs until they emerged in a narrow corridor. This level looked nothing at all like a five-star hotel. The ceilings were low, the plain white walls scuffed and dusty, and lined with sturdy metal doors. Instead of a subtle glow from designer sconces, harsh light glared from fluorescent bulbs.

The space was so tight, they couldn't have walked side by side if they'd wanted to. Emma stayed behind the steward until he stopped in front of a door near the end barely wide enough for an adult to pass through.

Inside the room was basic. A single bed was built into the left-hand wall. Across from it stood a small dresser, also physically connected to the wall. At one end, a narrow door led to a miniscule bathroom barely bigger than a standard shower. The whole thing was so narrow she could almost touch both walls if she stood in the middle and stretched out her arms.

"There's a wardrobe there." Jason pointed at a locker. "Your uniforms are inside. Annabel gave us the size. If they don't fit, let me know."

"Great." Emma's voice was flat. Jessica would be having a lot of regrets about what she'd signed up for.

"You're working the dinner shift," he continued, as if he hadn't noticed. "Get unpacked and changed and then come up to the bar when you're ready and we'll start training."

"Where's the bar?" Emma asked. She knew perfectly well it was on the top floor. But Jessica would have no idea. And Jason must be aware of that.

"Sorry." He flashed a toothy smile. "Just take the stairs to level six. You can't miss it."

He was walking out of the door when Emma thought to ask, "Wait. Where's my key?"

Jason turned back, his expression bland. "We don't lock doors on board. There's no need. Anyone who steals anything on the *Eden* would be thrown to the sharks."

She waited as he closed the door, listening until his footsteps faded before kicking her suitcase hard.

"Fuck, fuck, *fuck*."

Her heart raced as the adrenaline she'd suppressed during the meeting in Volkov's office flooded her system. Her lungs felt tight and airless. It took a moment for her normal breath to return.

She forced herself to calm down and assess her situation. She'd lost her phone, which was catastrophic, but she'd survived her first encounter with Volkov. The operation was in play. Also, she'd been inside his office, and so she knew there were no locks on the door. Best of all, she knew where the safe was.

The conversation with Ripley and Martha had been fortuitous. They would know she wasn't the one who'd initiated that call. They must have guessed the phone might have been seized.

As she went over the conversation in her mind, she remembered the comment Martha had made about shoes.

Grabbing the suitcase, Emma dumped the contents onto the bed. Out tumbled the outfits she'd tried on the day before, the dresses, the sandals.

The last thing to fall was a pair of trainers.

She picked them up and turned them over. They were brand new, almost painfully white. There was nothing overtly unusual about them.

Carefully, Emma ran her fingertip along the edge of the rubber soles. Then, loosening the laces, she looked along the edges of the fabric lining, following every inch of the stitching from the instep to the toe. Finally, her fingertips identified a loose section of fabric near the heel. Carefully, she teased it up. Neatly hidden underneath it was a SIM card.

Emma stared at the tiny golden chip with relief. The Agency really had prepared for everything. They knew her phone might get taken away. But with this SIM, any phone could become hers.

She just had to make sure nobody realized she had it.

Using the tip of her finger she slid the SIM back into its hiding place and secured it.

There was no time to linger. Jason would definitely be watching the clock, and she didn't want him to come back and put on his jolly boss act.

She unpacked quickly and changed, stowing the suitcase under the bed, then walked out into the narrow corridor. Before she closed the door, she pulled a hair from her head and placed it between the top of the door and the frame.

A few minutes later, dressed in the *Eden*'s uniform of khaki shorts and a dark blue top, and wearing the white trainers with the hidden SIM, she stepped out onto the top deck, and was dazzled by a wall of pure *blue*. Azure sky and turquoise water combined to create a stunning seascape so beautiful it took her breath. The city of Nice gleamed pink and perfect in a curve of shoreline across the bay, and a dozen other yachts bobbed gently in the distance.

It might have been an image of perfect peace were it not for the *thumpthumpthump* of dance music pouring from the speakers.

The yacht had two open decks. The larger one was just below this floor, and it held the two swimming pools and a hot tub. This upper deck was the bar and dining space. Double glass doors led to an interior lounge, which she could just make out through the opaque glass. The rest was out in the open air where built-in sofas and a dining table were arranged in a long rectangle on the polished teak flooring in front of a small bar.

Jason was behind the counter mixing drinks and talking to a tall, lanky blonde in a white minidress draped across a barstool.

Spotting Emma, Jason waved her over, all smiles. "Jess, come meet Madison." Turning to the blonde, he said, "You're going to love Jess."

Madison spun around on her stool. Slouching back with her elbows against the bar behind her, she eyed Emma up and down with lazy interest and said, "Wait. Where did *you* come from?"

Her husky voice had a flat, California accent. She was as slim as a dragonfly with high cheekbones and enormous blue eyes any camera would love. Her short skirt made the most of her long, tanned legs.

"Jess is the new Amy," Jason told her. "She just arrived today."

Nothing in his face betrayed the fact that he'd just watched Emma be interrogated and robbed of her phone.

"Oh my gosh, it's so nice to *meet* you! We're all so *sad* about Amy. She's so *sweet*. I really hope her mom is OK." Madison had a habit of emphasizing words at random.

"I hope so, too," Emma said. "I'm just really glad to be here. Working on the *Eden* is my dream."

"I don't blame you." Madison lowered her voice confidentially. "It's the most *beautiful* yacht I've ever seen. I adore it."

Her pupils were unnaturally large. Emma wondered what drugs she took.

Behind her, Jason raised the cocktail shaker above his head, showing off his biceps, and shook it violently for a few seconds.

Madison cast a languid glance at him over one shoulder before turning back to Emma.

"So, this is your first day. How exciting! Is it what you expected so far?"

Emma thought of her new boss looming over her in his office, his face dark with suspicion, and said, "It's unbelievable."

This response delighted Madison. "Isn't it? I really think you'll love it here. We're a small group but everyone works hard, and we all like to have a good time. All you have to do is relax and have fun, and you'll fit in just fine."

"And keep the cocktails coming." Jason placed a pink confection dead center on a white coaster in front of her. A pale pink flower floated at its heart. A vivid red strawberry was impaled on the lip of the glass.

Madison squealed and applauded. As she did, the huge diamond ring on her right hand caught the late-afternoon sun, sending tiny shards of light flying.

"That's perfect! Nobody makes a cosmo like you." She reached across the bar to squeeze his hand.

As she watched this, Emma kept her expression neutral but she wondered what Jason was thinking. Flirting with Volkov's girl didn't strike her as wise.

Clearing her throat, she said, "Where do you want me to start, boss?"

Madison snorted a laugh. "She called you 'boss.'"

"I *am* the boss, thank you very much," Jason retorted.

Madison gave him an amused look and picked up her cocktail. "Don't let Andrei hear you say that."

Emma thought she detected a hint of bitterness in her voice, but Jason seemed not to notice as he stepped out from behind the bar.

"Stay here. I'll be right back," he told Madison, gesturing at Emma to follow him.

"See you later, new Amy!" Madison called behind them, raising her glass.

"I'm going to get you started straightening the cabins," Jason said as he and Emma walked across the sun-soaked deck. "You'll do it every afternoon at around this time. When you're finished with that, Andrei should be up here for drinks and dinner and you can help serve."

"Is anyone else on board?" Emma asked. "Other guests?"

"Tonight it's just the two of them." Jason climbed down the stairs with the speed of practice, holding the metal railings and sliding over the last few steps, before turning to glance up at her. "We'll be sailing to Saint-Tropez soon, though, and more will come aboard there." He kept up the chat as they went down two more levels. "Most afternoons, all we need is basic housekeeping—empty the bins, close the curtains, turn down the beds. You know the drill. The main thing to remember is, no matter how many guests are aboard, Andrei's suite always has to be perfect. He's the one you have to impress."

He showed her where his office was on level three, and the storage cupboard where the supplies were kept. They gathered bin bags and cleaning cloths before heading back up to level four.

The main guest quarters were one floor below Volkov's office. The corridor on that level had a similar tasteful décor. The air was cool, climate controlled, and subtly perfumed.

Emma knew from the blueprints that there were twelve suites on this level. Jason stopped in front of the door marked "ONE," and tapped on it.

This door, Emma noticed, did have a lock.

"He's not in here, but always double-check," he told her, before pushing it open.

Volkov's suite was as masculine as his office. The walls and furniture had been done in various shades of charcoal gray. The bed was covered in a dark blanket. One wall was dominated by a floor-to-ceiling window.

The only sign of Madison in the room was a pale silk kimono flung across the back of a chair, and the makeup box open on the dressing table.

"All it needs is a quick straighten and turndown," Jason told her, picking up the silk gown and heading for the closet. "You get started here. I'll check the living room."

As he walked into the connected living quarters, Emma fluffed the pillows and folded down the duvet before hurrying to the sturdy oak dresser. She didn't dare open any drawers with Jason so near but a stack of papers had been left tantalizingly on top next to a heavy bottle of Creed cologne.

Emma picked up the papers and let them slip between her fingers so they fell to the floor.

Crouching low, she scanned each sheet as she picked it up. One was a bill for a wine delivery from a French company. Another was an eye-watering invoice from Boodles Jewelry shop in London. The third was blank save for a row of numbers, written in a series of angry slashes in thick black ink. It could have been a phone number, or something else. A bank account.

"What are you doing? Memorizing those?" Jason's voice came from behind her. The carpet had hidden the sound of his footsteps.

Emma's heart skipped, but she didn't flinch.

"Not exactly." She stood up, casually placing the papers back on the dresser with the Boodles invoice on top. "It's just there's a bill for a hundred and fifty thousand pounds for a diamond ring, and it blew my mind."

Jason laughed. "You get used to that stuff pretty fast around here. We've got some bottles of wine on board that cost fifty K. Each."

He seemed to accept her excuse but he stayed nearby after that, and she could sense him watching as she straightened

Madison's dresser, noting the small mirror that lay on top, smudged with white powder she'd be willing to bet was cocaine. Inside the open makeup case, half a dozen prescription bottles lay conspicuously among the lipsticks and mascara, and she glimpsed the names of painkillers and tranquillizers on the labels.

As she worked, she considered her options. She didn't want Jason to remember her looking at those documents. She needed to give him something else to think about.

She waited until their work was finished. When they walked out into the hallway, she rounded on him.

"You know, I didn't like what happened in Andrei's office," she said abruptly. "I was really scared, and you didn't do anything to protect me. I honestly don't know what to say except . . . I don't feel safe right now. At all."

For just a moment, Jason looked uncomfortable, but he quickly recovered.

"Andrei didn't mean to scare you." Seeing the disbelief in her face, he held up his hands. "I mean, you know who he is, right? Annabel must have told you he's one of the richest people on the planet. He's demanding. You have to expect some odd behavior."

Emma gave him a level look. "He stole my phone."

"He'll give it back," Jason said. "He just wants to be sure of you."

"I don't know what to think. Annabel didn't tell me there'd be any weirdness like this. But I don't have my phone so I can't even call her to ask what to do." Emma's voice quivered. "This is messed up. I really thought he was going to hit me. And you did *nothing*. You just left me alone." Tears spilled down her face and she turned away, her shoulders shuddering. "I want to go home."

This was the moment she'd been waiting for. A chance for Jess Marshall to melt down.

There was a long uncomfortable silence. Finally, Jason said,

"Look. I'll talk to him. You're right—he went too far. That was unacceptable. I'll get your phone back."

Emma could speak four languages fluently, but in the world of men, being able to cry at the drop of a hat had always been one of her most useful skills.

She drew a shaky breath. "Thank you," she said fervently.

"No worries. It's my job." He paused. "To be honest, it was a bit out of character for Andrei. I think he's been under a lot of stress lately."

"From what?" she asked, wiping the tears from her cheeks with her sleeve.

"Oh, I don't know," he said. "I think something happened in London. Someone working for him let him down—I don't really know the whole story, but he hasn't been himself since he came back."

Emma pretended to have only slight interest, and when he changed the subject, she let him. Jason believed she was who she said she was, and that was all that mattered. She could work on him. She needed to take it slowly.

Already he'd told her enough for her to be certain that she was on the right track. It was entirely possible the information they needed to put Andrei Volkov and Oleg Federov in prison really was somewhere on this boat.

Now all she had to do was find it.

11

When Emma walked back to her room that night, the door was shut tight but the hair she'd placed on top of it was missing. In the dresser, her clothes were not as she'd left them, and the suitcase had clearly been moved. As expected, her room had been searched.

They would have found nothing—the SIM card was inside the shoes Emma wore and she'd brought nothing else that could have identified her as anyone other than Jessica Marshall.

Emma hoped this would clear some of the suspicions around her, and to a certain extent that is what seemed to happen. The next day, Volkov was warmer to her when she served a bowl of iced caviar to him and Madison on the bar deck. And Madison treated her like an old friend.

But her phone was not returned. And Cal Grogan still watched her with open mistrust, especially whenever she and Madison talked or laughed. He seemed to see Madison as a weak point, and Emma agreed with him on this. She was chatty and a bit lonely, and Emma believed that, with time, she could build a relationship that would allow Madison to confide in her.

In the meantime, she focused on the staff. That night, she sneaked the cook, Conor, and Lawrence, his assistant, bottles of ice-cold beer from the bar after dinner service, winning them over instantly.

They proved to be useful allies. They didn't mind her asking questions, and they were definitely not huge fans of either Cal Grogan or Jason.

"He's a to'al bawbag," Conor declared of Jason, wiping his ruddy face with a towel as he leaned against the counter in the steamy kitchen. "He'd throw his own mother under a bus for twenty quid."

"Complete twat," agreed Lawrence, who'd perched on the stainless-steel counter with his Converse-clad feet hanging loose, his brown hair sticking up and damp with sweat after his shift. "Don't trust him."

Conor was a Belfast native in his forties, but Lawrence was much younger—no more than twenty-five and quite posh. In their first conversation he'd confided to Emma that working on a yacht was keeping him out of his father's London advertising firm.

"But Jason seems nice," Emma said.

"You think he's nice?" Conor scoffed. "It's an act."

Emma looked puzzled. "What's wrong with him?"

Lawrence explained, "He acts like he's everyone's friend, but he's Volkov's boy. He turned us all in for having a pool party for Conor's birthday while Volkov and Cal were in London a couple of weeks ago. No one ever would have known otherwise. Every single one of us got written up. We're all still on probation."

"There was no reason to do that," Conor interjected bitterly. "Jason was just currying favor. Making himself seem important.

And he ought to be more careful around Madison." He gave Emma a significant look. "Boss is particular about who touches his girl. Which Jason knows rightly."

"They're getting a little too cozy," Lawrence agreed, and took a long sip of his beer.

Emma had noticed the same thing. Jason and Madison were careful to keep a distance from each other whenever Volkov was at the bar, but the second he disappeared they took ill-advised chances. She didn't think there was really anything between them. It seemed to her that Madison wanted more attention from Volkov, who never left the boat but spent long hours locked in his office with Grogan, while she sunbathed alone on the pool deck. She was bored.

"I hope Jason can swim," Conor said, throwing his empty beer bottle in the trash. "Because if Volkov finds they're getting up to anything serious, that'll be the only way he's getting to shore."

Emma casually pressed the two of them about Volkov's business activities, but they made it clear they knew nothing about any of that.

"Nobody good owns a yacht this big," was all Conor would say. "This isn't an honest boat."

The only crew member who gossiped more than the cooks on the *Eden* was Sara, the fast-talking Liverpudlian day shift steward.

Handily, Sara's room was next door to Emma's. Her cabin was absolute chaos, strewn with clothing and clutter, and when Emma stopped by to introduce herself, she spotted a mobile phone and tablet left carelessly on the bed.

Sara bounded over to greet her, beaming with enthusiasm. "We're all going to miss Amy, but I'm so glad you're here! And not just because it means I don't have to do all the work by myself."

She'd chattered excitedly, offering to show Emma around, to teach her the ropes.

The next night, she knocked on Emma's door and held up a bottle of white wine and two glasses.

"I'm the welcoming committee," she announced with a broad smile that created deep dimples in her cheeks.

Emma invited her in, and as she poured them both a glass Sara surveyed Emma's orderly cabin with envy. "My God, Jess. Your room's as tidy as a nun's fanny."

"I haven't had time to mess it up yet," Emma explained, laughing.

There was no need for manipulation or cultivation. Over several glasses of wine, she found Sara very willing to share what she knew about basically everything.

"I think the girl's a vampire," Sara said of Madison. "I bring her breakfast in bed at two o'clock in the afternoon and she's got the shades down. Lying in that bed in a silk negligée like a princess. 'Leave it there, won't you?' she says." Sara made a languid gesture with one arm. "Doesn't eat a thing. I take it all upstairs again later. She lives on cocktails and cocaine. No wonder she's so thin. And have you seen that ring? The bling of it! It's bloody *gorgeous*. Almost worth shagging someone like him to get a rock like that." She paused before repeating with a shudder, "Almost."

"You're not a fan, then?" Emma asked, laughing.

"Of Andrei?" When she said his name, Sara lowered her voice to a whisper and glanced over her shoulder at the closed door. "He kind of scares me. Where does his money come from anyway? That ring must have cost more than a house. I know a dodgy bloke when I see one and he's got it written all over him."

It was after midnight by then, and they were sitting on Emma's narrow bed finishing their second glass. Around them, the *Eden* was heavily quiet.

"Have you ever seen anything *really* dodgy here, though?" Emma asked. "Annabel told me to be careful, so I figured something must be a bit off."

"Other than the drugs and the booze?" Sara shrugged. "Nobody's ever been shot in front of me, if that's what you mean." She paused. "Things have changed lately, though."

"What do you mean?" Emma asked, taking a casual sip of wine.

Sara thought for a moment.

"This place used to be a nonstop party, with people coming and going constantly. We'd never have a time when all the guest rooms are empty like they are now. And Andrei's always shouting at people, and locking himself away with Cal in his office — something's wrong, I think."

"Any idea what's happened?" Emma asked.

"Not a clue," Sara said. "All I know is, everything's been strange since Andrei came back from London. The only person who's come on board since then is you. It's like he's afraid of something, but I don't know what."

The next morning at nine o'clock, the *Eden* weighed anchor.

Emma woke with a start, aware that something had changed. The sense of quiet and stillness she'd grown used to was shattered by the growl of powerful engines. Waves struck the boat hard enough to make it shudder.

When she crossed to the small window to look out, the sky, which had been vivid blue until now, was sullen gray. Spray streamed across the glass like tears.

Emma threw on her uniform and headed up to the pool deck.

The boat swayed sickeningly, making walking complicated. Twice she lost her footing on the stairs and clung to the rail until she could find her balance again.

The *Eden* was a very different place when it was in transit. In the quiet harbor, Emma had at times forgotten she wasn't on land. But that was not a mistake she could make right now.

When she reached the deck, she stood at the rail, looking out over the empty water. The rain-soaked wind whipped her hair back, and the metal felt slippery beneath her fingers. She practiced bracing herself with her feet far apart, barely touching the rail as the yacht rolled with the waves.

"It's beautiful, isn't it?" The voice came from beside her, and Emma jerked around to see Madison walking toward her, her feet bare on the wet deck. Her white silk dressing gown flared behind her, outlining her slim figure. She moved gracefully, unbothered by the swing and sway of the deck, and her blond hair clung to her sharply defined cheekbones as she looked out across the water. "I love setting sail. You go from nothing to *something* all at once."

Emma thought that was exactly how it felt.

"It's like when a plane takes off," she found herself saying. "When the wheels leave the ground."

Madison glanced at her, her blue eyes alight with excitement. "That's it. It's weightlessness."

Thinking about her conversation with Sara the night before, Emma said, "It's been so quiet lately. You must be excited about going somewhere new."

"Oh God, it's been so *dull*." Madison's voice was vehement. "Andrei's obsessed about work and something stupid that happened in London and he's cut us off from all our friends for days now. I'm so sick of it."

Emma's breath quickened. This was what she needed. Before she could ask more, though, Cal Grogan emerged from the double doors behind them.

Her heart sank. The bodyguard seemed to follow Madison everywhere.

There had to be a way to get rid of him, just for five minutes.

Madison was in the mood to talk and Emma needed to find out what she knew.

Catching Madison's eye, she tilted her head in the guard's direction. "Do you ever feel watched?"

Madison looked where she indicated and the excitement left her face, replaced by fury. She spun around to face Grogan.

"Will you just fuck off, Cal?" she demanded. "I don't need you following me around like a dog."

Grogan didn't budge. "Boss says to keep an eye." He glanced from Madison to Emma.

An angry flush crept up Madison's pale face. "Oh come on. What's she going to do? Throw me overboard? Jesus, Cal. Leave me *alone*. Just get lost."

The two faced off: Grogan, muscular and hulking. Madison, slim and fragile, but fueled by righteous anger.

After a long seething moment in which the two glared at each other, Grogan held up his hands, his amputated ring finger creating a startling hollow space.

"Look after yourself then," he told her, and stomped back toward the doors.

When he was gone, Madison stood in silence at the railing looking out at the turbulent seas and spoke softly, as if to herself. "He goes too far sometimes."

Emma glanced at her. "Who? Cal?"

Madison shook her head. "Andrei. He says he wants to keep me safe. But really he wants to keep me prisoner. He doesn't want me to see anyone if he's not there. Or go anywhere." She met Emma's gaze. "He's obsessed with you, by the way. It's bizarre."

"With me? Why?" Emma asked.

Madison shrugged. "Because you're new. And Cal works him up. It seems like anyone new is a threat now."

"Now?" Emma pressed. "Why now?"

Madison's long hands flew up, the diamond ring flashing.

"Who knows? Since he came back from London he's been hideous. He's said crazy things, like he wants to stay on the yacht forever. Then yesterday, he announces he's moving back to Russia." She shook her head, wet blond strands swaying. "If he thinks I'll live in Moscow he's out of his freaking mind."

Shivering and near tears, she seemed suddenly fragile, and very young.

Emma reminded herself that Madison was only twenty-four. It would have been so easy for Andrei to seduce her. At the beginning, he must have seemed the height of international sophistication, someone who could buy magnums of the most expensive champagne, drop diamonds on her fingers, and get her into all the glitziest rooms in the world. And he *could* do that. But not for free. And Emma realized that the cost to Madison had to be high.

Maybe Madison didn't want to live in Moscow. But Volkov was organized crime. And one thing Emma knew for certain was that no one walks away from a crime syndicate unscathed.

"I'm really sorry things have been so grim lately," she said. "Has Andrei said anything to you about what happened in London and why he's so upset?"

Madison let out a long breath and met her eyes. "All I know is, something bad must have happened. I think Andrei's . . . scared." She glanced up at Emma. "You'll say 'scared of what,' and I don't know. But he believes someone's going to kill him."

Emma gave her a shocked look. "Who?"

"I wish I knew." Madison leaned against the rail, the wind whipping wet strands of hair back from her face. "He won't tell me." She lowered her head to her arm, and whispered, "Everyone's an enemy."

Hesitantly, Emma stepped closer and rested a hand on her thin shoulder. "I'm so sorry. This must be hard. I know you care about him."

"You're a kind person, Jessica." Madison put her hand on top of Emma's, pressing it. "I'm working on Andrei. I need him to like you as much as I do. Give me time. I'll win him over."

Emma suppressed a smile. Everything was going precisely as she'd hoped.

12

At its heart, spying is lying, but Emma had never much minded that part of the job. In fact, pretending to be someone else was exciting. The moment when she first convinced a target to accept her false identity, to believe the deception, however unlikely, was utterly exhilarating.

All of it was a challenge. To get into someone's life, you have to truly understand them—who they are, what they enjoy, what they hate. You need to know them as well as you know your dearest friends. It's the only way. If you can convince yourself you like them, then you can convince *them*. Once you're close enough to someone, you can take whatever you need from them. In fact, in many cases, they'll just hand it to you. It's that simple.

Almost no one is immune to this dance of seduction and betrayal. No matter how thick the shell someone erects around themselves, if you know them well enough there's always a chink in their armor where you can plunge a sword.

Emma rarely troubled herself with how her target might feel about it all. The only time she'd ever felt guilty was when she was fresh out of training, and she was assigned to befriend the daughter of the Russian defense secretary. At twenty-one years old, Kira Zakharova lived in an apartment in central London for which she'd paid over four million pounds. She had no job, but her offshore bank accounts held enormous sums. Her social media was a stream of selfies in exclusive shops buying designer clothes, on Bond Street showing off her designer bags, in chauffeur-driven cars on her way to the theatre or a nightclub.

On the surface there was nothing special about her: her father stole the money; she spent the money—the second oldest story in the world. All the same, the Agency ordered Emma to form a relationship with her. She wasn't told why. All Ripley said was, "Learn everything you can about her."

It had been incredibly easy to step into Kira Zakharova's life. She fancied herself sophisticated, but was actually vulnerable and eager to be liked.

Kira's pleasures were simple—she loved shopping and dancing. So Emma had arranged to run into her first at the upscale London department store Selfridges. The two spoke briefly as they tried on the same lipstick at a makeup counter. The next day, Emma had turned up at a nightclub where she knew Kira would be. The Russian girl had been thrilled to see her again. They'd danced all night.

Over the subsequent days, they'd lunched, gone to parties together, and shopped.

Emma had loved the deception. It had been exciting fooling Kira; convincing her they had friends in common back in Moscow. They agreed that their paths must have crossed on so many occasions, it was astounding they'd never met before.

While visiting Kira's flat for dinner and drinks, Emma searched it thoroughly, finding drug paraphernalia in the bathroom, and a second mobile phone in a bedside table. One MI5 didn't know she owned. On her computer she found a video of Kira having sex with her ex-boyfriend, which she'd copied and passed on to the Agency.

Emma memorized everything Kira told her: the money she spent, the names of all her friends, relatives, the men she'd dated. All of it went into her report.

The girl was innocent, really. She knew her father had money he shouldn't have, but she didn't know how or why he'd taken it. She didn't care about politics. She was a careless person. But she was not the thief. Her father was.

After reading her report, Ripley gave Emma one final assignment: she had to invite Kira to lunch at a restaurant in central London. Instead of meeting Emma though, she was going to meet him.

When Kira walked into the restaurant, she was directed upstairs to a private room. There Ripley, Emma, and three representatives from MI5 locked the door and showed her the evidence Emma had collected about her life.

Kira's terrified gaze had skittered from Emma to Ripley, to the officers he'd brought with him.

For the first time, Emma had felt nauseous with guilt. She had done this. She'd lied and dissembled, and now Kira was here. Cowering.

Ripley, though, had been emotionless. He'd told Kira, "We know your friends, your family, your lovers, your drug habit, your sex life. We know *everything* about you. You have no secrets left. We have enough evidence to arrest you and put you in prison any time we want. But there's no reason for us to do that. We don't want you. We want your father. So I need you to give him a message. Tell him if he doesn't stop laundering his government's stolen money through this country, *you* will spend years in a British prison." As Kira sobbed, he'd added, "Make sure he understands that we're serious."

By that point, Kira had been hunched over the table, her body curled as if braced for another blow.

Emma couldn't take it. She'd fled the room and stood outside for a long time, taking deep breaths, as if the air could purify her. But it could not.

Within days of that meeting in the restaurant, Kira had returned to Moscow, leaving everything she owned behind. She'd never returned to the expensive London flat again. Her father had also left the country, never to return.

Since then, Emma had taught herself not to feel guilt about her work. If she thought about the ramifications of her actions she wouldn't be able to do her job. She hadn't thought of Kira in years. But her conversation with Madison brought the memory back. The two were so alike. Both were surrounded by people who would use them to get what they wanted. The more she thought about it, the more she worried about Madison. The way Volkov and Cal Grogan treated her as if they owned her, and the way Madison pushed back against those restrictions, the money involved, the drugs . . . it was a dangerous game. One Madison was unlikely to win.

But she wasn't here to protect Madison. She was here to expose Volkov. He needed all of her attention.

The *Eden* arrived in Saint-Tropez harbor before noon, anchoring off shore. By then, the rain had dissipated, and the skies were a blinding Mediterranean blue. The city gleamed white and angular in the distance.

As soon as they anchored, Jason called the crew to the bar deck, and announced three hours of shore leave.

"For the newbie among us," he said, with a nod to Emma, "we have to leave one crew member on board at all times for security. If no one volunteers we draw straws." He looked around the circle of faces. "Do I have a volunteer?"

"Get away ta fuck," Conor called in his thick Belfast accent.

When no one else spoke Jason held out his hand, which

clutched white paper straws from the bar. "Right, then. Everyone take one."

One by one, the crew members pulled straws. Emma, Sara, and Conor pulled long straws. Lawrence's, however, was short. He stared at it glumly.

"Tough luck, pal," Conor said, patting his shoulder, as the others headed downstairs to get ready.

"The launch leaves for shore in fifteen minutes," Jason called after them. "Don't be late."

Emma, thrilled by this unexpected opportunity, didn't need to be told twice. Ten minutes later, in shorts and a vest top, she walked down to the aft deck, where the powerboat was tied up and ready to go. The others were already there—not just Sara, Conor, and Jason, but also the captain and first mate, whom she'd not yet been introduced to.

"Where's Andrei and Madison?" Sara asked, looking around the gathered crowd.

Before anyone could respond, Emma heard voices from above their heads. It was Madison, and she sounded furious.

"This is fucking ridiculous. I've looked forward to this for days. I came all the way to France because you asked me to and now I've been trapped on this stupid boat and you tell me I can't go ashore because *she's* in town? You didn't think to mention this before?"

Volkov's voice was a low rumble. Emma couldn't make out his words but Madison cut him off anyway. "You should have warned me. It's humiliating. Get out. I can't *stand you.*"

They all heard something crash against the wall, and then the sound of a door slamming.

The captain and first mate exchanged looks, but no one spoke. A minute later, Andrei Volkov and Cal Grogan emerged from the hallway onto the aft deck. Volkov's face was stony as he strode onto the boat.

There was a pause.

"Right, then." Jason clapped his hands. "Let's go."

One by one they filed onto the long powerboat. The air was heavy with unspoken gossip and unasked questions.

Emma glanced up at the *Eden's* snow-white upper decks, wondering if she should stay on the boat to try and talk with Madison. But that would be hard to explain. Besides, she needed to know what Volkov did on dry land.

This time, she was ready for the rise and fall and sway of the launch beneath her feet as she stepped aboard and took a seat between Conor and Sara. The air was hot, but a cool breeze blew off the water as Grogan started the engine and Jason slipped the lines.

The boat cut a swathe through the smooth blue water, heading for the clutter of ivory buildings lining the jagged shore. The day was perfect. The water, almost unbearably blue. Silver fish, startled by the boat's powerful motor, leaped in their path, glittered momentarily in the air, before disappearing again beneath the waves.

The ride to shore was brief, and Volkov sat still throughout it, his eyes hidden by sunglasses, the fingers of his right hand tapping a Morse code of unhappiness on the white leather arm of his chair.

Emma was intrigued about the decision to leave Madison behind. There had to be a reason he'd risk her fury, and she wanted to know what it was.

The marina was near the center of the town. As Grogan turned the boat around and backed it into place in the long row of white boats, the *Eden's* blue launch stood out. The second the motor cut off, Volkov leaped to his feet and walked away. Grogan followed.

Emma and the others climbed off. "Three hours only," Jason reminded them. "Meet back here at four o'clock sharp." Turning to Conor, he said, "I need you to help me order a few things for tomorrow before you go to the pub." The two of them headed away, talking quietly.

Sara turned to Emma eagerly. "Want to go to lunch? Or maybe shopping?"

Emma was ready for this. "Actually, I have a friend who lives here, and I haven't seen her in ages. We're going to meet up," she explained, apology in her voice. She'd never told Sara she didn't have a phone, so her story seemed plausible.

"Oh, of course." Sara sounded disappointed.

Overhearing this, the captain, a tall, dark-haired man in his early forties, leaned toward Sara. "Come with us." He motioned at the first mate. "We're going to a new place on the seafront. It's supposed to have amazing shellfish."

"Really?" Sara's face lit up. "That would be fab."

As they walked out of the marina together, Sara and the two men were talking but Emma barely listened. She was looking for Volkov and Grogan.

The second they reached the main street, she spotted them. Volkov was red-faced and gesticulating angrily. Grogan was nodding and holding his phone to his ear. Something had obviously gone wrong.

Pretending not to notice them, Emma said goodbye to the *Eden*'s crew and raced to a waterfront tourist information kiosk.

She spoke multiple languages but her French wasn't very good. Still, she gave it her best shot and asked the man at the counter, "Savez-vous où je louer une vespa?"

Pointing to a shop a few doors down, the man replied in perfect English, "That's the best place to rent a scooter."

Keeping her head down, Emma walked toward the row of parked scooters. In the car park, Grogan was still talking into the phone. Next to him, Volkov looked tense and frustrated.

They must be expecting to meet someone, but who?

Ten minutes later, Emma emerged from the shop with a set

of keys in her hand, just in time to see Volkov and Grogan get into the backseat of a long black Mercedes. Neither of them appeared to notice her as she pulled a helmet over her head and climbed onto a pale blue Vespa.

Saint-Tropez was filled with twisting, cobbled lanes crowded with tourists, and cars moved slowly. Emma positioned herself two cars behind the Mercedes and followed.

As they left the old town behind, Emma was forced to drop farther back in order not to be noticed, grateful every time another scooter sped by. She was a hundred yards behind the Mercedes when it slowed and turned in to the gates in front of an imposing white house. As she drove by, she had time to glimpse a circular driveway and a fountain.

She turned around and retraced the route, pulling into a parking spot across the street from the white house.

Keeping her helmet on, she watched as Volkov and Grogan got out of the car. A young boy ran over and hugged Volkov, who smiled and said something Emma couldn't hear. A woman in her fifties dressed in white linen stood a distance away, watching them with a controlled expression. When Volkov walked over to kiss her cheek, the woman stiffened.

As they walked slowly toward the house, Cal Grogan turned suddenly back to the street, his eyes searching the cars. It was uncanny, Emma thought. Almost as if he'd sensed her watching.

Hastily, she flipped the visor on the helmet down, and started the Vespa's engine.

By the time Grogan reached the gate, she was pulling out into traffic.

She drove for half a mile before stopping, and waited on a side street for ten minutes before driving back to Volkov's house. This time she parked and got off. By now, the metal gates had closed, and all she could see of the white house was the upper floor.

Jon had showed her pictures of Volkov's family, and she'd recognized the woman in white linen as his wife, Olga. The boy was his youngest son. But they were believed to spend all their time in Monaco. Volkov's house in Saint-Tropez was supposed to be empty, kept as an investment only. What were they doing here?

No wonder Madison had been furious. Unable to leave the *Eden* for even a few hours.

Whatever was going on, Emma had the feeling Volkov was going to be in that house for a while. She needed to make herself less conspicuous. In a nearby shop, she bought a top chosen at random and pulled it over the vest she'd worn on the *Eden*. It wasn't much of a disguise, but it was better than nothing. Choosing a café with tables on the pavement with a view of the house, she took a seat and ordered a *citron pressé* and waited.

Two hours passed without anyone emerging from the big house.

When she could no longer justify occupying the table, Emma strolled the neighborhood shops, searching for a burner phone, but they sold nothing that useful. Always, she kept one eye on the white house. But its tall gates gave nothing away.

Finally, at half past three, the gates opened and the black Mercedes emerged.

Emma, who had been leaning against a tree near the Vespa, jumped on the rented scooter, following the car back across the city until it pulled up in front of a large, unmarked building on the main street.

Again, she found a spot to pull over a short distance away, but this time she stayed on the scooter, watching in the side mirror as Volkov climbed out of the backseat of the Mercedes and strode into the lobby. Grogan got out as well, and stood outside, watching the street with a suspicious glare.

This stop was shorter. In ten minutes, Volkov emerged holding a briefcase he hadn't had before, and headed straight for the car.

His shoulders were tight, his mouth set in grim lines.

Emma longed to know what was in that building, but it was nearly four o'clock and she had to get back to the marina before Grogan and Volkov did.

From the center of town, it was easy to find her way to the waterfront, where she returned the scooter and helmet to the rental place. With almost no time to spare, Emma sprinted into the tourist shop next door. But the woman at the front desk shook her head when asked about burner phones.

"*Pas ici,*" she said, with a shrug.

Not here.

There was no time to find a place that might sell them. Instead, Emma grabbed a Saint-Tropez T-shirt off the rack and bought it with cash. Before walking out of the door, she took off the new blouse and stuffed it into the shopping bag with the T-shirt, emerging from the shop in the same outfit in which she'd left the *Eden* earlier that day.

By the time Volkov and Grogan arrived at the marina, Emma was chatting with Sara and the crew, the vividly colored bag obvious in her hand. Neither man so much as glanced at her when they walked onto the launch, Volkov clutching the briefcase tightly.

Emma felt a surge of triumph. They'd never spotted her and she'd followed them all day.

But the emotion didn't last.

There was so much she didn't know. If Volkov's wife had left their home in Monaco, then he must believe his entire family was in danger. But where did he think the threat was coming from? The British government? Or someone else?

13

The next morning, Jason announced that Volkov was throwing a party on the yacht later that day. Everyone was pulled in to help with preparations. At noon, Emma was prepping the bar while Sara stood on a chair, connecting festoon lights to poles mounted around the deck. Conor and Lawrence were busy in the kitchen, and Jason was in his office ordering last-minute supplies.

It was a hot afternoon, and the sea was so still the *Eden* barely swayed. In the unnatural quiet, broken only by the occasional swish and slap of the water against the hull, Sara and Emma could clearly hear Volkov and Grogan arguing on the pool deck one level below them. Volkov sounded furious.

"I'll go wherever I fucking want," he said, his voice rising. "It's not up to you what I do."

Emma stopped scrubbing to listen. Grogan said something in reply, his voice too low to register, but Volkov's response was clear.

"Remember who pays the bills around here, Cal. And get the

boat ready." There was a whump of air as he slammed through the glass doors heading for his office.

Sara caught Emma's eye, the string of lights dangling from her hands. "What is going *on*?" she whispered. "Everyone's losing it lately."

She wasn't wrong about that. When they'd returned from Saint-Tropez the day before, Volkov and Madison had had another blazing row. Madison accused Volkov of cheating on her. The two had screamed accusations at each other for half an hour before Madison locked herself in their suite and refused to come out.

"Last night, Andrei slept in cabin two," Sara whispered. "Jason sent me to make up the bed this morning. He said Andrei might sleep there again tonight."

Cabin two was the largest guest room. No one had slept in it since Emma arrived on the *Eden*.

Emma asked quietly, "How's Madison?"

"I don't know," Sara said. "She was comatose last night. Jason told me he had to help her into bed after she passed out."

Emma thought about how brittle Madison had seemed that morning in the rain, and her chest tightened.

"We should check on her," Emma decided. "Have you seen her today?"

Sara shook her head. "Jason took her breakfast down. He said she was fine, but . . ."

At that moment, they both heard the sound of a motor rumbling to life. Emma and Sara ran to the rail and leaned over just in time to see the *Eden*'s launch pull away from the aft deck and speed across the crystalline blue sea. Grogan was at the wheel. Madison sat in the back wearing a sleeveless dress and clutching a large straw hat to her head with one hand. Andrei was next to her in a designer suit.

"I guess she's well enough," Sara said, eyebrows rising.

"Where are they going?" Emma said, not hiding her surprise.

"There's a party in town, not that it's any of your business." Jason had walked onto the deck while the two of them peered over the rail.

He gestured at the dangling festoon lights and half-finished bar with irritation. "Why are you standing around gossiping? Why aren't the lights up? We've got six people coming aboard. Are the guest rooms ready?"

"We've been getting the bar ready," Sara said, defensive.

"Oh, is that what you're doing? Because it looked like you were gossiping." Sara opened her mouth to argue but Jason held up a hand. "There's no time for breaks. We could have a full house in a few hours. We need to get four bedrooms ready in case people stay over. And the table isn't set yet."

Sara's mouth formed a perfect "O" of outrage. "What are you going to be doing while we run our arses off?" she demanded. "You could pick up a sponge and help, you know."

"I'm supposed to be in my office getting the supplies arranged. I have had zero notice for this party and it's a bloody nightmare," he told her frostily. "I don't have time to do your job for you. If I were you, I'd get to work."

"Well, you're not me," Sara snapped.

"Look, it's fine. I'll go and do the bedrooms," Emma announced, before the argument could go further. "Sara can finish up here. No problem." Meeting Jason's gaze she said, "We'll get it done."

"Good." His tone was curt. "Get moving."

On the residential floor, Emma worked quickly, spreading fresh sheets and plumping pillows, setting out towels and scented soaps. She was hard at work when Jason walked down to check on her. He didn't stay for long.

"When you're finished, go back upstairs and help Sara," he told her. "She's off her game. I've got a problem with one of the suppliers. If you need me, I'll be in my office."

"OK, boss," Emma said, barely glancing up from her work.

She waited patiently when he left, finishing up the last few bits. As soon as his footsteps faded down the stairs, though, she left the bucket of cleaning supplies in the hallway and ran up one flight to the tastefully decorated hallway leading to Volkov's office.

Everyone was away or busy. This was her chance. She had to take it.

With one hand on the doorknob, she stopped to listen. She could hear nothing except the blood thudding in her ears.

Taking a deep breath, she opened the door in one smooth movement.

The huge office was just as she remembered it: the oversized desk at one end of the room beyond a set of sofas arranged around a heavy coffee table.

Nerves made everything seem much clearer. Emma noticed every curve of the pearl-gray vase on the marble-topped table, each shard of golden light that slid through the windows and crept across the carpet.

On her first day on the yacht she'd looked in every corner of this room and seen no cameras. No alarms.

It was hard to believe Volkov wouldn't have CCTV. But then again, he was a criminal, and it was safer for him to have nothing recorded, no proof of what he was doing in here.

She searched the desk first, looking through the papers on the leather blotter—some were in Russian, others in English, some in French. Some were receipts for supplies; others related to Volkov's companies. She recognized many of the names from Stephen Garrick's research, but the information in the documents was opaque—just rows of data. What she needed was something tangible and clear. Something that would prove Volkov was involved in dealing chemical weapons.

Putting the papers back where she'd found them, she began pulling open drawers and rifling through them. When she yanked opened the top drawer, something heavy rattled away from her. Reaching in, she pulled out a Glock semi-automatic handgun. Flipping it over, she popped out the cartridge. It was fully loaded. She sniffed the barrel, wrinkling her nose at the sharp, astringent scent of gun oil. It didn't smell as if it had been fired recently, but it had also clearly been cleaned.

She wiped her fingerprints from the weapon with the hem of her shirt before sliding it back, and moved on to the next drawer.

Nerves thrummed in her chest. The boat was heavily quiet around her, but every second in this room seemed too long. She had no idea where Jason was right now. He could be searching for her, and if he found her here she was finished. Still, there was one more thing she had to do.

She turned to the polished teak cupboard built into the wall. It had no handle, but she'd seen Volkov open it. She pressed her fingers against the edge as he'd done, and felt a latch give. The door sprang open with a click.

The sturdy briefcase he'd collected in Saint-Tropez was on a low shelf. She grabbed it and popped the brass latches. It opened silently.

Empty.

Disappointed, she put it back, and turned to the safe. It was black metal, two meters high, and solid. She ran her fingers across the cold, smooth keypad, and the numbers lit up. This safe was cutting edge; she could see the quality. It took a minute to find the brand, artfully inscribed near the bottom of the door.

"Dottling."

Of course. Dottling was a German company, famed for making some of the strongest, most expensive safes in the world.

"Oh, marvelous," Emma whispered with heavy irony.

Whatever she needed must be in that safe. Somehow, she had to get into it.

As she closed the cupboard doors, the faint whine of a motor split the quiet, and she swung around to look out of the window. In the bright glare of the afternoon sun, a blue boat with white trim shot across the water. The *Eden*'s launch was returning from Saint-Tropez.

It was empty except for Grogan, who hunched over the wheel, his thick arms bare, biceps bulging as the speedboat hurtled over the waves. As she watched, he looked up to the window and straight at her.

All the air left Emma's lungs.

She threw herself back into the shadows, her heart pounding.

He couldn't have seen her. Not from that distance. The light would have reflected off the glass. There would be glare. She hadn't been directly in front of the window anyway.

It was an illusion.

It had to be.

Moving fast, she closed the cupboard and straightened the papers on Volkov's desk. Using the hem of her shirt, she rubbed down the polished wood to remove fingerprints. Her hands were steady but her heart hammered against her ribs. The work took seconds but even that felt far too long.

By the time she closed the door behind her she couldn't hear the launch anymore.

She tore down one flight of stairs, snatching up the bucket of cleaning supplies she'd left earlier, before racing to the floor below. There, she paused for a moment to catch her breath before walking into Jason's small office.

The steward barely glanced at her. He was at his desk, muttering to himself as he read over a delivery list of supplies.

"Hey," she said casually. "The guest rooms are ready. We need more dusting spray, if you're ordering . . ."

"Not now," Jason said curtly. "I'm up to my eyebrows."

Emma set the bucket down and leaned back against the doorframe. Her heart rate had slowed to normal.

"How's it going?" she asked. "It looks so stressful."

"It's intense." Jason gestured at the laptop open in front of him. "Andrei is very picky about these parties and I'm not sure they've bought the right kind of oysters. I've been trying to call Conor but they must be unloading the stuff Cal just brought back. If it's not the kind Andrei likes, he'll hang my balls on the mast."

"Look," Emma ventured. "If you'd like, I could run up right now and check with the kitchen on the oysters. What kind do you want?"

He gave her a grateful look. "Actually, that would really help. Ask if they're Gillardeau oysters. Conor will know what I mean. Make him double-check. If they're not, tell him to send them straight back."

"Not a problem." Emma placed the bucket in the supply cupboard outside his office and ran up the stairs again.

When she stepped out of the staircase and onto the deck, Grogan was standing right in front of her. His thick arms were bare, muscles bulging. She noticed a tattoo on his forearm in Chinese symbols, and she wondered vaguely what it said. His thatch of dark hair was windblown, his scarred face ruddy from the wind and sun. His small, emotionless eyes watched her with suspicion. A snake observing a mouse.

Something seemed to press hard against Emma's chest.

"What are you up to?" Cal's voice held heavy suspicion. "Why isn't Jason with you?"

Emma gave a puzzled frown. "I just left his office. He sent me to check on the oysters."

"Did he now?" His expression didn't flicker.

He couldn't have seen me, she reminded herself.

"If you don't believe me, go ask him." She gestured at the door. "He's freaking out about the oysters being wrong. He says Andrei's very particular about them and if it's the wrong kind they have to go back straightaway." Her voice was exasperated, as if she didn't have time right now to defend herself. "Is there something else you want?"

There was a long silence. Then, abruptly, Grogan pushed open the double glass doors and walked away.

Emma let out a long breath. He'd seen nothing. If he had, she wouldn't still be standing here.

Her steps felt lighter as she turned and raced to the kitchen calling ahead, "Conor! About those oysters . . ."

14

J ust before six o'clock, a helicopter roared across the bay toward the *Eden*.

Emma, who'd been arranging flowers on a long table, shielded her eyes to watch as it skimmed the water, sending glittering ripples scattering across the quiet surface of the sea. Painted in the brilliant gold of the evening sun, the scene was stunning.

"It's the boss," Jason announced. "Are we ready?"

Emma glanced back at the deck. The festoon lights glowed. Low dance music played from speakers tucked out of sight. The table was set for eight, with crystal glasses and sterling cutlery. It looked like the cover of a décor magazine.

"We're ready," she said.

"All set," Sara agreed from the other end of the table.

"All right, places!" Jason clapped his hands. "Sara, get the champagne. Emma, pour the cocktails. Let's go!"

Behind his back, Sara caught Emma's eye and made a face. Emma suppressed a laugh.

By then, the roar of the helicopter was deafening as it landed on the helipad on the yacht's top level. The rotors were still turning when Madison leaped out, the full skirt of her dress billowing around her like a parachute. Four others climbed out after her with less grace—the men in expensive suits, and the women in flowing summer gowns. They'd all clearly been drinking. Emma could hear the laughter and jokes as they crowded into the elevator.

She walked over to where Sara was pouring champagne into tall flutes. Grabbing a jug of iced cosmopolitans, she filled cocktail glasses and set a cherry impaled on a toothpick in each.

By the time the guests poured out of the elevator and flowed from the inner lounge onto the deck, they were both standing by the door, each holding a tray of drinks.

Emma searched the faces eagerly. She'd hoped for Oleg Federov, Volkov's partner in crime and suspected arms dealer, but there was no sign of him. Instead, she recognized the distinctive pock-marked features of Sergei Krupin.

At sixty-five, Krupin was a despotic oligarch right at the top of MI6's most wanted list. Once close to the Russian government, he'd been on the outs since they discovered he'd drained a number of banks dry, funneling the money into his personal accounts in Dubai. Lately he'd been focused primarily on the drugs trade, moving heroin around the world.

It seemed to Emma that Volkov was spending time in truly terrible company.

Krupin was with a woman Emma thought must be his wife, as she wasn't beautiful enough to be a mistress. After them came a famous Russian footballer, whose name Emma couldn't recall, and his girlfriend. They were much younger than the others, and went straight for the cocktails.

"Perfect," the girlfriend said in heavily accented English as she plucked a drink from Emma's tray. "I'm so thirsty."

They gathered around at the rail, talking in rapid Russian and admiring the *Eden*.

"Oh, look," Krupin's wife exclaimed when she saw the flowers and lights. "It's lovely, Andrei!"

Red-faced and pleased, Volkov made vague comments in reply. At his side, Madison said nothing.

Emma noticed her blank smile, and the way she weaved slightly while trying to stand still. Her eyes were glazed.

She'd taken something.

As soon as everyone had drinks, Emma and Sara dropped their trays at the bar and picked up trays of canapés.

"What's wrong with Madison?" Sara whispered.

Emma shook her head. Apprehension tightened her stomach.

Lifting the tray of pink prawns curled around green slices of avocado, she headed straight for Volkov and held it out, her eyes on Madison.

"Canapé?" she said hopefully.

Volkov picked one delicately from the tray and popped it in his mouth.

Ignoring the food, Madison beamed at Emma. "Jessica!" She clutched her arm. "I missed you."

Aware that everyone was watching Madison stumble toward her, Emma gave her an easy smile. "We're glad you're back," she said. "Have a prawn! We're giving them away free."

To her relief, Madison laughed, and took one of the shellfish, holding it up to her eyes. "They're pretty."

Emma turned to the Krupins. "Canapé?"

She sensed the footballer and his girlfriend exchanging amused glances. But the moment passed, and soon everyone was talking.

Setting the tray down on a table nearby, Emma headed back to the bar.

"She's wasted," Sara whispered as she picked up a bottle of champagne.

Emma nodded, her lips tight.

While the others talked, Madison wandered over to the bar and draped herself across it. "Christ, I need a drink."

Emma wanted to give her water but knew better than to try. Instead, she reached for the cocktail jug. "Too much Russian?" she asked, very quietly, as she filled her glass.

Madison giggled. "Way too much."

She drank half the glass in one go, and then plucked an olive from the bowl at her elbow and tossed it into her mouth, catching it perfectly.

"How was the party?" Emma asked, sliding the bowl closer to her.

"Like this." Madison gestured at the cluster of Russians chatting and laughing. "For hours and hours." She closed her eyes, letting the sun hit her face.

Emma's gaze drifted across the chattering crowd, landing on Cal, who stood at the edge watching Madison with an expression of cool contempt.

Unaware of his attention, Madison straightened. "I think I'll go swimming," she announced. "I'm so hot and sticky."

Jason, who'd just walked in from the kitchen with another tray of food, overheard. "Is that a good idea?" he asked. "There's a party happening."

Madison gave a loose shrug. "No one cares if I'm here. They don't even care if I'm alive."

Blowing Jason a kiss, and shooting Emma a quick smile, she slouched across the deck. Andrei was listening to Krupin talk and barely noticed when she stopped to speak to him. Realizing this, Madison turned, and headed to the elevators.

She'd only been gone a few minutes when Jason pointed out across the water and said, "There's more coming."

In the distance, a long, white powerboat was cutting across the blue ocean toward them.

Soon, two more guests disembarked and appeared on the bar deck: a woman in her thirties with a plump, florid man in his sixties. Emma didn't recognize either of them, and longed for a camera. They greeted Volkov politely but were clearly more impressed by the presence of Sergei Krupin. As the champagne flowed, and silver bowls of caviar emerged from the kitchen, the guests encircled him, vying for his attention with nervous excitement. Whether the attraction was his money, his drugs, or his notoriety, Emma wasn't certain. But Volkov seemed almost nervous about the older man's presence on the yacht. His smile was stiff, and he straightened his shoulders every time Krupin looked at him.

Madison was still down at the pool. As soon as they'd noticed where she was, the footballer and his girlfriend had gone to join her. Glancing over the rail, Emma saw them laughing and chatting.

Glancing up, Madison saw Emma and waved up at her. "Bring some champagne," she called.

"Ooh, yes!" the girlfriend agreed, laughing. "We're far too sober."

With some reluctance, Emma grabbed a bottle from the cooler and held it up so Jason could see. "Madison wants this. Should I take it down?"

For a second he hesitated, but then he held up his hands. "Fine. Keep her happy."

Emma put the champagne in a silver ice bucket and carried it down the stairs. The pool deck held two oval pools and a hot tub. She could see the closed office doors through the glass.

Volkov hadn't been in it since she'd explored his desk. But she had a feeling Grogan checked everything, all the time. She wondered what had set off their argument that morning. There was still a tension between them. Volkov seemed to be ignoring Cal. And sometimes Emma caught Grogan watching his boss with a sneer.

When she emerged from the stairs into the sunshine, Madison ran over to her delightedly. "You're a lifesaver."

"That's what they tell me." Emma set the ice bucket on a side table and picked up the bottle, peeling off the gold foil from the cork.

"I'll open that." The footballer reached out and plucked the bottle from her hands with a good-natured grin. "It's my only job here."

His English was good, Emma noticed.

Madison draped an arm across Emma's shoulders. "Jess just started a few days ago," she told the couple. "She's lovely. She knows all the shit I put up with."

The two looked at her with new interest.

"I'm . . . just super excited to be here," Emma said.

The cork popped and everyone cheered. As the footballer filled glasses, Emma gently pulled Madison aside.

"Are you OK?" she asked. "You should eat something."

Madison put her hands on Emma's shoulders and looked into her face with sudden seriousness. "You are so nice. You really do care." Her huge blue eyes brimmed with tears. "I hate everything. But I'm so glad I met you."

Before Emma could think of anything to say in reply, Madison turned away and picked up her glass. "Champagne makes everything better," she announced, taking a long drink. Her tears had already disappeared. Emma watched her with concern, but there was nothing she could do except return to her work on the bar deck, and hope Madison stayed away from the party upstairs. She was too drunk to be careful about what she said.

But Madison wasn't alone in being drunk. By the time Andrei finally invited his guests to sit down for dinner at half past seven, most of the group appeared to be quite tipsy. Only Krupin and his wife seemed completely sober. He'd barely touched his glass.

By then, Madison had begun slurring her words, and she sat crookedly in her seat, gazing emptily as food was carried to the table.

"Don't you *dare* drop this," Conor warned, handing Emma two plates of oysters arranged artfully on a layer of ice.

"Aye aye, captain." She backed through the swinging doors, a plate in each hand.

She set one of the plates down in front of Madison, who was sitting across from Krupin and his wife. Madison wrinkled her nose at the sight of it.

"I despise oysters," she announced. "Take them away." Then, as if realizing who she was talking to, she giggled and touched Emma's arm. "Sorry, Amy. I didn't mean to sound like a dick."

Emma didn't correct her about the name. "Don't worry," she said, breezily sweeping the plate away and setting it in front of the footballer instead. "I'll bring you something else."

Conor stared at her with disbelief when she asked for a cheese sandwich.

"It's for Madison. She *has* to eat something," Emma told him, firmly.

"That girl cannae hold her drink," he grumbled, but he ordered Lawrence to make the sandwich.

However, when Emma set it in front of her a few minutes later, Madison barely seemed to notice. Her attention was focused on Volkov, who was talking eagerly with Krupin in Russian. She seemed utterly absorbed in the conversation, which didn't make any sense as Emma knew she didn't speak the language.

Later, when she brought in the main course, Emma overheard Krupin's wife having an excruciating conversation with Madison.

"You look so young, you must still be in school. What do you study?" the older woman asked.

"Sex and drugs," replied Madison, with a giggle. "Also booze. But never oysters."

Krupin's wife frowned and turned away.

Once everyone had been served their meal, a brief peace descended. The entire crew was on deck now; even the yacht's captain and first mate—who normally avoided all gatherings—were sitting with Grogan and the helicopter pilot in the inside lounge, talking and eating.

It struck Emma suddenly that if everyone was on deck, nobody at all was below.

Catching Jason at the bar, she said, "I need to dash to the loo. Is this a good time?"

With a glance at the diners, he nodded. "Go ahead. Take ten minutes. When you get back, tell Sara to go. Things will get busy again after they eat and I'll need you both up here."

Emma ran to the stairs and headed down to the staff quarters. She felt uncomfortable about leaving Madison unguarded, but she couldn't let this opportunity go.

Bypassing her own room, she headed straight to Sara's door. After casting a quick glance over her shoulder, she let herself in.

As always, the tiny room was chaotic—clothes were slung everywhere. A makeup bag had spilled out onto the dresser. But Sara's phone lay in its usual place on the rumpled duvet.

She sat on the bed and pulled off her shoe, teasing the SIM card loose from its hiding place. After removing Sara's SIM, she slid the Agency's replacement in.

When the device finished churning the screen looked exactly like the one on the phone Volkov had taken from her on that first day.

Only seven minutes remained before she needed to be back on deck.

Emma didn't dare call directly in case anyone happened to pass and hear her voice. Instead she sent a secure message:

Eden in St. Tropez. Gold Dust 1 met wife and son in town yesterday address 32981 Les Parcs. Wife may be in hiding? Access code required for Dottling safe. Found this partial number in GD1's bedroom: 086732. Meaning unknown.

Sergei Krupin is on Eden now. Could be Gold Dust 3, but no chemistry with GD1. No other possibles at this time. Request urgent response on safe.

The reply came back in seconds.

Message received. Await instructions.

Emma sat on Sara's bed, holding the phone very tightly. She had five minutes left. Less, if Grogan noticed she was missing and came looking for her.

The person at the other end of the phone could have been anyone at the Agency, but somehow she knew it was Ripley. It was like him to be methodical even under pressure. The Dottling code would be hard to find.

The air in the room felt suddenly close, and she wiped the sweat from her forehead.

"Come on, Rip," she whispered. But no message came.

When five minutes had passed, she didn't dare risk waiting any longer. Just as she was opening the SIM holder, though, a message opened.

Dottling code 10-01-09-1969. Krupin's presence a surprise. Files show no connections with Volkov. Keep watch. Is this phone safe?

Emma typed quickly.

Negative. Phone stolen, must return. Will try and contact again.

There was no time left. She pulled out the SIM card, dropping it on the floor in her haste and swearing as she picked it up and put it back in her shoe before returning Sara's SIM to the phone. The secure messages would leave no traces. It would be as if she'd never touched the device.

Seconds later, she was racing across the tiny room and out the door.

By the time she walked back up to the bar deck, the sun was dipping below the horizon, sending spectacular sheets of silken vermilion across the sea and the darkening sky.

She was three minutes late, but Jason didn't notice. His attention was focused on Madison. In fact, everyone was looking at Madison.

"All you do is speak Russian," she was slurring accusingly. "Russian. Russian. *Russian.*"

In the chair next to her, Volkov watched her with a look of disgust. "Don't be a child."

"Why not? You treat me like one." Madison waved an empty glass at him. "Might as well fulfill my role."

"Oh no," Emma whispered.

Sara sidled up to her and hissed in her ear. "She's losing it. Moaning about how bored she is. Andrei's mortified."

"Has she eaten anything?" Emma asked quietly.

"Not unless champagne is food."

"We have to get her out of here," Emma whispered.

Sara made a helpless gesture. They both knew Madison well enough to know she'd resist if they tried to intervene.

Emma turned to Jason, who was standing near the bar, watching the scene with a frozen expression of shock.

At the table, Madison demanded, "Why doesn't anyone speak even a little English?"

"I do." The footballer's girlfriend raised her hand, but her boyfriend batted it down quickly and whispered something in her ear. The two had seemed to be forming an alliance with Madison at the pool, but they were now distancing themselves from the damage.

All of the other Russians seemed to find the scene amusing,

until Krupin made the unfortunate decision to intervene. His wife watched doubtfully as he leaned closer to Madison.

"I'm sorry if we've been rude," he told her in careful English. "It's easier sometimes to speak a language you are familiar with."

If he thought this would help, he was wrong.

Madison held up her hand in front of his face. "I'm so *bored* of Russians." She looked at her empty glass and craned her neck to see the bar. "Refill please!"

Again, Emma and Sara turned to look at Jason, whose eyes were now focused on Volkov.

Meeting Jason's gaze, Volkov shook his head.

"No one is to serve her." Jason spoke quietly. Emma could see his hands clenching at his sides.

"I just want to have some fun," Madison informed Krupin. "Andrei's so boring. And you're all so dull. All you care about is money and stupid clothes." She looked at the woman next to her as if seeing her for the first time. "Do you care about anything except money?"

"What else is there?" The woman's voice dripped amusement and contempt.

"There's life," Madison cried, her voice high and emotional. "There's joy. There's love. What about love? You probably think this is love." She held up her right hand, where the huge ring Andrei had given her glittered like ice. "But this isn't love. It's a bribe. A bribe to forget. A bribe to behave. Well, I can't be bought."

Before anyone could stop her, she ripped the ring from her finger and threw it overboard.

There was a collective gasp as they watched the glittering jewel sail through the air and drop into the sea.

"Oh my God." The footballer's girlfriend jumped up and raced to the rail. "Where is it? Did it sink?"

"Enough." Volkov roared. He stood over Madison, who looked up at him with confusion, as if she'd forgotten he was there. "Are you mad?" His face was tinged purple. "Why would you do that?"

He motioned to Grogan, who stood impassively near the lounge doors, watching the scene play out.

"Madison is very tired," Volkov told him roughly. "She wishes to rest. Take her to the suite."

Grogan was beside Madison in an instant, grabbing her arm in a tight grip and manhandling her from her chair.

"No!" Madison's face turned scarlet as he dragged her up. "Let go of me!"

She struggled to wrench herself free of his hold, making the table shake violently, sending wine sloshing across the pristine white linen. The other guests scrambled out of their chairs and backed away as Grogan grasped Madison by her wrists. In the process she managed to scrape her nails across his cheek, leaving livid slashes. With an unpleasant smile, he lifted her bodily and began half-carrying her away.

"Time to leave the ball, princess," he grunted.

Madison screamed and reached for anything that would help her, smashing glasses and sending her chair flying onto its back with a crash that made everyone jump.

Sara gasped, reaching unconsciously for Emma's arm.

"Someone help me," Madison pleaded, twisting in Cal's grip to look back. Her eyes fixed on Emma's. "Jessica! Help me!"

Emma knew anything she did now might blow her cover, but she couldn't stand by. She ran across the deck and reached out for Madison, who gripped her hand.

"Help me," Madison whimpered.

"What the hell are you doing?" Grogan demanded, yanking Madison's hand free of Emma's.

"Just making sure she's OK," Emma said.

Grogan fixed her with a look of searing suspicion. "Why don't you mind your own business?"

As he strode away across the deck, they all clearly heard Madison pleading. "Please help me. I don't want to die."

Then Grogan wrestled her into the lounge and the doors closed behind them.

15

For a long, silent moment, nobody moved. Then Jason shoved a bottle of champagne into Emma's hands. His expression was fierce, almost desperate.

"Quick," he hissed. "Refill everyone's glasses. Sara, get the desserts. Go."

White-faced, Sara raced across the deck, the thumping of her rubber-soled shoes loud in the breathless quiet.

Emma headed straight to Krupin's seat. "More champagne?"

He glanced up, and she found herself looking into the coldest pair of eyes she'd ever seen. It was like staring at ice.

He held a hand over the top of his glass. "Just coffee, please." He glanced at Volkov, who was sitting silently a few feet away, his face dark and brooding. "I think everyone could use coffee."

"Not me." The footballer's girlfriend waved her glass at Emma merrily. "I need a drink after all that."

"Shush." Her boyfriend gave her a warning look, but as Emma filled their glasses she could see he was fighting back laughter. He added, "He'll hear."

"Oops." She covered her lips with her fingertips. "But surely he knows."

Emma drew in a breath. They were openly ridiculing Volkov in his home.

They spoke Russian now—Volkov's language. As if to make absolutely certain he understood every word.

She found herself feeling unexpected sympathy for the yacht's owner. With friends like these, who needed enemies?

Expressionless, she continued to make her way around the table, politely filling glasses. But Volkov's guests were only getting started.

"That was quite a performance," someone said. "Americans are so hysterical. I think they are spoiled."

"That ring wasn't real, was it?" Krupin's wife asked Volkov. "If it was real you could hire a diver . . ."

Volkov jumped to his feet abruptly.

Everyone turned to look at him. For a long, furious instant, he stared at them with loathing, before storming away, slamming through the double doors into the lounge.

Another startled silence swept over the group. Then, the footballer's girlfriend began to giggle. "I'm just so bored," she exclaimed, making a fair attempt at Madison's California accent. Soon the others were laughing, too. Even Krupin chuckled quietly.

"Such a performance," his wife clucked, shaking her head.

They were still laughing when Sara rushed back from the kitchen, her cheeks flushed, clutching a tray of tiny cakes. Her gaze skated from the Russians' amused faces to Andrei's fallen chair to Emma, who gave her a warning look.

"Dessert!" Sara announced, with desperate chirpiness, and began placing a delicate plate in front of every guest.

Conor had worked on the pastries all morning—each was a piece of art, accented with ruby glimmers of strawberries and thick swirls of cream.

Tucking the champagne bottle inside her left elbow, Emma paused next to Krupin. It seemed to her he had absorbed Volkov's humiliation like oxygen. He looked flushed and sated, a slight, cold smile lingering on his thin lips.

"I'll go and get your coffee now. Would you like espresso?" she asked.

But he shook his head and stood, dropping his napkin on his chair with disdain. "I have had enough. It was a mistake to come here." He had a powerful voice—a growl that carried above the shallow titters around him. "I thought Andrei Volkov was a serious man. I was mistaken."

At some point, probably when Madison had been taken away, the *Eden*'s captain and first officer had disappeared from the deck, but the helicopter pilot still sat at the table near the kitchen. Turning to him, Krupin made an authoritative gesture. "We're leaving."

His wife stood to follow him, along with the footballer's girlfriend.

"Give me a second. I'm going to eat this first," the footballer said, digging a fork into the delicate flesh of the cake. "I might as well get something out of this weird party."

Still laughing, the glamorous array of guests crowded onto the helicopter and the long, lean powerboat and headed back to Saint-Tropez and the mansions and hotels that glittered across the bay as if carved from glass.

When the thud of the rotors faded in the distance, a heavy quiet seemed to spread across the water. In the stillness, Emma could hear waves lapping against the sides of the boat, and she realized it was the first time she'd heard that sound since they'd arrived. Everything until now had been music, activity, and loud laughter.

She was alone. Jason was still on the helipad, while Sara had gone below to help people onto the powerboat. The kitchen crew were cleaning up in uncharacteristic silence.

The table still looked elegant beneath the cheerful festoon lights. From a distance the scene might have looked beautiful. But it was very ugly indeed.

Emma was certain of only one thing: Krupin was not in league with Volkov, and therefore not part of Gold Dust. In fact, he didn't appear to know Volkov at all.

That, at least, was useful information. The rest, though, was worrying.

Madison could be in real danger. Volkov was furious, and he and Grogan were capable of anything. If Volkov wanted revenge, he would take it. Brutally.

This put Emma in a difficult position. If she tried to help Madison, the whole operation could be exposed. There was too much at stake for her to take that risk. She had the code for the safe now. If she remained on the *Eden*, she might yet find proof of Volkov's weapons dealing and his involvement in Stephen Garrick's murder. She could discover who he was working with. That alone could save thousands of lives.

But the idea of doing nothing while something awful happened to Madison didn't sit easy with her.

"The boat is gone," Sara announced, emerging from stairs. "All the vipers have returned to the nest."

"Well," Emma said, glancing back at the detritus of the party. "That could have gone better."

Sara gave the table a mournful look. "Everything was so beautiful, too. What a waste." Picking up a tray from behind the bar, she began clearing plates. "God, those cakes were gorgeous." Glancing around first to make sure no one was near, she plucked a strawberry from one untouched plate and popped it in her mouth.

She closed her eyes and sighed. "It's utterly delicious. None of them even tasted it."

"That footballer did," Emma said, picking up a tray to help. "He was the only one I almost liked."

"Seriously, though." Sara paused and glanced at her. "I'm worried about Madison. I didn't like the way Cal dragged her out of here."

"What do you think they'll do to her?" Emma asked.

Sara's expression grew grave. "I don't know. But if I were her, I'd get off this boat and never come back."

By the time they'd restored the deck to its usual state, it was nearly ten o'clock.

A dark cloud seemed to have settled on the *Eden*. Volkov had retreated to his office and did not reappear. Grogan was nowhere to be seen. There was no sign of Madison.

Everything was dangerously still.

Emma walked with Sara to her room, lingering in the doorway as she picked her phone up from the bed to check her messages. There was no indication that she suspected anyone had been in here.

"Do you want to stay and hang out?" Sara asked hopefully. "We can get food from the kitchen and hide together."

"To be honest, I think I'm just going to get some rest." Emma stifled a yawn.

"I don't blame you. It's been a hideous day." Sara looked around the cluttered space as if seeing it for the first time. "God, my room is such a mess. My mum would be furious. Maybe someday I'll clean it."

Emma started to laugh but cut it short when she saw Jason striding down the narrow corridor, his face tense. He stopped on the way to knock on Conor's door.

"I need a word with all of you," he said, looking at Emma. "Can you come out here?"

Conor and Lawrence emerged from their rooms. Conor was still in his kitchen whites, but Lawrence had changed into shorts.

Sara and Emma joined them. The hallway was so narrow,

they couldn't cluster together, but had to arrange themselves in a jagged line.

"We're sailing first thing in the morning," Jason informed them brusquely. "We need to get the deck ready before we go to bed."

"You're joking." Conor's brow creased. "We just got here."

"And now we're leaving." Jason's tone was clipped. He looked tired and unhappy.

"Where are we going?" Emma asked.

He glanced at her. "Barcelona."

Emma's stomach lurched. They were heading farther away from what little support she had.

Sara stepped closer to Jason. "How's Andrei?"

"Exactly as you'd expect," Jason said curtly. "Not happy at all."

"What about Madison?" Emma asked.

Jason shot her an unfriendly look. "What about her? She's probably sleeping it off. Who cares?"

"Should we check on her?" Sara suggested. "I could bring her some food."

"Look," Jason said irritably. "She's not our problem. Let Andrei and Cal deal with her. I just need the kitchen and bar sail-ready before you go to bed." Softening his tone slightly, he added, "Once the deck is squared away you can all get some rest. There's no service in the morning. So get this done and then you can crash."

His message delivered, he headed back down the corridor. Behind his back, the four crew members exchanged long looks.

"Just another day in paradise," Lawrence said, turning toward his room.

"This is a madhouse," was Conor's assessment.

Sara glanced at Emma and sighed. "Let's get going."

On the darkened bar deck, they moved quickly, stowing loose objects away, removing vases of flowers from the lounge and putting them in cupboards. It was Emma's first time preparing to sail, and Sara guided her through the steps.

Locking down the bar proved to be a simple process. The shelves were all equipped with an inventive system of metal braces that kept the bottles in place so they wouldn't break in heavy seas. The entire bar was built on hinges, so it could be folded inward, leaving nothing exposed to wind and waves.

As they worked, Emma said, "This seems really sudden. Is this normal?"

Sara glanced over her shoulder to make sure nobody was near, before saying quietly, "I can't remember this *ever* happening. There's always warning before we sail." She gave Emma a dark look. "Andrei must really be losing it."

When they'd finished their work, Sara got some food from the kitchen and headed back to her room, but Emma lingered on deck. She filled time with last-minute jobs — finding small things to do that naturally led her down to the corridor outside Volkov's bedroom.

She paused beside the door and listened. She could hear nothing at all from within.

Tentatively, she reached out a hand and tested the handle. It was locked.

"Madison?" she hissed, pressing her face close to the polished wood. "Are you OK?"

No one replied.

Reluctantly, she wandered back up to the bar deck, taking her time. She knew she should go back to her cabin but still she lingered in the warm night air. Something wasn't right. She couldn't define it, but she could sense it.

She headed to the kitchen and grabbed an apple and a bottle of water. After a moment's thought, she unlatched a drawer and surveyed the contents before choosing a small, very sharp knife, which she slid into her right shoe.

After that, she settled on a chair on the pool deck, cloaked in darkness. And she waited.

Sound carries strangely across the water. For a while, Emma heard the soft whisper of music drifting on the breeze from another boat, or perhaps from the streets of Saint-Tropez. Sometimes she heard faint voices. But mostly things were quiet.

Just after midnight, a scream split the silence.

Emma sat up straight and held her breath. It sounded close, but it was impossible to know where it had come from. This boat? Another yacht?

Nearly twenty minutes passed before she noticed movement. More of a shift in the air than anything. And then a scuffing sound, like something being dragged.

Soundlessly, she stepped to the rail and leaned over, peering into the darkness below.

"Be careful," someone hissed.

The voice seemed to be on the lowest level, at the aft deck, just out of view. Emma leaned farther, hanging over the rail.

The *Eden*'s launch should have been raised out of the water, ready for tomorrow's journey, but it was still moored to the aft deck, as if someone was about to leave.

Emma tiptoed down the narrow walkway along the side of the vessel, until she was just above the speedboat.

A security light at the back of the vessel caught Jason's face as he walked from the aft deck onto the powerboat. He was holding something white and heavy. It sagged in his arms.

It took Emma a moment to realize she was looking at Madison, in her white silk dressing gown. She wasn't moving.

Emma's heart stuttered.

Jason was holding Madison's shoulders. As he backed onto the boat, he stumbled, and nearly dropped her.

"Watch where you're going, you prat." Grogan stepped into the light, holding her legs. "Put her over there."

They set Madison down at an angle on one of the smooth

leather seats. Her head dropped back; her face looked straight up at Emma. Her eyes were closed, and her perfect skin gleamed alabaster pale.

Emma could see no blood staining the white silk. No visible wounds on her hands or wrists. But she was so still.

For the second time that day, Emma felt trapped. Ripley would want her to stay right here, silent and watching. Grogan was already suspicious of her. She couldn't risk making that worse.

But Madison was, as far as she could tell, an innocent in this. If she was alive, Emma had to do something to help her.

She ran to the staircase and hurtled down it, rubber-soled shoes nearly silent on the steep treads. When she neared the aft deck, she stepped casually out into the light, running straight into Jason.

"Oh, hey," she said, as if surprised.

Caught in the act of untying the lines to the launch, Jason froze. His eyes shifted nervously to Madison's unconscious form.

Grogan looked up from the steering console. "What the fuck are you doing snooping around?" he growled, suspicious and hostile.

"I was upstairs and I heard voices. What's going on?" Emma's tone was loose and puzzled. Her gaze fell on Madison and she froze. "Oh my God. What happened? Is Madison OK?"

Before either man could stop her, she stepped onto the boat, running to Madison's side.

"Madison, can you hear me?" she said, grabbing her wrist.

The girl's eyes didn't open. Beneath Emma's fingers her skin was unnaturally cool. She couldn't feel a pulse.

Grogan slapped her hand away. "Get out of here," he growled.

Emma stood to face him. "What's the matter with her?"

"She's fine." Jason stepped between them, holding up his hands. "She took too many sleeping pills. Cal's taking her to Saint-Tropez to see a doctor."

Emma thought of the scream she'd heard, and wondered what they'd given her.

"I should go with her," she announced. "She'd want a woman there."

Grogan fixed her with a look that seemed to see through her and straight to the doors of the Vernon Institute back in London.

"I don't know what you think you're doing," he said evenly. "But you need to get off this boat before I knock you out of it."

Emma turned to Jason, but he shook his head. "You really should go to your room."

Still she hesitated. She could feel the metal of the knife pressing against her foot inside her shoe. She could use it, but what was the point? She could easily kill Jason, and if she fought Cal, she might win, but even if she did, her work here would be ruined.

And it was too late to save Madison.

Straightening, she walked back to the aft deck, with Jason right behind her. "I hope she's OK," she said. "I just wanted to check . . ."

Grogan still watched her with that emotionless stare. "It's not your job to check on anything except cocktails," he said. Then turning to Jason, "Release those bloody lines and let me get this over with."

Jason did as he was told.

Stepping behind the wheel, Grogan jutted his thumb at Emma. "I'll deal with you tomorrow."

The security light turned the expression on his scarred face into a gargoyle's leer as the engine started with a low, ominous growl. Grogan pushed up the throttle, and the boat shot across the water.

All Emma could do was watch in silence as the engine blurred into the sound of the waves, and then disappeared into the dark night.

16

As soon as the powerboat was gone, Jason rounded on Emma.

"It's one in the morning, for God's sake," he told her hotly. "Why are you prowling around?"

"I couldn't sleep," Emma said. "I went up to sit by the pool and do some meditation. When I heard voices I came down to see what was happening."

"Meditation." His tone was doubtful.

Emma didn't blink. "It helps me sleep." But she had questions of her own. "What did Madison take? Is she going to be OK? I know a thing or two about overdoses . . ."

He held up a hand, cutting her off. "She's going to a doctor. They'll handle it."

"Well, good," Emma said, after a long pause. "Because she looked terrible."

Perhaps realizing his anger wasn't helping, Jason suddenly turned on the charm. "Look," he said, lowering his voice confidentially. "Madison has a lot of problems. She takes too many drugs and she drinks too much. I mean, you've seen her, right? The stuff in her room? Today she went too far. Andrei just wants her to get the help she needs."

The nice act made Emma's skin crawl, but she kept her voice neutral. "Where is Cal taking her?"

He had his answer ready. "A private hospital on the mainland. Andrei's already called her parents to let them know." Jason ran a tired hand across his forehead. "It's a bastard of a situation, if I'm honest. I really liked her."

Liked. Past tense.

"Well, I'm glad she's going to get help," she made herself say. "Today was horrible."

"Yeah. It was pretty hairy." His eyes darted to hers and away. "Look, I've still got some stuff to do. You'd better get back to your cabin."

Emma didn't argue. She had something she needed to do, too.

She raced back upstairs. The narrow staff corridor was empty, but the fluorescent lights glowed brightly. For safety, they were never turned off. Leaning against the doorframe, she tapped on Sara's door.

"Sara?" she whispered. "It's Jess." Cautiously she cracked the door open. As she'd suspected, Sara wasn't asleep. She was watching TV on her tablet with headphones. When Emma stepped into the room, Sara nearly jumped out of her skin.

"Jesus on a *bicycle*," she gasped, her tablet sliding from her fingers to the floor.

"I'm so sorry." Emma held up her hands. "I didn't mean to scare you. But something's happened and you need to know."

Talking quickly, she told her about Madison, leaving out her suspicions that she'd been murdered. "Jason said she overdosed. They were taking her to a doctor but . . . she looked bad."

Sara's eyes filled with tears. "That poor girl. I just feel so sorry for her."

"I wondered if I could borrow your phone? Mine isn't working and I want to call Annabel right now and tell her what's going on," Emma said. "I know it's late but I think she needs to know."

She'd never told Sara that Volkov had taken her phone, so she had to make up an excuse, and this seemed as good as any.

"Of course." Sara grabbed the phone off the duvet and held it out to her. "Let me know what she says."

Emma took the phone to her room and closed the door. Kicking off her shoe, she pulled out the SIM and replaced the one in the phone, and dialed the emergency number.

The phone rang three times before Jon answered. "Emma? What's wrong?"

Emma's chest tightened. She hadn't realized until then how much she wanted to hear his voice.

"They took Madison off the yacht on the powerboat ten minutes ago. Cal and Jason carried her. I think she's dead. They said she overdosed, but I'm pretty sure I heard her scream. If she did overdose, I don't think it was her idea." The words poured out in a rush. "They said they were taking her to hospital, but I don't believe them. I think they're going to dump her body. Someone needs to notify French police, coast guard—"

"Slow down, slow down," Jon interrupted. "Why would they do this? Did something happen today?"

Emma pressed her fingertips against her temple. "She caused a scene at Volkov's party today. He was furious. She humiliated him in front of Sergei Krupin."

Jon swore softly. "Right," he said. "We'll get French police and coast guard on it straightaway. We'll also call the hospitals. What about you? It sounds like it's getting rough out there."

"I'm fine for now," she said, hoping it was true.

"What about Grogan?" Jon asked. "Is he still buying you as Jessica?"

Emma hesitated, thinking of the way the bodyguard had glared at her.

"He's suspicious," she said after a moment. "But I think I'm safe."

There was a brief silence before Jon said, "If you need to come off the *Eden*, can you get this phone again?"

"Yes," she said. "I can get it when I need it."

"Good." There was a faint hint of relief in his voice. "Is there anything else I should know?"

Emma's throat was so tight it was hard for her to speak. "I couldn't save her," she said softly. "I couldn't do anything."

"Listen, Emma. You did the right thing." Jon's voice was low and steady. "Whatever happened to Madison, it's not on you. We're dealing with a much bigger cause here."

Emma pressed her fingertips against her eyelids. "I just felt . . . helpless."

"You did everything right. And you're still on the boat. The operation is still in play," he reminded her. "We need proof about the chemical weapons Volkov is peddling. We have to know who's helping him. We can stop them. *You* can stop them. We could save many lives." He paused. "And we don't know that Madison is dead. Give me time to find out what I can."

Emma didn't argue. But she'd seen the awful blankness in Cal Grogan's face. She'd felt the stillness of Madison's veins. And she knew the truth.

After she returned the phone to Sara, they talked for a long time, both of them unnerved.

"What did Annabel say?" Sara asked.

"She's horrified," Emma told her. "She's going to speak to Andrei and find out what happened."

Sara pulled a pillow into her lap and held it tightly. "I'm starting to hate this place."

"Yeah," Emma said. "Me too."

It was nearly dawn by the time she returned to her room. She was climbing into bed when she heard the rumble of the power-boat returning.

She ran to the window to look out. The sky was silvering with the first hints of light. In the faint glow, she saw the launch, empty, save for Grogan, his broad, muscular shoulders hunched over the wheel as he stared straight ahead.

When she woke later that morning, she sensed something was different. In the hazy unreality between sleep and wakefulness everything in the tiny bedroom looked just as it should. Except the hairbrush on the dresser was moving.

As she watched, it shifted to the left. And then, a second later, it slid back to the right.

The bathrobe hanging from the back of the door swung gently, as if caught in an invisible breeze.

The *Eden* was moving.

Emma dressed quickly, slipping the knife into her shoe before heading upstairs.

The bar deck was deserted. She lurched to the rail and stood gazing out across the blue sea. The beauty made her chest feel hollow. The last time she'd done this, Madison had been with her.

She was surprised by how hard this was hitting her. She felt it like a personal failure and more. In any other circumstances, she might have found a way to save her. But out here, there'd been no way.

As she watched, the waves seemed to take on a new form, arcing and diving like living things. Emma's breath caught. It was a school of dolphins—swimming ahead and around the bow of the yacht, moving with power and tremendous grace, as fluid as the water.

The sight was breathtaking.

Madison would have loved this, Emma thought. The realization seemed to fire some emotional alchemy inside her, and her pain turned to anger. Grogan and Volkov were running away from their crimes again.

She would stop them. She would do whatever it took to make them all pay.

Straightening her shoulders, she let go of the rail.

In the kitchen, the cooks had left breakfast out for the crew, although there was less of it than usual—just cereal and fruit. Emma poured herself a strong cup of tea.

Although she had little appetite, she made a bowl of cereal, spilling the milk everywhere when the yacht pitched to one side. She had to hold her tea up to stop it slopping as she cleaned up the mess she'd already made. She was just finishing when the ship's captain, in full white-and-blue uniform, walked through the door with easy balance.

"Oh good," he said, seeing the mug in her hand. "I'm dying for a cuppa."

Emma gestured at the kettle. "It's all yours.

"I'm Jess, by the way," she added. "I don't think we've been properly introduced."

"Robert." He reached out to shake her hand. Intelligent blue eyes considering her cautiously before he turned to switch on the kettle.

"Do I call you Robert or Captain?" she asked, forcing a light tone. "I don't know the etiquette."

"Robert is fine unless you're on the bridge. There, I'm Captain to everyone." His voice was pleasantly deep.

In her briefing, she'd been told Robert kept his distance from Volkov, and wanted to know nothing about his employer's activities. But it seemed to Emma, if he was accepting Volkov's money, Robert was part of Volkov's operation, whether he liked it or not. And he needed to know what had happened.

"I was just wondering if the launch made it back last night," she asked as he placed a teabag in a mug.

Robert looked puzzled. "Back from where?"

"I don't know. Cal took it out last night. Very late." She took a sip of tea. "Also, I don't think Madison's on board anymore."

"Right," he said, his jaw tensing. "Someone needs to update the manifest before we reach Spain. I wasn't informed anyone had left." His tone was deeply disapproving.

"So, you don't know where Madison went?" Emma asked.

"I do not." He added milk and a level teaspoon of sugar and stirred. "Although it's no bad thing that she's gone."

Emma was surprised. "Why do you say that?"

"You were there yesterday." He dropped his teabag in the bin and turned to face her. "Look, you're new, so that's probably the first time you've seen her like that. But it was not out of character. In fact, she's been worse."

"How much worse?"

"Five weeks ago she jumped over the rail in high seas. She could have died," he said. "She needs real help. And she won't find it on the *Eden*."

"Did she see a doctor? Did anyone take her to hospital?"

Robert met her gaze directly. "Andrei Volkov can't have people knowing his mistress tried to kill herself, can he?"

He picked up his mug and headed for the door. "Well, I hope she's gone somewhere better than this place."

The door had closed by the time Emma replied, quietly. "Me too."

The *Eden* arrived at Port Vell outside Barcelona just before noon. The sun was high and hot when they anchored well offshore, and the water was such a sharp shade of blue it hurt Emma's eyes as she stood on the empty pool deck taking in the sprawling city in the distance. In the marina, hundreds of snow-white yachts bobbed in long, glittering rows.

This far out from shore, it was peaceful; the sounds of the city could be heard only faintly in the distance, so the loud voices coming from the stairwell were very clear. It sounded as though Robert was arguing with someone.

Emma moved closer to the doors.

"He's a bloody idiot and I'm risking my career by working for him," the captain was saying furiously. "You can't make up your own rules in one of the most crowded yacht harbors in the world."

"Look, I get it. But it's his boat. And he says we stay offshore." Jason seemed to be struggling to stay calm.

Robert laughed then, a bitter, angry sound. His voice dropped, and Emma stepped closer to the stairs to hear.

"If he thinks he can avoid the law by keeping this boat out of safe harbor, he's wrong. If what he's done is as bad as all that, they could catch him in space."

There was a silence, and then Jason said, "I'm sure I don't have to remind you that you have a contract."

Robert's response was instant. "I've given my notice. In two months, I'm out. Good luck finding a replacement."

Emma could hear the thud of his feet as he walked away.

A few minutes later, Jason's voice came through speakers, flat and emotionless. "All crew to the bar deck for a shore announcement."

Emma took the stairs two at a time to the bar, meeting Sara along the way. The kitchen crew were already there when they stepped onto the deck. Conor stood at the back, his arms folded sullenly, as if he sensed bad news.

The mood was tense—there were no smiles or jokes. Everyone watched Jason warily as he took his spot near the bar. Nobody except Emma knew the truth about Madison, but it was as if they all sensed that something terrible had happened.

Jason kept his expression steady. "We'll be in Barcelona for at least two days," he announced. "The boss has already gone ashore, so you've all got leave."

This was a surprise. Emma glanced over to where Grogan stood at the edge of the group, watching them as Jason continued, "Anyway, you all know the drill. We can have a volunteer to stay aboard or we can draw lots."

Emma thrust her hand up. "I'll stay."

Sara gave her a look of surprise but Emma held her hand steady.

Jason hesitated, but when nobody else's hand rose he nodded slowly.

"Right," he said. "We have our volunteer. Everyone else, meet me on the aft deck at thirteen hundred hours."

"Thanks, Jess." Conor patted her on the shoulder. "I was going to throw Jason overboard if he tried to make me stay, so you saved a man's life."

As the rest of the crew trooped away, Sara turned to Emma. "Why did you volunteer? Are you mad?"

"It only seems fair. I'm newest," Emma explained. "Everyone's in such a bad mood, I thought it might make things better."

Sara couldn't really argue with that. "Well, let me know if you want me to bring you back anything." Then, spotting the captain heading across the deck, she brightened. "What do you think? Should I invite Robert to lunch in town? I have *such* a thing for a man in uniform, and he was so nice in Saint-Tropez."

Emma considered Robert, who'd already removed his uniform and changed into jeans and a button-down shirt. He was handsome in a square-jawed way.

"You should go for it," she decided. "He'd be a fool to say no."

Sara gave a hop of excitement. "I'm going to do it. No guts, no glory." She waved one arm and dashed away. "Robert! Wait a minute."

Emma waited until she was out of sight, and then raced down four flights into the claustrophobically narrow corridor of the staff quarters, where she ran past her own cabin and opened Sara's door.

Everything was just as cluttered as it had been the day before. The tablet had been thrown on the pillow as usual. But the phone was nowhere to be seen.

Hurriedly, Emma shook out the rumpled duvet, and felt beneath the pillows. Nothing.

They weren't allowed phones on deck; it had to be here. Dropping to her knees, she moved blankets aside and noticed a cable snaking down the wall. The phone lay on the floor, where it must have fallen during the night.

She slipped it into her pocket and hurried to the door. As she opened it, she heard voices. The rest of the crew was coming downstairs to get ready.

Forcing herself not to run, Emma walked casually to her room, opening the door just as Conor emerged from the stairwell.

"Hey," he said, waving.

Emma lifted her hand in reply, and then stepped inside, closing the door behind her.

She felt no compunction about taking Sara's phone. She was about to be alone on the *Eden* all afternoon and she intended to use those hours very wisely.

It was time to find the evidence she needed to bring Cal Grogan and Andrei Volkov down.

17

Through the door of her cabin, Emma could hear the others talking and laughing.

A short time later, Conor called from the end of the hallway, "Hurry up, Sara! We're heading out."

Sara shouted back, "Coming. But I've lost my bloody phone."

Other voices joined in with sympathy and advice. But Sara said resignedly, "God knows where it is. It's my own fault—the place is a mess. I'll just have to stick with you lot, I guess."

There was a knock at Emma's door and Sara cracked it open. Emma was on the bed, holding a book.

"Sorry to leave you alone, lovely," Sara said. "Sure you'll be OK?"

Emma held up the book. "I'll be fine. Have fun."

The door closed and the voices faded as they headed down to the launch. A few minutes later she heard the unmistakable rumble of the powerboat engine.

Emma watched through the small cube of a window as the long blue boat swung into view. She ticked the passengers off her list: the captain, the first mate, the two kitchen crew, Sara, and, at the wheel, Jason.

No Cal Grogan.

Emma's stomach dropped.

She watched as the boat cut a white curve in the cobalt sea and powered toward the marina.

Grogan was becoming more of a problem. The fact that he'd decided to stay on the *Eden* was unlikely to be a coincidence. His suspicions about her must have grown after last night.

She leaned back against the wall, her thoughts racing. This had been her best chance to get into Volkov's office. How could she do that with Grogan on board, watching her every move? He was the one person on the boat she was afraid of. He had the training and the bulk to defeat her.

But she couldn't let him stop her from doing her job.

There's no way to teach someone not to be afraid. Fear is an intrinsic part of us. But there are ways to make people forget their fear. Soldiers are taught to think of their enemy as something other than human. Spies are taught to think of their enemy as a traitor.

This training had been particularly effective in Emma's case because even before she joined the Agency she already despised traitors. Her father had been betrayed by someone in Russia he trusted, and that betrayal had led to his execution.

To Emma there was no sin worse than betrayal.

She had a fierce loyalty to her colleagues, and a deep love of her country. In the way of many immigrants, she was more loyal to her adopted land than some whose families had lived there for generations. She didn't feel even slightly Russian. Despite the fact that she spoke the language fluently and Russia had been part of her life since she was born, she was British to her core.

As far as she was concerned, Cal Grogan was a traitor. He was as British as she was, but had spent a decade working for Russian despots. He'd sold whatever soul he had long ago. Something in him had been lost, and he'd filled that space with money and violence.

She had to stop him.

In her mind, she went over the layout of the yacht. Volkov's office was on the same level as the pool deck. Grogan tended to spend his time in the lounge, one level up.

Gradually, a plan began to come together.

Moving quickly, she changed out of her uniform and into a bikini and a pair of shorts. She slid the phone, now containing the Agency's SIM card, into one pocket, and the knife into the other. Grabbing her sunglasses and a book, she slipped out into the corridor and up to the pool deck, where she stretched out on a deckchair.

Now, she just needed Grogan to find her.

Apprehension seemed to make Emma's hearing more acute. Everything sounded loud. The breeze blowing against the upper decks. The jangling of metal against metal. Water splashing. Gulls cawing overhead. The rumble as other boats sped by. And Cal Grogan's heavy footsteps as he walked across the deck toward her.

"Making yourself at home?" he asked with contempt.

Emma lowered the book and looked up at him in surprise. "What are you doing here? I thought you'd gone with the others."

"Thought I'd hang around. Keep an eye on things." He fixed her with a long look that seemed to see all of her plans.

Emma reminded herself that he was an expert in deception. But then, so was she.

"Great!" she said brightly. "The boat's a bit creepy when it's empty."

There was a long pause. "It was kind of funny you coming down to the aft deck last night," he said.

Emma met his gaze. "Funny isn't the word I'd use."

"Uncanny timing, then," he said.

The tension between them thickened until Emma could almost see it in the air. He didn't trust her but he was still trying to understand why, and she wasn't about to help him figure it out.

"Is Madison OK?" she asked, sitting up. "What did the doctors say?"

He looked at her steadily. "They said she needs to get sober. They're going to help her."

"When is she coming back?"

There was a pause.

"I don't see how any of this is your business. They're taking care of her. She's not our problem anymore." Grogan's Adam's apple bobbed as he swallowed.

"It's my business because I like her. We all want Madison back, safe and sound," Emma said pointedly.

"Well, I doubt she's ever coming back after her little performance yesterday. And don't go telling the crew what you saw down there." He thrust a thumb toward the stern of the boat. "Madison wouldn't want people knowing she was like that."

"Sara already knows," she said. "I told her last night."

Grogan stiffened, his scarred face darkening. "Why does every bitch on this boat have such a big mouth?"

His fury was so instant and visceral, it took effort not to flinch in the face of it.

Emma gave him an icy look. "If you need me for anything," she said, with slow deliberation, "I'll be here for the rest of the afternoon."

She leaned back and opened her book.

Still Grogan didn't leave.

Refusing to look up, Emma stared at the page until the words swam.

At last, he turned away. As soon as his heavy tread faded into the stairwell, Emma sat up again. Finding the pool deck empty, she dropped the book to the floor.

In theory, she could walk across the deck, through the glass doors and straight to Volkov's desk. But she didn't dare. Not yet. She needed to know where Grogan had gone.

Leaving her book and sunglasses on the chair, she headed to the staircase. He could have gone down but there was nothing there for him. She was willing to bet he'd gone to the lounge.

She climbed the steep stairs, her bare feet silent.

The bar deck was deserted. Emma strode out across the teak flooring, warm beneath her toes. She tried to see through the dark glass into the indoor lounge but the glare of the light made it impossible. She headed to the kitchen, as if that had always been her destination.

Conor and Lawrence had left it spotless. The appliances gleamed. Emma poured herself a glass of orange juice, taking her time as she listened for any sign of Grogan on the silent boat.

Where was he? If he wasn't up on this deck, she didn't dare break in to the office.

When she walked out on deck a few minutes later, she took her time, stopping to lean against the rail and take in the view of the city across the water. Sara's phone was a dead weight in her pocket, a constant reminder of what she was meant to be doing. What she could not do with Grogan right there.

It could be weeks before she was alone on the *Eden* again.

She had to do it now. If she had to fight Grogan, so be it.

As she turned back toward the stairwell, she heard a voice coming from the lounge.

Through the tinted glass she could just make out Grogan's shape on one of the sofas in the air-conditioned room, a phone pressed against his ear. She couldn't hear what he was saying, but she walked deliberately slowly, making sure he could see her sipping from her glass of juice before retracing her steps to the staircase.

As soon as she reached the stairwell, she broke into a run, flying down the steps to the pool. She set the juice glass on the deck next to her sandals, and dashed through the glass door into the shadowy hallway. The carpet was velvet soft beneath her bare feet as she opened the double doors into Volkov's office.

The adrenaline rush made her head feel light. Doing this with Grogan right above her was insane. But he'd probably be there for at least a few minutes, and she had to take the risk.

Bypassing the desk, Emma headed straight to the cabinet on the wall.

The Dottling was thick-walled and dark. When her fingertips brushed the keypad, the numbers lit up in pale blue.

Every safe has a back-door code—a way to open the device if the owners lose or forget the code they've created. A way for a spy to see what's inside. Ripley had given her the code for this one.

Holding her breath, Emma typed in the sequence she'd memorized yesterday: 1001091969.

For a breathless moment, nothing happened. Then the device whirred and the safe door unlocked with an audible metallic *clunk*.

When she pulled the heavy door ajar, the first thing she saw was money. Lots of it. Multiple thick stacks, all of them bound with paper strips. It had a smell—a kind of sweet-sour scent, like sweat. This, she thought, must be what Volkov had collected in Saint-Tropez.

She reached for a stack of green hundred-euro notes. As she picked it up, two small plastic bags fell out from the safe, landing at her feet. Emma picked them up gingerly. Each held fine white powder.

Emma thought of the mirror on Madison's dresser, with its white powdery residue.

Pulling Sara's phone from her pocket, she took a photo of the drugs and money together. As she worked, she constantly listened for any sound, but this office was well soundproofed, the carpet thick enough to absorb footsteps.

Whatever happened, she wouldn't hear Grogan coming.

She needed to work fast. She'd been in here two minutes so far. She could allow herself no more than five to get what she needed.

Hurriedly, she began pulling documents out of the depths of the safe. Tucked away behind the first stack she spotted her phone, but she left it where it was and worked quickly through the documents, taking pictures of any that looked useful. Most of the paperwork documented the movement of money. Hundreds of thousands of pounds in one account. Millions in another. Some based in London, but others in Dubai, in Moscow, on Jersey.

There was no time to read. She shot each one that looked useful and moved to the next. Still, it was time-consuming work. By the time she finished the first stack and started on the second, the five minutes were up and her nerves were on edge.

But she couldn't go now.

There had to be something incriminating in here. Some proof of the chemical weapons Volkov was selling.

She was flipping through a stack of papers when one document stopped her. It looked like a ledger of sorts. Everything had been written by hand—as if the person keeping track hadn't wanted to put the information on a computer. It held nothing but a series of transactions. The amount of money involved was stunning. Tens of millions of pounds.

Emma took a picture of it, before slowing down to read it.

It looked to her like a register of recent payments. Each line held an amount, who it came from, a code in the middle, and which account it went to. The biggest single transaction was a transfer of fifteen million pounds from a bank in Iran.

The other countries on the list of those making payments to Volkov's company read like a roster of the despotic nations—Iran, Russia, Syria, Brazil, North Korea.

She was sure this was it—the ledger of his sales. This was why Garrick hadn't found what he needed. Because it wasn't on a computer. Volkov had wisely decided no computer was safe.

Even here, though, on paper, the chemical names were in code—he was that cautious.

MI6 could break the code. But one thing was abundantly clear already: nobody would be safe when he was finished with these deals. These were the kinds of countries that wouldn't just buy banned weapons—they'd use them.

As she turned the page, a piece of paper fell out and fluttered to the floor. When she picked it up, Emma noticed it didn't look like the other documents. It was on thicker paper, and the handwriting was different. It looked as if it had been shoved inside the ledger by mistake.

It held a note scrawled in Russian: "I'm getting tired of cleaning up your messes. This must finish it. There's too much at stake." It was signed "Oleg." It was dated two days after Stephen Garrick was murdered.

Gripping the phone tightly, she photographed it.

It had to be from Oleg Federov. Former director of the Russian spy agency, smarter by far than Andrei Volkov, and much more ruthless. This was tangible proof that Federov had given Volkov money directly. Proof that both men knew something had gone wrong. Proof that they were working together.

But was it enough?

Before she could answer the question, a sound stopped her. It was very faint. If she hadn't been standing still, she might have missed it. But in that instant of silence it was clear and unmistakable.

It was the *ding* of the elevator arriving.

18

Working quickly, Emma put the stack of documents back inside the safe, set the money on top and rested the drugs among it. She couldn't hear anything from the hallway. Her own breath seemed so loud to her, she could hear nothing over it as she closed the heavy metal door and typed in the code, her fingers flying across the keypad, begging herself not to make a mistake now.

Maybe he's just going to the pool, she told herself. It's on this level.

Even if he was, that wouldn't save her. There was no way out of this room that wouldn't take her straight to him. She had to hide and wait. But the sleek leather sofas were raised on legs that would expose her if she hid behind them. She wouldn't fit inside the shallow cabinets.

There was only one option.

Carefully, she pushed back the sturdy leather chair and ducked beneath Andrei Volkov's desk.

It was an ostentatious piece and heavily built. It should hide her. But, like the sofas, it was raised off the floor. Her feet would be visible to anyone who walked in. It wouldn't work.

Across the room the air shifted, and she heard the soft shushing sound of the door beginning to swing open.

Bracing her back against one side of the kneehole, she pressed the soles of her bare feet against the other side and raised herself until she was suspended above the ground.

Time seemed to stop. Emma was conscious of the muscles in her legs holding her up. Of her back and her palms pressing hard against the cool wood of the desk. And of the soft sound of someone walking across the room toward her.

Her lungs felt thin and airless.

If he walked behind the desk he'd see her. Odds were he'd kill her. Or at least, he'd try.

She froze. Her heart hammered against her ribs so loudly she was certain he'd hear it.

The footsteps stopped on the opposite side of the desk. For a moment there were no sounds of movement. Just the quick, tight rhythm of his breathing.

The air-conditioning chilled the sweat that ran down Emma's face and dripped onto her torso as she used every sinew to hold herself perfectly still.

A faint tapping sound came from above her head. She frowned as she tried to place it.

It sounded like Grogan was . . . tapping his fingers.

Suddenly, he spoke, his tone harsh. "What are you doing?"

Emma suppressed a gasp.

Then he spoke again.

"You're still outside? Is Volkov in the room with him?" Grogan asked.

He was on the phone.

"Don't let him out of your sight. He'll fucking wander off and it'll be my arse in a sling," Grogan growled. After another pause, he said, "Yeah, I've got to babysit some bint on the boat." A pause and then, "Why? Because she might be babysitting *us* for someone. I'm still trying to figure it out. Anyway. Got to go. Let me know as soon as he comes out."

Emma held her breath as he strode away from the desk.

There was a long pause. The door didn't open.

Why didn't he *leave*?

Emma's legs had begun to quiver from the strain. Droplets of sweat fell from her face and pattered on the carpet beneath her like rain. In the quiet, it sounded far too loud.

Across the room, Grogan muttered something she couldn't make out.

A second later the air shifted. And then, at last, the door clicked shut.

Relief flooded through Emma. Her muscles were burning.

Still, she didn't move. For three long minutes she remained suspended, listening.

Finally, hearing no sound of movement, she dropped her feet to the carpet and crawled out from beneath the desk. The room was empty.

Shaking her legs to try and ease the muscle spasms, she limped to the door and pressed her ear against it. She could hear nothing but the low hush of the air-conditioning and the rumble of a boat passing by. Carefully, she opened the door.

The hallway was clear. Grogan had gone.

Emma paused, deciding what to do next. She couldn't go straight back to the pool—he might see her come out, and she had no reason to be in here.

Instead, she raced to the stairs and skidded down the steep steps to the staff level, and ran to her cabin. In the tiny bathroom, she flushed the toilet, ran water from the tap at full strength, and sang a song loudly.

As the water ran, she took the phone from her pocket and quickly forwarded all of the pictures she'd taken of the documents, money, and drugs to Jon.

She didn't dare call him in case her voice was overheard. In-stead, she messaged him briefly.

I think this is the ledger of chemical weapons sales. Can we break the code?

Jon's reply came back within a minute.

Good work. Passing these to Ripley and the team now. Where are you?

Barcelona. Anchored offshore. Alone on the Eden *with Gro-gan,* she wrote. *Everyone else went into town.*

There was a pause before he responded.

Why is Grogan there? Does he suspect you?

It was an extremely astute question. Emma considered her reply for a moment before typing one word.

Maybe.

The true answer, she knew, was *Yes*. But if she said that, Jon would likely cancel the operation, and it was too soon. She had to find the evidence to stop Volkov. It was worth taking risks for that.

But if she thought a vague reply would satisfy Jon, she was wrong. Barely a second passed before the phone lit up with his response.

Come ashore tomorrow. We need to talk.

Emma swore under her breath. She'd hoped to have another chance to search the yacht. She knew better than to argue, though.

Copy that. Any word on Madison? she asked.

Again, the tell-tale pause before his response.

Nothing. French police are aware.

Emma hated that she'd been right about this. She'd never wanted to be wrong more.

As angry as she was, there wasn't time to say more. Grogan would be looking for her.

She turned the phone off and headed back up the steps, emerg-ing on the pool deck into the full strength of the afternoon sun.

She put on her sunglasses and stretched out her legs, ordering herself to relax; intentionally loosening her tight muscles, un-clenching her hands.

By the time Grogan pushed open the doors and strode out onto the deck fifteen minutes later, she *was* relaxed, her eyes closed, her head resting on the soft cushion of the long, low chair.

"There you are." His tone was accusing.

"What do you mean?" Emma removed the sunglasses and met his stony gaze with a look of confusion.

"Where were you ten minutes ago?"

Her brow creased. "Cal, I've been here all day. The only time I've left the pool was to use the loo and get something to drink."

As she reached for the orange juice glass, his empty eyes stared at her fixedly.

"I've been meaning to ask," he said. "I don't suppose you know anything about Sara's missing phone?"

Emma's stomach clenched but she answered without hesitation. "Not *again*." She gave her voice an exasperated note. "She loses her phone more often than my mum loses her glasses." She raised a hand to shield her eyes. "It's probably in her room."

He didn't blink. "Yeah, well, I've looked in her room. It's not there."

That must be where he'd gone after leaving the office. That would mean he knew she hadn't been in her room, either. She forced her breathing to stay even.

"How can you tell? It's such a mess. It's usually under her bed."

The phone in her pocket suddenly seemed to weigh ten pounds. Why hadn't she returned it before she came upstairs? That had been a mistake. If he insisted on searching her, she was screwed. It still had the Agency SIM card inside. She had to distract him.

"Speaking of phones." Emma swung her legs around and sat up straight, looking at him directly. "I'd like *my* phone back. Andrei said you'd give it to me when we were in port."

He considered her, a slight smile twisting his mouth.

"I don't trust you," he said. "And people I don't trust don't get to use phones on this boat."

"That is ridiculous—" Emma began, but he didn't let her finish.

"If you stole Sara's phone and I find out, you're fired." His voice was as emotionless as his eyes.

"Oh, for God's sake. I didn't steal anything. You're paranoid. And I'm so tired of you pushing me around." Emma jumped to her feet and strode toward the stairs. He let her go, but his mocking voice followed her, like an icy breeze.

"Where are you going to run, Jessica? There's nowhere to go but the sea."

Emma wondered if he'd told Madison the same thing.

She stayed out of his way for the rest of the afternoon. When she got the chance, she returned the phone to Sara's room, leaving it just where she'd found it. After that, she kept to her cabin.

Only when she heard the launch returning, just after six o'clock, did she head up to the bar deck. By then, the low sun was washing the sea and the distant city in an apricot light that gave the day an unreal feel.

Through the open stairwell door, she could hear Sara, Conor, and Lawrence chattering as they climbed up. She was heading over to meet them when the elevator doors opened in the lounge to her right. Volkov stepped out first, followed by Grogan, and then Jason. The three men noticed her at the same time. Everything that followed happened in an instant. Volkov visibly recoiled. Jason gave her a look of cold recognition. But it was Grogan's expression that made Emma's breath catch.

Cal Grogan was smiling.

19

The next morning, the *Eden*'s crew were called to the top deck just after ten o'clock.

Emma hurried up the stairs with the others. After running into Volkov and his henchmen, she'd been too unsettled to rest. Their behavior hadn't made sense. Volkov had seemed almost afraid of her. Jason had been cautious. But Cal Grogan was the one who worried her most. He'd looked triumphant.

Something was very wrong. It was as if, all at once, they all knew she was lying. But how could that be?

The group that gathered on the deck today was smaller than it had been yesterday; Robert and the first mate had both stayed the night in Barcelona. This was normal for them, but their absence somehow made the *Eden* seem more threatening.

Emma wasn't the only one who'd noticed a change. The air was already beginning to simmer, but the mood on deck was chilly.

"I don't want any messing about," Conor announced when

he and Lawrence joined them. "They need to let us off this boat and into a pub."

As he spoke, Grogan and Jason walked out of the lounge together. Grogan positioned himself in front of the double doors as if making certain nobody could escape. Jason stood by the bar, leaning casually against the sun-warmed polished wood in neatly ironed chinos and a Ralph Lauren polo shirt, with the collar raised behind his neck.

Emma had come to loathe his smug, sun-tanned face.

Jason avoided her gaze, focusing his attention on Conor and Lawrence as he said, "We have a new rule for shore leave starting today. Andrei and I will now choose a designated person to stay on board the boat, rather than a volunteer." He paused. "Today that person is Sara."

"What?" Sara's face reddened with instant fury. "I have plans!"

"This is the rule from now on," Jason said evenly. "If you've got a problem, take it up with the boss. Everyone other than Sara, be on the aft deck in an hour. Don't make us wait."

With that, he walked over to join Cal. When the two went inside, Jason looked over his shoulder at her, and Emma saw something furtive in his gaze.

This new rule couldn't be a coincidence. Something had happened yesterday to change things. She'd seen the same warning in their expressions last night. Had Grogan discovered she'd been in Volkov's office? Or was it worse than that?

"Can you believe this?" Sara was distraught. "I was going to meet Robert. We have a date. I hate this place. We're like prisoners on this stupid bloody boat." Fury made her Liverpool accent thicker, sharpening every word. "I've had it, Jess. I bloody have." Turning on her heel, she fled toward the stairs. Conor and Lawrence ran after her, shouting, "Oi! Sara, wait!"

Emma didn't follow. Instead, when they'd gone, she headed

toward the lounge where she could see Grogan and Jason were still talking.

She had to know what they suspected. Or even worse: what they *knew*.

The glass door was still ajar, and she slipped inside, silent as a breeze.

The lounge was the same size and shape as Volkov's office, with long walls of windows through which sunlight spilled onto white carpet and sleek, pale sofas.

The two men stood by the elevator doors, partially screened by a column. Moving soundlessly, Emma stepped closer.

"Why don't we dump her in town and leave her there?" Jason was saying quietly.

"Because first we need to know what she knows," Grogan replied. "Then we can get rid of her."

The cool air turned Emma's skin to ice.

They didn't suspect. They *knew*.

The realization made her feel unsteady. She couldn't seem to breathe. She'd been so careful. There was nothing in her cabin to identify her as anyone other than Jessica Marshall. She had a history—a full legend. The internet was full of Jess Marshall.

And yet, somehow, they knew.

"Why can't *you* watch her?" Jason asked. "You know I'm not good at this part."

"Andrei's business partners are both in town," Grogan said. "Things are a bit tense after London. I have to be with him at the W in case there's trouble; these guys don't fuck around. We need you to handle her."

"Handle her how?" Jason sounded frustrated, maybe even a little scared. "If she is who you say she is—"

"I don't give a damn what you do with her." Cal's voice sharpened. "Take her to a bar. Take her shopping. Get her drunk and fuck her. Not my problem. Just keep an eye on her until we decide what to do with her. I know what I want to do but Andrei's partners insist on being involved. They're still pissed off about London. Like *they* would have handled it better."

The elevator opened, and the two men stepped inside. As their voices faded, Emma leaned forward to catch their last words.

"Why can't she just stay on the boat?" Jason asked. "We could keep an eye on her here."

"Because I don't *trust* her on the boat," Grogan snapped.

Then the doors closed, and they were gone.

An hour later Emma stepped out onto the aft deck dressed in khaki shorts and a short-sleeved top like an ordinary tourist. But there was nothing ordinary about this day. And her knife was in her shoe.

She'd had time to think through the conversation in the lounge and to understand just how screwed she was. The last British agent who'd got in Andrei Volkov's way had ended up folded in a suitcase. The memory of Stephen Garrick's tortured face still sickened her. She couldn't go out like that.

But her choices were all bad. There was only one thing to do: pretend to suspect nothing until they got to land, and then run like hell.

Her skin felt cold. All her senses were alert. She felt every breeze like a razor blade against her skin. Whatever Grogan had said to Jason, she knew they could kill her at any time.

When she walked up to Conor and Lawrence, the chef jutted his thumb at the bag hanging from her shoulder. "Careful with that. There are pickpockets on every bloody corner in this town."

"Oh." She had to force herself to be Jessica Marshall. She had to remember that until she got away, the game was still on.

Feigning concern, she looked doubtfully at him. "I've never been to Barcelona before. Is it dangerous?"

Conor opened his mouth to launch into more details of the city's criminal element but Jason spoke over him. "Actually, Conor's right. This place is pretty rough. Why don't you stick with us? We'll protect you."

Emma, who had suspected this was coming, pulled a travel guide from her bag. "Sara loaned me this. She told me some places I should visit. I think I'm just going to mosey around."

"We can mosey with you," Jason said, his smile betrayed by the firmness of his tone.

Before Emma could refuse, Volkov and Grogan stepped out of the hallway onto the deck. In a suit and tie, Volkov was over-dressed for the heat and his skin was already reddening as he swept past them. When he saw Emma, the piercing recognition in his eyes made her stomach clench. She'd never felt more exposed.

She followed numbly as the others filed onto the launch. The powerboat bobbed beneath their weight, but she was used to walking on water by now.

Grogan took the wheel at the back of the boat. Volkov sat in the smooth leather seat nearby.

As Emma stepped to the front, she could feel Volkov's eyes boring into her back.

As soon as Jason released the lines, Grogan opened the throttle and the boat leaped away from the *Eden*. The roar of the motor made conversation difficult, and Emma welcomed that. She stared at the city in the distance—the crowded beaches, the block-like apartment towers—barely seeing any of it. Her thoughts were racing.

The main question she had was, if Volkov suspected she worked in Intelligence, why hadn't he killed her already? She was certain now that they'd known since last night. She'd seen the look in Volkov's eyes. A kind of furious knowing. The logical thing would have been to kill her immediately, but they hadn't, and that mistake was all she had to hold on to.

How they'd found out didn't matter right now. What mattered was surviving.

She sat stiffly, her hand gripping the arm of the seat, staring straight ahead until the whine of the motor told her Grogan was maneuvering the powerboat into a space between other similar vessels moored alongside a long pier.

Emma dropped one hand toward the knife in her shoe. If Volkov and Grogan were going to grab her and take her somewhere for questioning, it would happen now.

The second the boat stopped, though, the two men strode away without a word.

Emma watched as they headed into the heat, Volkov's hand-tooled shoes gleaming against the damp concrete.

Every molecule in her body told her to run then, but the second she stepped off the boat, Jason bounded up to her with a wide grin. "Ready to see the city?"

He stuck to her side, relentlessly, as she, Conor, and Lawrence walked across the port and out into the tangled city streets. There, they were instantly surrounded by crowds of tourists. Emma searched for a means of escape but, as if he knew what she was doing, Jason stayed right beside her, keeping up a steady line of patter.

Obviously, he was taking Grogan's orders very seriously.

Traffic roared and rumbled in the busy streets and the air had the smoky tang of diesel exhaust, fried food, and brine. After days of isolation on the *Eden*, it was a kind of sensory overload.

All around them, elegant nineteenth-century buildings with their chunky balconies in sun-faded shades of terra-cotta and lemon stood shoulder-to-shoulder with featureless modern structures, squeezing the narrow boulevards.

Emma saw and discarded multiple options for losing Jason. She could have simply run, but she wanted some deniability, just in case she had to go back to the *Eden*. She had to be more subtle.

"It's a gorgeous day. Where should we go?" Jason raised his voice to be heard above the noise. "Bit of sightseeing?"

Conor and Lawrence exchanged glances. "Uh . . . we're going to the pub," Lawrence said.

"Oh, come on," Jason chided, his smile tightening. "It's not even noon. We have to show Jess a bit of the town before we start drinking."

"You do that," Conor said. "We'd prefer to cut to the chase."

"You should go," Emma agreed. "I'm very happy to explore on my own."

But Jason wouldn't back down. "Let's get a taxi and take Jess to a museum first," he suggested. "It'll be fun."

As the three argued with a superficial good humor that barely disguised a distinct underlying bitterness, Emma spotted her chance.

Two tour buses had stopped on a narrow side street just ahead. A large crowd in shorts and T-shirts milled around as one bus unloaded and another prepared to depart. The two slow-moving groups were blocking the way so that other pedestrians had to navigate around them where the two streets met.

A woman in a blue top with a tour company logo displayed prominently on her chest stood near the loading bus desperately urging her group to board.

Jason was still arguing with Conor and Lawrence, who looked increasingly frustrated.

Emma's attention focused on two women talking near one of the tour buses. Both were middle-aged, wearing shorts and tops similar to Emma's. A tour identity badge on a lanyard hung out of a bag thrown carelessly over the shoulder of the woman on the left.

There was no time to plan. Emma had only seconds if this was going to work.

While Jason was distracted by Conor, she darted into the crowd near the tour bus.

"I need everyone on if you're going to the next stop," the tour leader pleaded. She had a British accent, and her short dark brown hair was frizzing in the Spanish heat. "We're already thirty minutes behind schedule."

Pretending to stumble on an uneven paving stone, Emma jostled into the woman with the bag over her shoulder, smoothly slipping the ID out of her bag and into her own pocket.

"I'm so sorry," she said.

"Don't worry." The woman waved the apology away. "This is all such a mess."

"It's incredibly crowded," Emma agreed as she joined the group at the door of the bus.

The woman rolled her eyes. "It's a ridiculous place to park a tour bus, if you ask me."

As they reached the tour guide, Emma flashed her ID very quickly, but the guide didn't even glance at it. "Yes, please hurry," she urged, as Emma climbed the steps.

The other woman dug through her bag. "It must be in here somewhere," she muttered. "I just had it out."

"Never mind. I recognize you. We have to get going." The tour guide rushed her on board and called to the rest of the group behind them, "Please everyone, the bus is leaving."

Within seconds, Emma was in a seat. At the front, the anxious tour leader rounded up the last stragglers. Some were still in the aisle when the doors slammed shut and the tour bus juddered into motion. The relieved tour guide stood at the front.

"Thank you, everyone," she said, wiping her forehead with the back of one hand. "We'll reach our next stop in about ten minutes. After that we have an hour's break. I appreciate your cooperation."

The woman next to Emma nudged her shoulder.

Braced for a confrontation, Emma turned to find a round-faced woman in her sixties, with curly blond hair and glasses, her eyes dancing.

"Can you believe this? Poor Julia," the woman whispered, tilting her head at the tour leader. "This whole tour has been a nightmare."

"It really has," Emma agreed.

The bus rolled past Conor, Jason, and Lawrence, who stood on the corner, looking around the crowded street. Jason was on the phone, his face red with fury.

Emma sagged back into her seat.

She was free.

20

Thirty minutes later she stood on the Plaza de la Sagrada Familia waiting for her burner phone to boot up. Across the verdant square, Gaudí's flamboyant cathedral soared, its extraordinary steeples stretching up toward the sky like beseeching fingers. All around her the square was thronged with tour groups.

She was finding tourists extremely useful. It was so easy to disappear among them.

The screen lit up, and she dialed quickly.

"Yes." Even in that one syllable she recognized Jon's distinctive Scottish voice.

"It's Emma," she said.

"*Emma.*" The surprise and relief in his voice sent a rush of unexpected warmth through her. "Where are you?"

"Barcelona." She lowered her voice. "Listen, I'm burned."

There was a brief silence, and then Jon spoke again, just one word. "How?"

"I don't know. I don't think it was me," she said. "I was careful."

"I don't understand," Jon said. "How else could they have found out who you are? Volkov must have discovered you were in his office."

But Emma had gone over this in her mind again and again, and kept coming back to the same thing—that moment when Volkov, Grogan, and Jason looked at her as they came out of the elevator, after their day out in Barcelona. At that point, Volkov hadn't had a chance to go to his office and find anything moved or changed. They'd only just returned from the city. And they already knew she wasn't who she was pretending to be. She'd seen it in their eyes.

"Whatever happened seemed to occur when Volkov went into Barcelona yesterday," she said. "It's like someone he met that day told him who I was."

"Oh, come on." Jon's voice was dubious. "Who would do that? Are you saying someone on our side betrayed you?"

Emma hesitated. He was right to be skeptical. Only a handful of people in the world knew she was on the *Eden*, and it simply wasn't possible that Ripley or Field would betray her. No, she had to be wrong about that. But then, that raised more questions she couldn't begin to answer right now.

"Look, all I can tell you is, Volkov and Grogan know." Her voice was tight. "I don't know how they found out but I can't go back on the *Eden*. This operation is blown."

"Fuck." He let out a long breath. "Right. I'm going to have to call London. We'll come up with a plan. Where are you exactly?"

Emma looked around. "Near the Sagrada Familia." She told him the name of the street.

"Stay put," Jon ordered. "I'll arrange a pickup. We'll bring you home. And don't worry—we'll find out what happened."

"Actually," Emma said, "there's something I want to do first. I think Volkov has a meeting at the W Hotel here in Barcelona at three o'clock. I want to go."

Jon's response was instant. "Absolutely not. If you're burned we have to get you out."

"I think this might be worth the risk," Emma said. "I overheard Cal talking to Jason. He specifically said Volkov was meeting business *partners*. He used the plural."

"You think it's Gold Dust," Jon said.

"I think all of them are right here in Barcelona today. If I go to this meeting I might see who the third man is." She talked low and fast, her words coming out in a rush. "Look, I know it's dangerous but if we really want to find out what Stephen Garrick discovered, *this* is where we do it. I've got the documents. Now let me get the people."

She was sure Jon would see what she saw. They couldn't pass up this opportunity. He would understand that.

When he spoke again, though, his voice was firm. "No. Stay where you are. We'll arrange a pickup."

The phone went dead.

Emma was stunned. It didn't make sense to pull her out just before that meeting. Yes, it was dangerous, but everything was.

She paced the large, rambling square in front of the eccentric cathedral, barely noticing the heat, the dust, or the crowds. She kept hearing Jon's voice in her head. *"Are you saying someone on our side betrayed you? Who would do that?"*

Who *would* do that?

If someone had told Volkov who she really was, it had to be someone she worked with, and that simply wasn't possible.

Except, a voice in her head reminded her, *you don't trust Ed Masterson. And he has access to everything.*

She recoiled at the thought that Ripley's deputy could do something like this. It seemed insane.

But try though she might, she couldn't let go of the idea.

What if? What if he really was a double agent?

Only once in her career had she ever doubted that she wanted to be a spy, and that had happened last winter during the disastrous operation to rescue the adult son of a Russian scientist. She'd felt betrayed that night. Betrayed by the Agency. Betrayed in particular by Ed Masterson, who'd left her alone with a Russian assassination squad intent on killing her.

She blamed him for the jagged scar on her shoulder that reminded her every day of how close she'd come to death in his naked grab for power.

He'd do anything to have Ripley's job, of that much she was certain. But would he betray his country? And for what? To make Ripley look bad? Or to make a few million pounds? Was he *that* duplicitous?

It wasn't impossible. People had turned traitor for less. Ripley always said that people betrayed their nations for two reasons: money or ideology. The most famous traitors were ideologues, in love with some mythical vision of communism. But the bog standard, everyday kind of traitors—they all did it for money. And there were hundreds of them. It was something the government was always on the lookout for. They searched for it constantly because it happened *all the time.*

A civil servant from the Foreign Office meets a pretty girl who claims to be Polish and eventually turns out to be Russian, and offers him money in exchange for "just a few papers."

Of course, if he hands over the papers, then he's in it for life. Because now the Russians can blackmail him, forcing him to give more and more information, with a constant threat of revealing his illegal actions should he refuse.

But Ed Masterson wouldn't fall for that. He was smart. If he was working for another government, he'd make sure the money was hidden in a safe place. After all, it was his job to investigate people who took and hid Russian money. Who better, then, to know where to hide it himself?

Emma's thoughts were interrupted as a tour bus rolled to a stop nearby and unloaded its burden of tourists in shorts and T-shirts, clutching phones and water bottles, onto the already crowded pavement.

As Emma watched them, she noticed an SUV crawling slowly toward her.

She couldn't say what drew her attention. Somehow it didn't fit in with the normal city traffic. It looked too expensive. The windows were blacked out and she couldn't see the driver.

In his briefing file she'd seen images of Volkov's fleet of vehicles, and this looked exactly like one of his cars.

Emma's pulse began to race.

There was no way he could know where she was, she reasoned with herself. This wasn't a small city. It wasn't his car. All the same, she lowered her head and stepped into the tour group, following them toward the plaza, losing herself in the throngs.

Out of the corner of her eye, she watched as the black Range Rover drove by without slowing.

It was nothing, she told herself when it was gone. But she wasn't entirely convinced of this. There might be a tracker in her clothes—she wouldn't put it past Grogan. Trackers could be very small, and easily planted in a seam. Either way, she couldn't just stand around waiting for Jon to call her back. And she didn't want to leave this town without doing every single thing she could to convict Volkov.

There was only one person on the planet who would understand why she felt like this.

Grabbing the burner phone, she punched in a number only she knew.

Ripley answered without saying hello. "I understand you're burned." The thin layer of frost in his voice was noticeable. "What happened?"

Some part of her wanted to tell him her suspicions about Ed Masterson, but she knew better than that. Ripley was blind when it came to his deputy. He'd forgiven him for what he'd done that night last year, and he expected her to do the same. If she went to him with vague allegations, he'd be furious. She had to take a different approach.

"All I can tell you is Volkov didn't know who I was when he went into Barcelona yesterday, but when he came back he did," she said, adding recklessly, "I think someone told them."

She heard the sound of Ripley's lighter click, the flare of the flame against one of his Dunhill cigarettes, the draw of air. When he spoke, she could hear the smoke in his voice.

"Emma, I'm going to be honest with you, the most likely answer is that you bollixed it."

She flinched as if she'd been slapped. "I didn't. I was careful."

"Everyone makes mistakes. And usually the person making mistakes is the last one to see the breadcrumbs they left leading straight to them." The sympathy in Ripley's tone took the edge off his blunt words. "Cal Grogan is good—we knew that from the start. One small error would have been enough. A paper left in the wrong place in Volkov's office would have done it. It could happen to anyone."

Emma fell silent. There was truth in his words. She'd been methodical, but there hadn't been time to double-check. Still, she just didn't believe this was what had happened.

When she didn't reply, Ripley continued, "Anyway, you must realize that if you screwed up that would be significantly better than the alternative. Because if there's a mole inside our operation we can't trust a single person we work with." He paused. "Jon told me about the Gold Dust meeting at the W Hotel. He's very firm that you shouldn't go. Too dangerous, he says. And I can't say I disagree."

"I know it's risky," Emma said. "But, Ripley, this might be our only chance to find out who Volkov's working with. I've got the documentary proof we need to go after him and Federov. But we need the third man. We need more. We can't pass this up. It's too important."

"Perhaps." Ripley didn't sound convinced. "Jon thinks you're too close to the case. Being burned is a gut-punch. It can throw you off-kilter. He and Andrew think we need to bring you back in now, and find a new approach."

Emma's shoulders slumped. "That would take months. Maybe years. And we're so close. I can handle this. You know I can. Come on, Ripley," she pleaded, "they're meeting in a public place. It's just surveillance. I could do it in my sleep. All I need to do is find out who meets with Volkov then I'll head straight home. None of them will ever know I was there."

She didn't tell him she suspected Cal Grogan had put a tracker in her clothes. She didn't want to confuse matters right now. She could take care of that part. She could take care of everything. She just needed permission.

Ripley fell silent.

"Please," Emma said, with sudden passion. "Those weapons they're selling will kill so many people and someone in our government might be helping them. Let me get the proof."

There was a long moment when she could hear Ripley smoking. Then he said, "If you're certain this is something you wish to do, I need you to take precautions. You must be invisible. They cannot recognize you. If they know who you are, they'll kill you. It's that simple."

Energy rushed through Emma's body.

"I'll be careful," she promised fervently.

"Good. What do you need to make this work?" he asked.

She looked down at her shorts and white sturdy shoes. "I'll have to change my appearance so I can blend in, but I've got time. The meeting isn't for another couple of hours." She paused, thinking of Ed Masterson. He'd want to know what the plan was, in case she crossed lines with Spanish Intelligence or MI6. Ripley would normally tell him everything.

"Listen," she said, "I'd like to keep this meeting need to know."

"Emma." Ripley's voice sharpened. "You can't start doubting your own side without proof."

"I'm aware I might have been burned because of my own actions." Emma chose her words cautiously. "All the same, I want to keep this afternoon off the books. It's only a couple of hours."

"You realize, if we do this, you're on your own? No backup. I can't even tell Jon what you're doing."

"I've been working without backup for *days*," she reminded him with some asperity.

"Touché," he conceded. "But I have conditions. You'll be there for surveillance only. All we need are photographs, so get those and get out. No matter who you see there. You can have no interaction with any of the targets. I'll book you on the five-thirty flight to London. I'll tell Andrew and Jon it's all under control. But you're to take no unnecessary risks. Break that rule and it's your job. Understood?"

Despite the hot day, Emma felt suddenly cold. Ripley didn't make idle threats.

But all she said was, "Understood."

"I expect you in my office at eight o'clock tonight for a debrief," he told her. "Do not be late."

21

The W Hotel was a glass exclamation point of a building on a flat spit of land directly adjacent to the main marina. It was so close to the rows of moored yachts where Emma had first arrived on shore that morning that through the taxi window she could see the *Eden's* distinctive blue-and-cream powerboat tied up on the long pier.

She turned away, straightening the lines of her jacket. After talking to Ripley, she'd headed to a department store and replaced all of her clothing with an outfit that would fit in with the five-star hotel's monied clientele.

She'd dumped her clothes, her bag—everything—in a street bin, in case a tracker had been placed inside them. The only thing she kept was the knife, which she'd tucked into the pocket of the cropped blazer that she wore with snug designer trousers.

The second the cab stopped, a porter raced to open the car door. "Checking in?"

"Just meeting a friend," she told him, giving her voice an American accent. "Thanks, though."

She walked straight through the huge glass doors. The hotel lobby was long and narrow, with soaring ceilings. The scent of roses filled the cool air as she scanned the faces around her. She saw nobody she recognized.

It was a good start.

A young receptionist holding a tablet hurried up to her. "Can I assist you?" she asked, brightly, in English. A name tag pinned to her shoulder identified her as Mina.

"No, thank you," Emma told her, still in a California accent. "I'm meeting a friend for drinks."

Mina hurried away and Emma perched on the edge of a white leather sofa in a shaded corner of the long room and pretended to wait patiently.

It was nearly three o'clock. Volkov's meeting would be starting soon. Of course, there was always the chance he'd decided not to meet once they'd heard about Jess's disappearance. But that seemed unlikely. As far as Volkov was concerned, Jess had no idea where he and his partners were gathering today, and they would have even more reasons to meet now.

The only question was, where in the hotel were they? In a place this size there would be private dining rooms, corporate meeting rooms, and hundreds of guest rooms. They could be anywhere. Somehow, she needed to get into one of the hotel's computers. But the open-plan lobby was too busy and public and the door into the hotel office could only be opened with a swipe card.

Mina seemed to be the main receptionist on duty. She spoke to every person who came in, typing their details into an electronic tablet, which she carried everywhere. She was young and energetic, her dark hair flying as she raced back and forth across the room. When things were quiet, she chatted with anyone who would give her the time—the desk workers, hotel guests, anyone who caught her eye. Twice Emma saw her set the tablet down on a table and walk away from it. Both times, though, there were too many people around for her to risk taking it.

When Mina headed down a wide hallway at a brisk pace, Emma decided to follow.

She kept her distance, but needn't have bothered; the Spanish girl never looked back before turning in to the ladies' toilets.

When Emma walked in, Mina was in a cubicle, humming to herself. The restroom was large and spotless, with a row of rectangular sinks set in front of a long mirror. A glass shelf above the sinks held neat stacks of white cotton hand towels. And Mina's tablet.

Emma grabbed the device and tapped the screen. It wasn't locked.

Mina was still humming as Emma typed Volkov's name into the search bar.

The device churned. The thick walls of the room must weaken the Wi-Fi signal.

The toilet flushed. She could hear the rustle of fabric as Mina begin fixing her clothes.

"Oh, come *on*," Emma whispered.

The screen opened a new window.

Client: Andrei Volkov
Location: EC 26
Time: 15:00 to 17:00
Guests: 3

Mina stopped humming. The cubicle door unlocked with a click.

Hastily, Emma closed the search window and dropped the tablet down on the shelf just as Mina stepped out into the room.

Leaning forward and studying herself in the mirror, Emma smoothed her hair.

Mina walked to the sink and turned the water on. Reaching for the soap, she glanced at Emma with interest.

"Is your friend late?" she asked in Spanish-accented English.

On the shelf, the tablet screen was still glowing, but she didn't notice.

"Always." Emma made her tone weary. "She's just one of those people, you know?"

"I have friends like that." Mina chattered nonstop as she washed her hands and dried them with one of the cotton towels. When she'd finished, she picked up the tablet and tucked it under her arm without ever glancing at it. "Well, I must get to work. I hope your friend comes soon."

"Thanks," Emma said, with a rueful smile, then she paused. "Oh, by the way. A friend of mine had a meeting here recently, and I was thinking of booking the same room. Could you tell me where the EC rooms are?"

Suddenly all business, Mina swung the tablet into her hand. "The EC rooms are great! Very spacious and fully serviced. They're up by the bar on the top floor. Would you like me to show you around? I'm expected at the front desk now, but in about ten minutes . . ."

"No, thank you, that's not necessary," Emma said. "And I'm going up to the bar anyway, so no need to show me. I'll talk to my husband and see what he thinks and then I'll get back to you."

"Well, if you'd like a price list, just let me know." Producing a business card from her pocket, Mina handed it to her. "The top-floor rooms are very popular, so don't leave it too long."

As soon as she was out of sight, Emma headed back to the lobby. Just as she reached it, the front door of the hotel swung open. The man who walked in was solidly built. He wore an

190 I AVA GLASS

expensive suit and a silk tie. His face was milk pale, and his dark hair was threaded with steel gray.

In short, Oleg Federov looked in person exactly as he did in the photograph on the cover of his MI6 file.

Instantly, Emma changed direction, ducking behind a nearby column and pulling out her phone.

Federov had a heavy stride and a slight limp, as if his left leg had been broken at some point and hadn't healed properly. Watching him, Emma tried to remember everything she'd read in Federov's MI6 file. The limp was the result of an injury he'd received when he was in the military, in Chechnya. He'd received a medal for bravery in an assault on a rebel position inside a school that had left dozens dead.

After that he'd risen through the ranks of Russian Intelligence to deputy head of the FSB spy agency. Ten years ago he'd abruptly resigned and joined the shadowy world of Russian finance, making unbelievable profits on investments. Since then, he'd traveled the globe selling drugs and weapons in shady deals that were virtually impossible to trace.

He was fiercely intelligent. And absolutely ruthless.

Mina darted over to him. "Can I assist you, sir?" she asked brightly.

"I have meeting," he told her curtly, his Russian accent thick. "Upstairs."

As he turned and lumbered for the elevators, Emma took his picture and forwarded it to Ripley.

Gold Dust 2 had arrived.

She watched as he pushed the up button and stood waiting, hands loose at his sides.

Tension thrummed in her chest.

Federov was the key to everything. He was the main weapons dealer. The master manipulator. The brains behind the whole operation. This might be her only chance ever to speak to him.

But Ripley had been firm—no engagement. So she watched as the doors opened and he stepped into the elevator.

The second the doors closed she ran to the bank of elevators and punched the up button hard.

A couple walked up just as the elevator arrived. Emma hit the button for the top floor, drumming her fingers impatiently against her leg as the car stopped on the tenth floor to let them off before resuming the climb to the top floor.

The penthouse bar was hypermodern, with curved lip-shaped sofas and an extraordinary view of the sea from enormous windows. Later tonight it would be packed, but right now only half the seats were filled, and the thumping dance music was low.

She spotted Federov almost immediately, limping slowly across the room, one hand clenched as if suppressing pain.

Pretending not to notice him, Emma walked straight to the long bar and sat on a tall stool with her back to the room.

She opened the small bag she carried and pulled out a compact. In the mirror, she watched Federov's reflection as he shuffled with that distinctive, uneven stride toward a door.

Picking up her phone, Emma began taking pictures of the reflected images as Federov opened a sliding door. Andrei Volkov stood just inside. As Federov walked in, he turned eagerly. Aside from the two of them, the room appeared empty.

A waiter carrying a tray of coffee cups walked up to the private room. The two Russian men stepped aside to let him enter.

That was when Emma noticed a shadow of movement at the very edge of her view, and a flash of navy blue, as someone just out of sight moved farther away. Then the door closed and her chance was gone.

Excitement thrummed through her. Quickly she typed a message to Ripley.

Volkov and Federov both here with one other.
Unable to ID 3rd man. Will continue to watch.

She sent it, along with a photo of Volkov and Federov shaking hands.

Ripley's reply was just three pointed words.

Keep your distance.

For over an hour Emma nursed cups of coffee and watched the closed door. Occasionally a waiter passed in or out with food or wine. Each time the doors opened the men were out of view, or the moment was too fleeting. Then the doors would shut and she would be closed out again.

She longed to hear what was happening but she couldn't invent a pretense to go inside—Volkov knew her. Somehow, though, she had to get closer.

Ripley had said not to engage, and she wouldn't. But she would at least make an effort to learn more.

Rising from her chair, she drifted closer to the room, pressing her phone to her ear as if she'd just received a call.

No one paid any attention as she leaned casually against the wall near the sliding doors, listening to raised voices from inside speaking in Russian.

A guttural voice growled, "You cannot expect the British to simply take this without responding. I told you to leave them alone. If you'd listened we would not be in this situation. *You* caused this."

And then Volkov's voice, defensive, "I did what I had to. You do nothing and they kill you. Better to kill them first."

The guttural voice, exasperated and angry, snapped, "Yes, and now the British are so far up our arses they can see out of our eyes. We are in a trap and you cannot see it."

"So for that you took revenge." Volkov's voice was suddenly hot with anger. "You killed my girlfriend. Isn't that enough? Do you need more?"

"This is pointless." A third voice interrupted the two of them. "What's done is done."

Emma's breath caught. This voice spoke Russian with a British accent.

"You need to let this go, Andrei," the voice continued. "You will not win this fight."

There was something familiar about the voice, but in the noise of the bar—the voices and music streaming from speakers—it was impossible to place it. She just couldn't hear it well enough.

She listened intently as the argument in the room continued.

"You think you can tell everyone what to do when you've ruined everything," Volkov snapped. "Both of you have destroyed—"

"Can I help you?"

Emma looked up to find a waiter watching her with a quizzical expression. His eyes moved from her to the door and back again.

"Yes, I'm looking for the ladies' room." It was an absurd statement given where she was, but it was the best she could come up with.

"It's in the corridor beyond the entrance," he told her. "I can show you where."

"Please," she said, biting back her frustration.

She followed him across the bar where he pointed down an empty hallway to a door on the left.

Emma walked toward the door, stopping once the waiter was gone.

She lingered in a shadowed nook, where she could observe the bar at a distance. One hand drifted to the pocket containing the knife she'd stolen from the *Eden*.

The snippet of conversation she'd overheard had confused her. Had Volkov not wanted Madison killed? What had he meant when he'd said the other two men had killed her? Neither of them had come on the *Eden* the night Madison died.

Before she could figure it out, the sliding doors slammed opened and Volkov stormed out in a fury. His jaw was tight, his face red. He headed straight toward the elevator, never glancing in her direction.

Emma's first instinct was to follow. But she needed to know who else was in that room. This could be her only chance to identify the third man.

With some reluctance, she stayed in her hiding place.

Seconds after Volkov walked into the elevator, Federov emerged. His expression was smooth as he walked with his curious lopsided gait to the elevator where he stood, his hands in his pockets, until the elevator arrived.

As Federov disappeared into the elevator, Emma kept her attention fixed on the meeting room. The sliding doors still stood ajar. Nobody else had come out.

The third man must still be in there.

But time passed, and nobody emerged. As Emma watched with increasing puzzlement, a waiter walked into the room, a tray tucked under his arm. A minute later he reappeared, the tray heaped with cups and plates.

Emma stared at him, frowning. A sense of apprehension crept up her spine.

She ran back into the bar, heedless of the attention she might attract, heading straight to the meeting room and stepping inside.

It was empty. Three chairs had been pushed back and left at odd angles. Dirty plates and cups were scattered on the white linen tablecloth, along with half-empty glasses of wine.

Emma's gaze swung to the back of the room, and a door with a green sign marked "SORTIDA."

Sortida. Exit.

Swearing under her breath, she ran across and shoved the door open. Even before she saw it she knew what she'd find — a fire escape spiraling down into the shadows.

"*Dammit.*" She slapped her hand hard against the wall.

A waiter walking in with a tray gave her a startled look. She pushed past him and headed straight to the elevator.

She'd been so close. But she'd been outsmarted.

As the elevator carried her to the ground floor, Emma tried to understand what had just happened. How had they chosen that room? And how had the third man known to go to the trouble of taking the stairs down twenty flights rather than use the elevator?

The preparation, the forethought—it was too good.

Federov had to be behind it all. The canny FSB veteran was taking charge now, and that was going to make everything harder.

She kept thinking of that flash of navy blue, the third man sliding into the shadows at just the right time, and she wanted to punch something. That had been her one chance.

When the elevator doors opened, the lobby looked just as it had earlier—the same mix of wealthy tourists and distracted business travelers. Nobody suspicious. Nobody she recognized.

She didn't even know who to look for.

She'd lost the third man, Volkov, and Federov. It was over. It was after four o'clock. Ripley had booked her on a five-thirty flight to London. The only thing she could do was go home and admit that she'd failed.

With a sigh, she walked out of the hotel's huge front doors.

The second she stepped into the muggy afternoon, a hand grabbed her arm with an iron grip. A familiar voice spoke into her ear.

"Hello, *Jessica*."

Cal Grogan draped a heavy arm across her shoulders. "We need to have a little talk."

22

Holding her in a vicious grip, Grogan dragged Emma swiftly toward a gleaming Land Rover.

Emma struggled to get free. There was no way she was getting into that car. If she did, he was going to kill her.

Her arms were twisted behind her back; she couldn't reach the knife in her pocket. Instead, twisting her body, she swung her shoulder up toward his nose, but he anticipated this, ducking to one side and wrenching her arms hard. Pain streaked down her shoulder, and she cried out.

"Do that again, you bitch, and I'll break your fucking arm. Now get in the car." Grogan's voice was a low, threatening growl, his breath hot against her skin as he yanked the door open and shoved her into the back.

Emma sprawled inside, almost landing on top of Andrei Volkov.

Expressionless, Volkov snatched her bag from where it had fallen on the floor and threw it to Cal, who caught it before he slammed the door and locked it. Through the dark windows,

Emma saw him rifling through it. There wasn't anything incriminating in that bag—the burner phone was still tucked in her pocket with the blade.

"What is this?" she demanded.

Volkov didn't reply. His stony gaze remained straight ahead, as if she weren't there.

Grogan slid behind the wheel and slammed the door.

"Bag's clean," he announced, dropping it onto the passenger seat.

Volkov gave a tense nod. "Let's go."

Grogan started the car and pulled out into traffic.

By now, despite the fear that had tightened its grip on her, Emma was piecing everything together. Grogan had to have been in the hotel the whole time, keeping an eye out for trouble. He must not have recognized her right away or he would have done something earlier. He'd probably placed her when she was in the bar, trying to listen.

That would explain the abrupt end of the meeting. The way Volkov had run out, red-faced and furious. Grogan must have phoned him and told him Jessica Marshall was in the bar.

"What do you want?" she asked, playing Jessica Marshall, her voice quivering. "I don't understand what's happening."

Her hand touched the knife in her pocket. She could leap over and stab Grogan. But then Volkov was right next to her, and she didn't think she could take both of them.

"Are you MI6?" Volkov asked bluntly. He spoke without looking at her. His eyes were fixed on the back of Cal's head.

"That's ridiculous," Emma said. "You know who I am."

She affected bafflement, but her heart was beating fast. This was a conversation she'd hoped never to have.

"Don't lie." Volkov's hand lashed out, grabbing her wrist and pulling her so close she could smell the green scent of his cologne. His flat eyes bored into hers. "I have no time left for lies."

Emma knew she should keep being Jessica, but what was the

point? She could cry or plead, but it wouldn't matter. They knew. Best to say nothing at all.

The pain from his grip made her eyes water.

Realizing, perhaps, that she wasn't going to speak, he let go.

When Emma dropped back, the shape of each of his thick fingers was outlined against her skin in livid red.

She wasn't sure what to do now. There was no rulebook for this. Most spies who found themselves in this position ended up in prison or dead.

"My partners say you're MI6." Volkov jutted his thumb at the front seat. "He says you're MI6. So I ask you again. Are you MI6?"

He obviously knew she wasn't who she said she was, but Emma wasn't about to tell him the truth. Instead, she played for time.

"Look," she said reasonably, "you've seen my passport. Annabel checked me out. She called my references—"

"I don't know this Annabel." Volkov cut her off angrily. "She could be spy too." He gave a morose sigh and looked out at the sunny city. "Everyone is spy now, I think. Everywhere are spies."

A kind of melancholy settled over him, replacing the rage that had simmered moments earlier.

Emma gave him a puzzled look. He wore the same suit from that morning, and the same polished shoes. But the fight seemed to have gone out of him. There was defeat in the slump of his broad shoulders as he looked past her.

"Look," she told him, softening her voice. "I just ended up at the same hotel as you. It's a coincidence."

"Coincidence?" He swung his weary face in her direction. There were deep bags under his eyes as he considered her pulled-back hair and expensive blazer. "I don't believe in coincidence. Do you?"

She didn't, in fact.

Cal Grogan glanced at Volkov in the mirror. "Are we going to the place we discussed?"

The two men exchanged a long look. Volkov was obviously unhappy now. His hands twitched nervously, tapping his knee, his chin, the door.

Emma's stomach twisted. The place they'd discussed would undoubtedly be a good spot outside the city to torture her for information. Somewhere her screams would not be heard.

She watched the Russian man with trepidation.

But then, Volkov straightened. "No," he said firmly. "We go to Blue Room."

In the mirror, Grogan frowned. "You sure? That's not what we agreed."

"Don't question me," Volkov replied irritably. "We go to Blue Room."

There was a long silence. Volkov stared at the back of his bodyguard's head with real loathing. Grogan's hands were tight on the wheel.

Finally, Grogan spoke, disapproval in his voice. "If you say so. We'll go to the Blue Room. It's your funeral."

At the next corner, they turned right, and after that left, then right again. Emma tried to memorize the route, but they were in the Old City where the streets weren't always signposted and soon she was lost.

On the other side of the dark glass, Barcelona shimmered in a golden afternoon haze. Tourists took pictures; locals rushed home after work. Inside the Range Rover the tension hung in the air as thick as smoke.

After ten minutes, the car stopped in front of a rambling building. On the ground floor was a shoe shop and, next to that, a restaurant with tables on the pavement surrounded by planters filled with bougainvillea that dripped and flowed in waves of magenta. The door next to the restaurant was outlined in blue lights. Volkov got out and motioned for Emma to follow.

As Emma left the car, Grogan grabbed her elbow, yanking her toward the door, but Volkov stopped and held up one hand.

"Just Jessica," he said firmly. "You stay here."

A look of rage creased Cal's damaged face. "That's not a good idea. *Boss.*" He said the last word with contempt.

Volkov's expression hardened and he rounded on Grogan with such instant fury, Emma took an instinctive step out of the way.

When he spoke, his voice held a threat beyond his words. "You will wait here. When I come back, remember who owns the boat."

The two men stared at each other. Finally, Grogan released his hold on Emma.

"As you wish. You should search her. But I suppose you know better about that, too."

Ignoring him, Volkov turned toward the blue door. Unlike the bodyguard, he didn't try to restrain Emma, or physically pull her. He simply indicated that she should walk with him.

By now, she was curious about what could have driven the two men apart in the few hours they'd been off the *Eden*. One thing was clear—Volkov was off-roading. And Grogan didn't like it one bit.

The blue door swung open and a large man in a dark suit stepped out, looking at Volkov with surprise.

"Andrei!"

He and Volkov shook hands warmly. The man glanced at Emma with mild curiosity and then back at Andrei.

"I wasn't expecting you today, but I see you have your reasons," he told Volkov in Russian. His smile was teasing. "I thought you were dedicated to Madison?"

"Madison is out of town." Volkov's voice sounded hollow.

With a wide, diplomatic smile, the man motioned for them to enter. "Come in and have drink, my friends," he said, switching to heavily accented English.

Inside, they found a narrow hallway. A wash of blue light illuminated a staircase directly in front of them. Volkov headed up, and Emma followed. As they climbed, the insistent throb of music grew louder with each step.

The bar at the top was large and surprisingly elegant, with clusters of tables and sleek leather chairs, most of which were empty. A stage at one end held a strippers' pole and a DJ booth. Nobody was dancing, but the DJ was in place, headphones around his neck, fiddling with buttons. A backlit bar provided the only golden light—everything else was flooded with pale blue, flickering like water.

Emma and Volkov walked to a table in a corner. He lowered himself heavily into a chair, motioning for her to sit next to him.

"My friend Sergei owns this bar," he explained. "It's very successful. But private." He waved at the empty seats. "We can talk here."

A waitress in a tiny skirt and perilous stilettos set cocktail napkins in front of each of them.

"Beer," Volkov said shortly, and then gestured for Emma to order.

"White wine," she told the waitress, who turned for the bar.

"White wine," Andrei scoffed, his eyes on the empty stage. "Girl's drink."

"Wait." Emma waved the waitress back. "Vodka please. No wine."

Andrei swung his gaze to her. "Better."

He leaned back in his chair and studied her, his eyes narrow and piercing. "Now the truth. Your story about the hotel—it makes no sense. You are MI6. Yes?" Seeing her expression, he gestured at the room. "No Cal here. Just you and me. The truth."

Emma hesitated. This entire thing could be a setup. Volkov and Grogan might have arranged to pretend to fight in front of her to make her think she could tell Volkov about herself. But somehow she didn't believe that was the case. Volkov's unhappiness seemed real, and he was no actor.

If he was disenchanted with his partners, he could be useful. More than useful. He might be able to get her out of here.

"All I can tell you is I work for the British government," she said. "You are not completely wrong."

Volkov's expression didn't change. "You investigate me for drugs? Or something else?"

"Drugs," she lied. If she admitted what she knew about the chemical weapons, she didn't think he could let her live.

He watched her intensely, as if he could sense deception. Emma had rarely seen him so focused. For the first time he looked like a man who might actually have billions of dollars hidden in accounts so complex governments couldn't trace them.

His scrutiny was unpleasant, and she was relieved when the waitress returned and set drinks in front of them. Emma's vodka was served in a chunky cut-glass bottle nestled inside a bowl made of solid ice. She couldn't tell whether the ice itself was blue, or if the lights in the club just made it look that way. A small matching glass sat next to it.

Volkov took a long swallow of beer, and then gestured at the vodka. "Drink."

Hoping it wasn't drugged, Emma poured a sturdy measure into the glass and downed it. The glow of the alcohol warmed her stomach and spread through her veins like bravery.

As soon as she set the glass down, Volkov leaned forward and spoke quickly. "If you are MI6, help me. Please. I need your help."

Emma stared at him. "I'm sorry. Could you repeat that?"

Volkov's eyes darted nervously around the room before he spoke again. "Please tell your people I know things. A lot of things. And I'm in trouble. I need their help."

Whatever she'd expected him to say, it wasn't this. Now it made sense why he'd left Grogan outside. He was trying to turn himself in to British Intelligence and if Cal heard him do that, he'd kill him.

That raised the question: if he didn't work for Volkov, then who did Grogan work for, really?

The answer was instant. There was almost no contest—it had to be Oleg Federov.

Federov had a ruthless reputation, and endless connections in the Russian government. If Grogan worked for him, and kept Volkov passive through the supply of money, girls, and drugs, that would explain a lot. Federov was known by many intelligence agencies. But he could use Volkov's identity and bank accounts to transport chemicals, money, drugs—whatever he needed moved.

She'd heard of shell corporations, but never a shell man. It was so twisted, she suddenly believed it completely.

If she was right, Volkov was not a player in this operation. He was being *played*. He was a pawn.

Ripley and Field had put her on the wrong boat. Federov was behind it all. Volkov probably had killed Stephen Garrick, and Federov was furious about it because he knew MI6 would come for him. He understood what it meant to kill an MI6 officer, even a low-level one.

Now Federov was planning to get rid of Volkov, and Volkov needed help.

Emma leaned forward. "We can help you. I need to make a phone call. But first tell me this, did you kill Stephen Garrick?"

Volkov picked up the beer and then hesitated before taking a drink.

"I didn't want to do that. Cal said we had to. I was stupid to agree."

The pause. The over-explanation. The way he reached for the beer and then changed his mind. Then picked it up and took a drink anyway.

He was lying. But there was another question Emma needed to ask.

"What about Madison?"

Volkov's face changed, every line and crag deepening. "That was *Cal*." He spat the name with venom. "He killed her. He did it and then told me when it was over. I would never do that. Never. Madison did not deserve that. She hurt me but I would never hurt her."

He seemed to be genuinely sad. Had he actually loved Madison?

It was hard to believe but the proof was written on his face.

"They will kill me, too, I think." He spoke softly, as if talking to himself. "I messed up. And someone must pay. They took Madison. They will take other things." He looked up and met her gaze. She saw no fear in his eyes, only a kind of exhausted resignation. "I think Cal might kill me. That would be the easiest for them. Please," he pleaded. "You must help me if you can. I know many things."

In her pocket, Emma's fingers found the burner phone, and then withdrew.

As if he sensed her hesitation, Volkov leaned closer to her, his small eyes holding her gaze. "I know about you. You are being betrayed. Someone told me who you are. I can help you, if you help me."

Emma went still, searching his face and finding nothing there except desperation.

"Who is it?" she demanded. "Tell me that and I'll help you."

Volkov shook his head and leaned back in his chair, folding his arms. "Protect me first. Then I'll tell you everything."

Andrei Volkov didn't deserve her protection. Everything that had happened to him was his own doing. The weapons he was selling illegally across the globe were used to kill tens of thousands of people. The drugs he sold would kill many as well. He'd killed Stephen Garrick. He did not have a conscience.

And yet he did know things. And he could bring down Oleg Federov, who was much worse than him. And that was the way things worked. It was a market of morality. A very bad man gets to live in exchange for a monster, who does not.

"I want to help you, but to do it, I need to make a call." Emma pulled out her phone and held it up. "Is that OK?"

Volkov gave her a long look. She could see in his haunted eyes that he understood what his future would be if he sold out to the British government. Federov would not rest until he was dead. And even if Federov were caught, others would take up the hunt.

The authorities would do their best to protect him, but many Russian men who'd found sanctuary in the UK had been assassinated while thinking they were finally safe.

But if he surrendered, at least he stood a chance.

He flicked his hand. "Do it."

Emma began to call Ripley, but stopped. This was Jon's operation. He was the one with the local connections who could sort this out quickly. She should go to him first.

He was not going to be happy to find out what she'd been up to, but that could all be dealt with later.

As Emma dialed the number, the moment—the bar, the *thumpthumpthump* of the music, the Russian bar owner keeping a tactful distance—it all felt unreal. She'd gone from failure to success in a matter of minutes.

As of right now, she had her man. All she had to do now was bring him in.

The phone rang, and Jon answered. "Emma? Where are you? You're supposed to be catching a plane."

"I'm in a bar called the Blue Room in Barcelona with Andrei Volkov," Emma told him. "I can't explain how, but Volkov wants to turn himself in. He wants to help us."

"What the hell." There was shock and anger in Jon's voice. "I don't understand what you're telling me. How did this happen?"

Volkov was watching Emma intently.

"I don't have time to go into it," she said. "Right now, Volkov is in danger and so am I. We need to get him to the UK for a debrief. I need a lifeline."

"Give me a wee second, I'm trying to absorb this." Jon's Scottish accent thickened when he was caught off guard. "So, you're saying you have him now?"

"Yes," Emma said. "But Cal Grogan's outside. Can you send someone?"

There was a pause. "It's tricky taking him from there—we don't have an arrangement with Spanish Intelligence. He could end up in a Spanish prison and we'd be hard pressed to get him out." Jon was thinking it through. "We need to get him to France. Can he get back on the *Eden*?"

Emma turned to Volkov. "Can you get on the *Eden* and sail to France? Will Grogan allow that?"

He thought for a long moment, his hand cupped around his jaw. "Yes. I think so." He gave her a look. "But Cal will not let you go."

Emma looked around the bar. The stage was still empty, although more drinkers had arrived. It was a very contained room. "Does this place have a back door?"

Volkov glanced over her shoulder, and she turned to see a green lighted sign tucked in a corner. *Sortida*. Exit.

Emma lifted the phone to her ear. "He can get on the *Eden*."

"Good. Tell him to go back to Nice. I'll meet him when he's in French territorial waters. We'll bring him in from there. Is that clear?"

"Clear," Emma said.

"And get yourself to the airport, right now," he ordered. "There's a seven o'clock flight. Be on it."

"Copy that." There was no way she was going to be on that flight, but she could explain that later.

She slipped the phone into her pocket and turned to Volkov. "It's done."

"Just like that?" He looked doubtful.

"There are details to work out, and those will take quite a while. But they've agreed to bring you in, which is the main thing. First, we're going to need to lose Cal Grogan, and get back to the *Eden*." She was itching to get Volkov out of here. If they were alone she was certain she could convince him to tell her who the third man was. She glanced back to where the bar owner stood talking to the waitress. "Could your friend get us back to the marina without Cal seeing us?"

Volkov looked at Sergei, and then pushed back his chair. "Give me a minute."

As Emma watched, Volkov spoke to the bar owner. Sergei listened and nodded, his face growing serious. At the end, he clapped a hand on Volkov's shoulder and said something before walking away.

When Volkov walked back, he looked pleased.

"It's settled," he said, sitting back in his chair with relief. "Sergei is an old friend. His driver will bring a car to the back door. Five minutes he says."

Emma watched the bar owner speak to someone on the phone before opening a door marked "PRIVATE" and disappearing.

In theory, this was all fine. But something about the moment filled her with foreboding. She didn't know anything about Sergei. He might be trustworthy or he could be a complete liar. There was no way for her to judge.

For his part, Volkov appeared thoughtful—even a little emotional. "I should tell you something," he said gravely. "Thank you for helping me. Thank your government. I am . . ." He touched his chest with his fist and searched for the English word. ". . . grateful."

Emma didn't want his gratitude. Andrei Volkov was a murderer and a chemical weapons peddler. She was not about to forge a friendship with him.

The music grew louder so suddenly it made them both jump. The blue lights dimmed, and a woman in a sheer negligee walked out on stage and began sashaying around the pole.

The bar was filling with customers. Clearly this was when the evening's entertainment usually kicked off. The more people there were, the less safe it was.

"We should go," she told Volkov, raising her voice to be heard above the music.

Before he could reply, though, the main door flew open and Cal Grogan strode toward them, one hand in the pocket of his sports jacket. The ruthless fury in his expression made Emma's heart sink.

Volkov saw him at the same time, and his face darkened.

Both of them jumped to their feet. Volkov grabbed Grogan's shoulder and shouted something at him. The music carried most of it away, but Emma heard the last words: "I will kill you."

As Emma watched, Grogan pulled a gun from his pocket and pushed it against Volkov's ribs. His body shielded the weapon from the others in the room, but Emma could see the metal glitter coldly in the blue light.

Grogan put his face close to Volkov's and spoke too quietly for her to hear.

Volkov shook his head hard but his shoulders slumped. It was over, and he knew it.

He turned to her and his eyes held nothing except despair.

Grogan pointed the gun at her and shouted something. The music drowned out his words but she could read his lips in the pale blue light.

"Let's go."

23

Traffic was heavy on the wide boulevard in front of the Blue Room as the three of them walked stiffly to the black SUV. Nobody in the rush-hour crowd spared them a glance. The passing drivers couldn't see the gun Grogan shielded inside his jacket, so they had no idea that it was pressed against Emma's ribs as his fingers sank bruises into her arm.

Automatically, she memorized the faces of the people around them—a woman in her twenties with a child. A couple looking in a shop window. A man with a beard on a motorcycle stopped at the corner. She couldn't risk trying to run or fight now. If Grogan fired blindly any of them could be killed. So she kept walking, conscious of the knife in her pocket. Waiting for her moment.

When they reached the car Grogan shoved her inside for the second time that day.

"Stop doing that," Emma spat.

Grogan locked the door and climbed behind the wheel.

In the front passenger seat, Volkov stared straight ahead, his face drained of color and emotion.

Emma looked frantically for a way out of this. The doors were locked through a central system and Grogan was utterly alert, one hand on the wheel and the other holding the gun.

Her options were slim. She still had the knife. She could leap over the seat and slash his throat, forcing him to crash the car. But odds were he'd shoot her dead. Even if she succeeded, an out-of-control SUV on these crowded streets would be a death machine. She couldn't take the risk of someone else getting hurt.

In the end, there wasn't time to do anything before the long rows of white yachts appeared in front of them, and the Range Rover turned in to the marina.

When we get out of the car I'll have a chance, Emma thought.

As if he could hear her thinking, Grogan met Emma's gaze in the mirror. "Don't do anything stupid. It won't work and you'll just embarrass yourself."

When the car was parked, Grogan and Volkov got out first.

The second Grogan opened Emma's door, she swung a kick at his knees, the knife already in her hand, ready to deliver a killing blow. But he'd anticipated this. With lightning-quick reflexes, he dodged the blade and struck her across the face with the butt of the pistol. For a second, Emma's world went dark. By the time her vision cleared, he had her by the arm and was dragging her from the car. The knife fell to the pavement where it glittered malevolently out of reach.

"*Bitch*," Grogan growled. "Try that again and I'll slit your throat." He shoved her hard.

Still dizzy from the blow, Emma lost her balance. Volkov righted her with one hand, his eyes on Grogan, who still held his gun half-hidden by his jacket. The barrel was, Emma thought, pointed as much at Volkov as at her.

In grim silence, the three of them trudged down to the long

pier. Blood streamed from Emma's temple, blurring her vision, but she made herself walk steadily. She didn't want Grogan to know it hurt.

Jason waited for them at the powerboat. His gaze took in the gun and the blood streaming down Emma's face. His expression went instantly blank.

Not for the first time, Emma wondered what else he'd seen during his time on the *Eden*. Was she the first bloodied woman he'd ferried to the yacht? Unlikely.

With a twitch of the gun, Grogan directed Emma to the seat in front of the steering wheel. "Sit there."

Emma had little choice at this stage, so she did as she was told. Volkov lowered himself heavily into the seat next to her.

In silence, Jason threw off the lines and Grogan took the wheel. The motor started with a growl.

As the shore slipped away behind them, a knot of ice formed in Emma's chest. She wasn't going to come back from this alive. She'd used up all her luck today.

It was too late for anyone to save her. Jon and Ripley would guess something had gone wrong when she didn't catch the flight, but by then she'd be far out at sea. And Grogan would have all the time he wanted to torture her the way he'd tortured Stephen Garrick.

Her only hope was the burner phone still in her pocket. But they'd search her, she was sure of it, and they'd find it. She could try and hide the phone on the powerboat now in hopes of re-trieving it later, but Grogan was right behind her. He'd see, or Jason would.

No. She had to come up with something else.

But what? Nobody on the yacht was going to be able to do anything, and she didn't want Sara or Conor to get into any trou-ble trying.

She didn't understand Volkov. He just sat there, staring straight ahead, his face blank. He'd done nothing to help her since Grogan walked into the Blue Room, and she couldn't be certain that the whole scene in the bar hadn't been a well-designed trap to get her to admit who she was. And yet. Volkov had seemed genuinely frightened of his partners, and what they might do. He'd wanted her to save him. But if she was going to have any chance of doing that, she needed his help now.

Standing abruptly, she covered her mouth with her fingers and said thickly, "I'm going to be sick."

She ran to the side of the boat and with her hair shielding her face, put her finger down her throat and threw up the vodka.

"Christ," she heard Grogan grumble. "What next?"

When she returned to her seat, she lost her balance and half fell across Volkov, and slipped her phone into the pocket of his suit jacket.

He gave her a startled look as she straightened. "Sorry," she said, holding his gaze.

She saw him reach into his pocket and touch the phone. Watched his expression change as he realized what it was. And then his face smoothed and he stared straight ahead. She had no idea what he might do with it. But if he would only dial one of the numbers on it, tell Ripley where she was, what was happening . . .

It was long shot. But it was worth a try.

It was evening now, and the sun sent vivid ribbons of gold across the water. The beauty seemed almost aggressive as the white hulk of the *Eden* loomed ahead of them. The sight made bile rise in Emma's throat again.

She would not die on that boat. She wouldn't be another body they dumped in the sea before sailing away to some new exotic port. She couldn't go out like this. She wouldn't let them do this to her.

When it all goes to hell, fight harder, she reminded herself. But how?

. . .

The second they reached the aft deck, Volkov leaped from his seat and strode onto the yacht without a backward glance. Grogan did nothing to stop him. He didn't have to: this boat was a prison; the sea was its walls.

"What do we do with her?" Jason asked Grogan, tilting his head at Emma. It was the first time he'd acknowledged her presence.

"Search her. Then put her in the storeroom," Grogan growled. "I'll deal with her later."

Jason shoved Emma across the aft deck into the corridor and held her against a wall. He ran his hands through the pockets of her blazer, and felt her hips and down her legs.

"She's clean," he told Grogan.

"Good." Grogan put the key from the powerboat into the locker by the entrance and slammed it shut. "Now get her out of my sight."

Jason dragged Emma down the corridor to a metal door and shoved her into a dark room. As soon as he let go, she spun around to face him.

The steward stood in the doorway, framed in light.

"I don't know what kind of game you're playing, luv," he said. "But you chose the wrong boat."

Emma met his gaze unflinchingly. "I guess one day we'll find out who here made the worst choices."

Jason slammed the door and the room descended into total darkness. She heard a key turn in the lock, and then the sound of footsteps walking away. After that, nothing.

24

When Emma first joined the Agency, much of her training involved learning methods to avoid ever getting trapped. If someone is held prisoner long enough, and put in sufficient pain, eventually they'll talk. The best way to avoid all of that is to never find yourself in a locked room unable to escape.

Most of the time, Emma found she could get out of trouble before the door was ever closed. She could negotiate, reason, dissemble, apologize, barter.

Sometimes, though, none of that worked.

The first time it failed, it was two in the morning, and Emma was in an abandoned warehouse in east London, facing three men with machine guns.

It was a simulated attack. The men were all soldiers, pretending to be terrorists, but it didn't feel fake at all. Emma's job was to negotiate the release of a hostage, also a soldier, tied to a chair.

The second she walked into the decrepit, stinking building

with her hands above her head, one of the soldiers fired at her. She heard the buzz of the bullet as it flew by and slammed into the wall behind her. That was their hello.

"Get down! Put your hands behind your head! Don't look at us. *Don't look at us!*" Voices shouted at her from everywhere.

It was December; the air in the old building was frozen. Emma could hear traffic on the M25 motorway nearby as she knelt on the icy concrete and put her hands behind her head, trying not to shiver.

"I'm not here to hurt anyone," she said, as she'd been taught.

The men had burst out laughing.

"We're terrified," one of them sneered.

"Yeah, please don't hurt us," another one said, and kicked her hard enough to send her flying backward.

For half an hour they'd punched, kicked, and taunted her as she used every bit of her training to try and convince them to give up, until finally they dropped a bag over her head and locked her in a side room alone.

It took ten minutes to work her wrists free from the cable ties, and by the time she succeeded her hands were wet with blood. Ignoring the pain, she pulled the bag from her head, and began looking for a way out.

She had few options. The door was padlocked from the outside, and the freezing room was windowless, lit by a single incandescent bulb that dangled from the high ceiling, casting shadows that seemed to skitter around the edges of the dank room.

She tried kicking the door, using a screw she found on the floor to unscrew the hinges—but nothing worked. In the end, she grabbed a chunk of masonry that had fallen from the old walls, and used it as a sledgehammer, pounding the door near the handle. Her hands were so numb she couldn't feel her fingertips when, at last, it gave way.

When she stepped out of the room, shivering, her hands bleeding, she received a round of sardonic applause from the "kidnappers," who were gathered in the next room, eating sandwiches and drinking tea with their hostage.

"Forty-three minutes," one of the soldiers observed, glancing at his watch. "Not bad."

"Bet it felt longer," the one who'd kicked her said with a teasing grin.

"What was the fastest anyone ever got out?" she asked, accepting the steaming cardboard cup of tea he held out to her.

The three men considered this seriously.

"Was it Kate? She was fast," one of them asked, but the first one shook his head.

"Adam got out in seventeen minutes. No one could beat that. But he was Special Forces. And they cheat."

After that experience, Emma decided that she would cheat, too.

She learned to pick locks until she could open almost anything in seconds. She watched tutorials on the internet, and practiced until she could open a padlock in under a minute. She kept lock picks with her always.

She learned to target the weakest points of doors and windows. The best way to break through anything that would otherwise hold her in. All she needed to get out of any situation was a few simple tools.

None of which she had now.

When Jason closed the door he left her in darkness so total she could see nothing at all. She fumbled across the room toward where she thought the door should be, her head still throbbing viciously from the blow from Grogan's gun. Disoriented in the pitch black, she tripped over something and fell, landing hard on what felt like a heavy cardboard box.

After that, she shuffled, moving slowly with her hands outstretched until they finally touched the smooth surface of the wall.

It took more time to locate the door, which was locked solid, and a few long seconds of feeling the wall around it before she located a light switch.

When the lights at last came on they were so blinding her eyes watered as she took in her situation. She was in a long industrial storage room. It held very little—some metal shelves stacked with life jackets and pool-cleaning equipment, a scattering of unmarked boxes, and what looked like a car under a tarpaulin.

Looking at the car, Emma gave a hollow laugh. "A gun would have been more useful."

The door was metal and the lock was modern. There was nothing she could easily break there. Still, the scattered boxes gave her hope. Almost anything can be a weapon. A chopstick can put someone's eyes out. A butter knife can be sharpened into a shiv in an hour.

All it takes is a little imagination and the right attitude.

One by one, she ripped the boxes open. This was clearly a space where things that didn't fit elsewhere were kept. She found kitchen pans, medical supplies, lightbulbs, napkins, batteries, flashlights—the kinds of things you want on a long voyage, but nothing that could unlock a door.

At least an hour passed before she'd gone through every box and examined every shelf. As she stood surveying the chaos of torn cardboard, she felt a faint vibration beneath her feet. Cut off from everything familiar, for an instant she wasn't sure what it was. But then the boat began to tilt, and then rise and rise before dropping with a shudder.

The *Eden* was heading out to sea.

A wave of despair washed over her. She was alone in the middle of the ocean with a sociopath trained to kill and a dissolute oligarch who had long ago sold his conscience to the highest bidder. Even if she found a way out of this room now, where would she go?

Slowly, she sank to the floor and dropped her head to her knees. What was the point of even trying? Without weapons or a phone, she didn't stand a chance.

Her breath came fast and shallow as fear dug its claws in. Along with fear came regret. She should have listened to Jon. He'd told her to go to London. He'd warned her to stay away. But no. She had to be the one to bring in Volkov and Federov, and crack the Gold Dust operation. She had to be the hero. All of this was her own fault.

When she'd given Volkov the phone, she'd hoped he'd understood the unspoken message: *If you can get me out of here, we'll still protect you.* But she'd seen the confusion in his face, and odds were he'd handed it over to Grogan to curry favor. Maybe he'd help carry her body to the powerboat.

The voices of failure rose to a chorus, and she pressed her hands against her ears.

"*Stop.*" She shouted the word, and it echoed hollowly in the huge room.

She would *not* lose today. Not like this. Not to these people.

There had to be something in this room that she could use.

She went back to the first boxes she'd searched and started going through each one again. But she'd been thorough in her first pass, and she found nothing. She was tired and desperately thirsty.

She had no watch and, without windows, it was hard to gauge the passing of time, but it must be late by now. Hours had passed while she'd been locked up.

Somewhere above her, Sara was talking with Conor and Lawrence, Jason was lying about what had happened to Jessica. They would have no idea she was here, a few levels below them, locked up.

As she imagined their conversations, her gaze fell on the car.

It was the one thing she hadn't searched. She ripped the cover off in one sweeping movement, so it billowed like a parachute before falling to the floor.

Beneath it was a pristine canary-yellow Ferrari.

Emma circled it slowly. It looked brand new. She hadn't seen it listed in Andrei Volkov's MI6 files.

It was a ludicrous machine. Unlikely to hold anything useful. But it also wasn't locked.

The car was so low, when she opened the door she had to kneel on the floor in order to see inside it properly. It smelled deliciously of new leather and plastic.

There was nothing on the floor. Nothing on the seats. The glove compartment held only a handbook. Emma felt around the dashboard until she found a lever. When she pulled it, the hood of the car popped up.

More curious than hopeful now, she peered underneath it. There was no motor, as Ferrari engines are at the rear. Instead, she found a carpeted storage space, about the size of a small suitcase. It was completely empty save for a small leather bag branded with the Ferrari logo of a rearing horse.

When she opened it she found a set of gleaming tools resting against black leather, like jewels in a velvet case.

"Bingo," Emma whispered.

It was the first piece of good luck she'd had in hours.

Grabbing a screwdriver and a small, sturdy wrench, she headed straight for the storage-room door.

It was metal and bifold style so it could fold open into the hallway, which itself opened out onto the aft deck. That's how they would have got the car on in the first place.

The hinges were mounted on the outside, so Emma tackled the lock. But it was modern and well designed, and the screwdriver did nothing but gouge it.

She was attempting to force the screwdriver between the door and the wall when she heard a voice from the hallway on the other side.

"Stop," it ordered gruffly. "You'll break something."

Emma jumped to her feet as she heard the distinctive metallic hiss of a key sliding into the lock.

Bracing herself, she raised the wrench above her head as the door swung open.

Andrei Volkov looked from her to the wrench and didn't flinch.

"You have to get out of here," he told her. "Cal's coming to kill you."

25

"What are you doing?" Emma found herself asking, so bewildered by this turn of fortune that for a moment she couldn't grasp her situation.

In response, Volkov held out his hand. In his palm was the phone Zach had made for her weeks ago in London. Her heart kicked, and she looked from it to his ruddy face without moving.

"Your other phone was shit," Volkov told her bluntly. "This looks better. It's fully charged."

Emma took it from him and turned it on. The screen lit up, and all of Zach's fake apps appeared.

She didn't know what to say. She still didn't trust Volkov, but here he was. He'd understood what she needed, and he appeared to be rescuing her.

"Thank you," she said. "I'm grateful."

As she spoke, Volkov's gaze slid past her and rested on the Ferrari, shining gold in the drab gray room.

"I bought that for Madison," he told her. "It was a present. I was going to give it to her on her twenty-fifth birthday. She would have loved it." He turned back to her. "Oleg and Cal told me they killed her to protect me. But it's a lie. She drew attention, and Oleg didn't want attention."

He spoke in his usual blunt way but Emma could see the true emotion beneath the words, and suddenly she believed that he'd really loved Madison. Federov had gone too far when he'd had her killed. He'd miscalculated.

And now Andrei Volkov, murderer and international weapons dealer, was saving Emma's life, as revenge.

Volkov turned his attention from the car to her. "We have deal, yes?" he demanded. "In the bar. We made agreement. I will help you with your problem; you help with mine."

"Yes," she said without hesitation. "We have a deal. Come with me. We'll go to England."

His heavy brow creased. "You said France," he reminded her. "You said go to France."

"Yes, but . . ." She looked around the long room. "Can you do that? With Cal here?"

Volkov lifted one shoulder in an expressive gesture that briefly and startlingly reminded her of her mother.

"Technically, he works for me." His wry smile told her they both knew the person Grogan really worked for, and it wasn't Volkov. "I'll handle him."

"Yes, but—" she began, and he cut her off.

"It's my problem." The quick chop of his hand signaled an end to the discussion.

The *Eden* swung high before crashing down, and the two of them adjusted their balance instinctively, legs wide and braced.

"I'll have to take the powerboat," Emma told him.

"Of course." Volkov followed her down the corridor to the locker near the door.

The smell of the sea met them halfway. Emma inhaled

deeply. Her hunger, thirst, exhaustion—it was all gone. She felt wide awake and ready for all of this.

"I don't suppose you can unlock this?" Emma gestured at the box.

Volkov shook his head. "Cal has the key."

"No problem." Emma pulled the wrench from her pocket and swung it at the lock. The sound of metal against metal was lost in the loud rumble of the yacht's engine. Two blows did the trick. The small locker swung open.

She grabbed the powerboat keys from the hook and headed for the aft deck.

"I'll meet you in France tomorrow, yes?" Volkov said. He pointed at her phone. "I have your number."

"Yes. Tomorrow," she told him. "In France."

"What the fuck do you think you're doing?" Grogan stepped out of the shadows behind them. He'd changed out of the clothes he'd worn in Barcelona and was now in a black T-shirt and dark trousers, the same clothes he'd worn the night he'd killed Madison and dumped her body in the sea.

Emma swung around, the wrench clutched in her fist, but before she could strike a blow, Volkov pushed past her and lumbered toward his bodyguard.

"She's leaving now. That's it," he announced. "I've decided."

"*You've* decided?" Cal's tone was contemptuous. "Who do you think you are, old man? You don't make decisions. You do as you're told and you get paid. That's the arrangement."

"That's not the arrangement anymore," Volkov said.

"Your memory's going, mate." Grogan pulled a gun from behind his back and leveled it at Volkov. "Try harder."

Volkov didn't flinch.

"You think you frighten me?" He stepped closer to Grogan until the gun was pressed against his abdomen. "You're the one who doesn't understand. You're not the boss. You're a tool. The tool shouldn't threaten the hand."

Grogan raised the weapon. In a lightning-fast move, Volkov grabbed his wrist and twisted it. The gun went off with a deafening roar.

Emma ducked. Grogan pounded on Volkov with his fists, but it was like hitting concrete. Volkov didn't seem to feel the blows as he swung his own punch at the bodyguard, connecting a solid left to the jaw.

Emma couldn't see the gun anywhere. Grogan must have dropped it.

She took a quick step forward, hoping to find it, but in the melee it was impossible to see beneath their feet. Volkov was relentless, all swinging thick fists, but Grogan was a canny fighter, aiming a kick at the older man's knees.

Volkov stumbled and that was all Grogan needed. He grabbed the Russian by the neck and slammed his head into the wall with a thud Emma could feel.

Volkov slid to the ground, unconscious.

Emma lunged toward the aft deck.

"No you don't, *Jessica*." Stepping over the prone body, Grogan grabbed her by the neck.

Spinning on her heel, Emma twisted loose and swung a whirling kick at his shoulder, connecting with satisfying force that sent him reeling back. But he caught his balance before he could fall.

"You bitch." He snarled the words and swung a punch at her head. But her unexpected attack must have thrown him off, because he misjudged the distance and his fist brushed past her, hitting only air.

Emma aimed another kick, this time at his face. Her heel connected with his jaw and his head snapped back.

He made a surprised *oof* sound and fell back against the wall.

Emma followed, punching him with the hand still holding the wrench. The move would have knocked a normal man unconscious, but Grogan was anything but normal. Ignoring the blood streaming over his ear, he grabbed her, slamming her body against the wall, knocking all the air from her lungs.

He raised his fist to hit her again, but she was ready for him, dropping to the floor before his fist could connect, and rolling to her left, leaping back to her feet behind him. Bracing herself in the doorway to the storage room, she swung kick after kick at him—sometimes connecting, sometimes missing, but it didn't really matter, she was forcing him to stay back and defend himself from the constant attack.

Eventually, though, she began to tire, and Grogan seized the advantage, grabbing her arm, dragging her to him, and locking his forearm across her throat.

The wrench slipped from her fingers and fell to the floor.

"What the fuck did you think you were doing?" he whispered in her ear. "Did you think we wouldn't figure out who you were?"

Emma's breath was cut off but she had enough air to reply. "How many of us do you think you can kill?"

He tightened his grip. "As many as it takes."

"I don't think so." In one smooth move, Emma lifted the screwdriver she'd taken from the Ferrari and plunged it into his shoulder, near his neck.

Grogan grunted in pain and he released his hold on her, reeling away as if propelled by some unseen force. Emma felt hot blood on her wrist.

She paused, looking down the hallway to where Andrei Volkov still lay unconscious. He'd freed her, and if there was a way to do it, she'd save him now. But there was no way she could lift him, and there was no time.

She had no choice but to save herself now, and hope she'd get the chance to do the same for him later.

Leaving him there, she hurtled out onto the aft deck where the launch was tied up out of the water. She crouched low and fumbled with the knots that held the powerboat in place. Her breath came in short tight bursts. She was almost there. Almost free.

"Where do you think you're going?" The Australian-accented voice came from the shadows.

In the harsh glow of the security light, she saw Jason standing behind her.

"Don't get in my way, Jason," she warned. "I don't want to hurt you. I'm leaving. That's all. Pretend you never saw me."

There was just enough light for her to see his expression: the arrogance, the ignorance.

"Cal says you're MI6," he told her.

"Look," she said evenly. "Just step away, and let me leave."

He stood still for so long, she thought he'd listened. She was wrong.

"I can't do that," he said. And lunged for her.

Emma sidestepped and Jason almost stumbled off the deck into the roiling sea, catching himself at the last minute on the powerboat.

The engines seemed louder now—an angry roar. And the seas were growing rougher.

"Come on, Jason," Emma pleaded above the noise. "Don't do this."

But he wasn't about to listen. Instead, he turned and ran at her again, bull-like, his head down.

Emma grabbed him by the shoulders and rammed his head into the wall. She heard the crack as it hit, and felt his body go slack. He sank down to the deck and lay still.

"You idiot," she told him, and left him there.

The cool night breeze blew her hair into her eyes and sent a shiver through her as she worked loose the last knots.

The boat, which had been tied high for the journey, dropped down to the water with a thud. Emma leaped aboard. Caught in the wake of the *Eden* and thrown by high waves, it swung violently. Emma clung to the steering wheel as it spun out of control. Water poured over the side, puddling at her feet until she feared the boat might capsize.

Gradually, though, the yacht began to pull away, and the powerboat steadied.

And soon Emma was drifting alone on the Mediterranean Sea.

26

As the lights of the *Eden* moved away, darkness curled around the powerboat like a threat.

Emma was utterly exhausted. Every part of her body hurt. Her knuckles were shredded and she stank of blood.

But she was free.

Waves tipped the boat back and forth like a toy, and she held on to the side while she pulled out the phone and checked the screen. No signal.

The phone made her think about Andrei Volkov. He'd genuinely surprised her tonight. She hoped he was still alive. They needed him to tell them what he knew.

But first, she had to get to shore.

Gripping the steering wheel with wet fingers, she slid the key into the ignition.

When the engine roared to life, her heart leaped with it. She kept learning over and over again that there was nothing more exhilarating than survival.

She pushed the throttle forward and the boat shot across the water.

As Emma's eyes adjusted, she realized the sky was alight with a silvery icing of stars, more stars than she'd ever seen in her life, and a half-moon hung low. The night was not so dark after all. In the pale, ethereal glow she could make out the outline of the shore in the distance. There was no sign of a town, but that didn't matter. All she needed was dry land and a clear phone signal.

At first, as the boat plowed through the choppy sea, the roar of the ocean and the growl of the boat's engine made it hard to hear anything else. Gradually, though, Emma noticed that a new sound had joined the cacophony.

She turned to look over her shoulder.

Gradually, she made out the dark shape of what looked like a small boat moving across the water toward her.

Where did that come from?

It wasn't a fishing boat. It was tiny, no bigger than a dinghy.

As she watched the small boat being tossed about by the ocean, she suddenly remembered the lifeboat bound to the side of the *Eden*. Jason checked it before every voyage. But it wasn't Jason in that boat. She was sure of that.

It had to be Cal Grogan. Nobody else was that determined. Nobody else was that crazy.

Fury flared inside her.

"Damn you," she shouted into the wind. "Why aren't you *dead*?"

She pushed the throttle as far as she dared, bending her knees to take the blow as the powerboat soared up a wave and crashed down the other side.

The lifeboat didn't have anything like the engine power of the launch, and it was soon far behind her.

But she couldn't keep up the speed once she neared the

coast. Jagged rocks glistened treacherously. As low cliffs emerged from the shadows, Emma's heart sank. She had no idea where she was. She didn't even know which country she was approaching. She had no compass, no guidance, no light.

But she didn't dare stay on the water too long. Even with the light of the stars, she couldn't see well enough. And Grogan was out there, looking for her.

When she spotted what looked like a stretch of beach, she decided to head toward it.

There were no signs of life as she steered cautiously toward the horseshoe of sand. It looked safer than the rock-strewn coast around it. But as soon as she reached the small bay, she realized she'd been wrong. There were rocks under the sea here, too. Their dark shapes loomed treacherously out of the shadows.

Emma eased up on the throttle, but it was too late. The launch crashed hard against something and flew upward, tilting violently.

Thrown off balance, Emma lost her grip on the wheel, and tumbled against the gunwale.

She picked herself up just as a wave hit the boat with a heavy, gut-twisting thud. This time, though, she managed to grab the back of a leather seat and hold herself up.

The key was still in the ignition. But when she turned it, the motor sputtered and died. She tried again and again but it was futile. The boat was dead.

Taking the phone from her pocket she checked the screen—three bars of signal.

"At last," Emma whispered.

Jon answered on the first ring.

"*Emma?*" There was an urgent note in his voice that she felt in her chest like warmth. Like hope.

"It's me," she said. "I'm off the *Eden*."

"What the hell happened? How did you get this phone? Your

tracker came on about an hour ago. The signal was so erratic I was afraid—"

His voice broke off but she could hear the unspoken words beneath the surface: *I was afraid you were dead and they'd dumped you at sea.*

"I took the powerboat," she said. "I think Cal is following me. I injured him earlier, but not enough. I'm near the coast but I've hit something and the engine's dead. I'm going to have to swim for it, which will kill the phone."

Jon absorbed all of this with admirable calmness. He didn't ask what had happened, or why she wasn't on a plane or how she'd ended up on the *Eden* again. They both knew there wasn't time for that now. All he said was, "Are you close enough to make it if you swim?"

Emma squinted at the dark shoreline. "Yes," she said.

"Good. What about Cal? Where is he?"

"I don't know. I think I lost him. But he'll find me."

"Just get to shore," he ordered. "Don't worry about the phone—I've got a peg on your location now, so you don't need it. Find a good hiding place and stay in it. I'll come for you as quickly as I can."

Emma's brow creased. "Aren't you in Nice?"

"Emma, I've been looking for you for *hours*," he told her. "Trust me. I'll get there. Just do me a favor and don't drown, OK?"

Her bruised face hurt when she smiled. "I'll do my best."

As she set the phone down she thought she heard the sound of a motor above the crash of the waves against the rocks, but when she twisted around she could see nothing but ocean.

Still, she hurried, ripping off her jacket, stripping down to her underwear and kicking off her shoes. At the last minute, she remembered the screwdriver and retrieved it from her pocket, holding it in her fist as she jumped over the side.

The water was deeper and much colder than she'd expected. Kicking hard, she broke the waves and drew a gasping breath.

Clutching the screwdriver, she swam toward the rugged outline of shore she could see ahead. She kicked with dogged steadiness until she felt pebbles and sand beneath her feet, and dragged herself onto the beach.

The night air felt warmer after the water but she shivered as she assessed her situation.

The cove was surrounded by rocky cliffs. She'd need to find a footpath out of here.

She walked along the stony beach until she noticed the faint marks of a path through a small, tangled wood and hurried toward it.

Crack.

The gunshot was so unexpected, for a moment she thought she'd dreamed it. Then she heard the whiplash echo of the bullet ricocheting off the rock face, and threw herself down to the stony ground, her breath hissing between her teeth.

Grogan hadn't got lost. He hadn't hit a rock and foundered. He'd always been coming for her. And Jon was never going to get here in time.

A second shot rang out, sending chips of rock cascading to the ground from the cliff face.

Swearing under her breath, Emma raised her head far enough to see a jagged black boulder gleaming in the faint light a few meters away.

She crawled toward it across the rocks and sand, scraping the skin from her knees and torso, scrambling behind the boulder just as Grogan fired again.

Emma pressed her back against the rough stone and forced herself to calm her panicked breathing. Two deep breaths, and then she leaned over to look at the beach.

Cal Grogan was at the far edge of the cove, the gun in his hand. Behind him, a small rigid inflatable boat lay on the rocks.

He must have used a paddle and pushed himself to shore silently. As she watched him point his gun at the boulder, Emma felt a curious mix of loathing and admiration for the bodyguard. His refusal to give up was remarkable. She wished he was on her side.

"Cal, what are you doing?" she called above the sound of the waves. "Stop this. Get out of here."

"You think you can stab me in the back and walk away?" His voice was hoarse. "You don't know who you're dealing with."

"I know exactly who you are. And you know I'm a British intelligence officer," she shouted. "You also knew who Stephen Garrick was when you killed him. You're looking at a life sentence in a British jail. My people are on their way. Get out of here while you can."

His arm swung up and he fired five shots in quick succession. Emma huddled behind the tall, weathered boulder, flinching as the bullets carved chunks off the stone.

There was no chance of a rescue now. Somehow, she would have to take Grogan out with no gun. No knife. Just a sodding screwdriver.

As she shivered, a cloud moved in front of the moon, sending shadows across the sand. Shielded by the darkness, Emma peered out from behind the boulder and got a good look at her opponent.

Grogan was walking in an oddly jerky way. The hand holding the gun was steady, but the other arm hung loose at his side, and he was unsteady on his feet.

He was badly hurt. She must have done real damage when she'd stabbed him earlier. Odds were she could take him. The only problem was the gun. All he needed was one clear shot.

As she looked down at the screwdriver in her hand, a plan began to form in her mind.

"Come out, *Jessica*," he called. "You seemed to like fighting earlier. Let's do it again."

Emma didn't reply.

The waves hit the sand like a punch, and then withdrew with a hiss. But she barely heard them now. She was listening to the shuffling sound of Cal's footsteps drawing closer.

Using the sound as her guide, she moved cautiously around the boulder in the opposite direction until she was behind him.

From this angle she could watch him approach her hiding place, the gun pointed straight ahead.

Gripping the screwdriver in her hand, Emma waited until the waves crashed again on the beach, drowning out all other noise. Then she lunged at him. Her bare feet were silent against the sand and stones, but his instincts were as sharply honed as any predator's and he must have sensed movement. At the final second, he turned and fired.

Emma threw herself down and rolled her body into his legs. Grogan fell hard.

The gun fired again when he hit the sand.

Emma leaped to her feet.

Still on his back, Grogan raised the gun but she kicked his hand with her bare foot, sending the pistol flying. Dropping to her knees, she twisted his injured arm behind him.

His scream sent a chill down her spine. She pressed the screwdriver to his jugular vein.

"You should have never come here," she hissed into his ear. "You should have stayed on the *Eden*."

"You whore." He spat the words at her.

Emma dug the screwdriver into his neck until the skin dimpled. She could see the artery moving blood beneath his skin, the rhythmic pulsing of life. A life she could take right now if she chose to. "Tell me one thing," she asked. "Did you sell your soul for money? Or did you not have one to start with?"

His scarred face turned and those empty eyes met hers.

"You don't get to win this." He thrashed in her grip, but her hold was tight.

As they struggled, Emma noticed a noise above her head. A thumping sound—similar to the waves on the stony coastline—but louder, more insistent.

A blinding light swung over the ridge of the promontory as a helicopter roared overhead.

Emma looked up, a smile spreading slowly across her face.

"I'm sorry to disappoint you, but I do get to win after all," she said, raising her voice to be heard above the noise of the rotors.

Emma didn't let Grogan move a muscle as the helicopter descended. She ducked her head, protecting her eyes from the sand that flew through the air like needles.

When the rotors finally stopped, her ears rang so loudly she didn't hear Jon calling her name, but it didn't matter. He was at her side in seconds.

"I see you caught something," he said, crouching beside her, a set of plastic handcuffs dangling from his fingers.

"Fuck you," Grogan snarled, squirming in Emma's grip, but his face looked pale as his eyes met Jon's. "You can't do this. You know—"

"Tsk," Jon chided, digging his fingers into Grogan's bad shoulder. "Manners."

After that, Grogan fell into a sullen silence as Emma and Jon handcuffed him and half carried him to the chopper, strapping him to a seat.

Talking quickly, Emma told Jon about Volkov and the fight on the *Eden*.

"He might be dead. If he is . . ." she said.

"We've got Cal Grogan and that's not nothing." He glanced down at her bare legs. "Now. We need to get you some clothes."

Until that precise moment, Emma had forgotten she was wearing only her underwear. She'd been too busy to care.

"We don't have much in the chopper." Peeling off his own jacket, he handed it to her. "This will have to do."

When Emma pulled it on, it carried a hint of his clean scent. She pulled it tighter around her.

Jon's gaze searched her bruised face, and then traveled down to her hand, scraped and bloody, and still clutching the screwdriver.

"You can let that go now," he told her gently. "It's over."

But she didn't drop it. She slipped it into the pocket of the jacket.

"Just in case," she said.

He touched her chin lightly with his fingertips, tilting her face up to examine the cut above her eye.

His touch sent a flutter of nerves swirling inside Emma's chest.

"Looks like he gave you a rough time," he said.

"I've been better." She made herself keep the tone light. "But I've also been much worse."

In reality, now that she was safe, she felt exhausted. Her legs trembled as she turned and climbed into the chopper. And she collapsed into the seat with relief. She wasn't sure she'd ever been more tired. Every part of her felt drained.

"Let's go," Jon told the pilot, as he climbed in after her.

Even as the rotors began to spin again, he didn't leave Emma's side, crouching beside her seat, one hand on the armrest, his eyes holding hers.

"You're going to have to tell me how all this happened, you know," he said, raising his voice to be heard above the noise of the chopper. "I'm going to need more details."

"Really, it's all Ripley's fault," she said, and closed her eyes. "You can't blame me at all."

PART THREE

THE
THIRD
MAN

27

When Emma joined the Agency, she soon discovered that having a personal life when you're a spy isn't completely impossible. It's just *nearly* impossible. Because you have to lie to everyone you know. It's bad enough with friends and family. It's even worse when you're dating.

She and Rob Murphy had served together in Army Intelligence in Germany, and they'd always got on well. When they were both back in England, he'd called her.

She knew him to be honest and utterly trustworthy. And yet she told him the same story she'd told her mother: that she worked for the Foreign Office, accompanying officials on diplomatic missions. He accepted this completely, and somehow that made it worse.

As the months went by, Emma began to hate herself for deceiving him. How could their relationship work when she was forced to lie to him over and over? Often the lies had to be invented quickly. She was rarely given notice when the Agency wanted to send her somewhere. Normally, she just received a secure message with an address, and the order to "go now."

Everything fell apart when she got one of those messages on the day Rob's best friend was getting married.

When Emma told him that she'd been called in to help a diplomat returning from abroad, he'd given her a look of absolute disbelief.

"I can't believe you're doing this again." He'd sat up, pulling the bedsheet around his bare waist. "You've known about Cam's wedding for weeks, and at the last minute you're just bailing on me? What will I tell him?"

"I said I was sorry," Emma said, but his dark eyes fixed her with a look of accusation and hurt, and she got out of bed mostly so she could stop looking at him.

She walked over to where her clothes had been strewn across the floor the night before, and began picking them up.

It was morning, and the sun streamed through the window at the end of Rob's studio apartment. The place had a particular smell in the mornings, which Emma had always liked—a mixture of oiled floorboards and scorched dust as the ancient radiators rattled into life. Emma's dress—a dark blue confection she'd bought especially for the day—hung from the door of the wardrobe, with her shoes just below. She'd brought them over the previous night, so they could get ready together before heading to the ceremony.

She looked at the dress with regret, and then pulled on her bra, hooking it firmly in place.

"I really wish I could go. I like Cam and Rachel. I'm sorry I'll miss it."

"I'll tell them how sorry you are while I'm sitting alone for four hours," Rob said coldly. He watched her dress, a look of suspicion spreading across his even features. "Sometimes I wonder where you really go, you know that?" He sat up straighter. "We've been seeing each other for months. You cancel on me all the time, always at the last minute, always because of work. I mean those diplomats really get around, right?"

Emma buttoned her jeans and turned to face him. She kept her voice measured. "I'm really sorry I can't go to the wedding but I think you're making this a bigger deal than it is. It's just a party, really. You'll know lots of people there. You won't be alone."

"That isn't the point, Alex." Rob got out of bed and walked up to her. He moved with the grace of a panther; his long legs still had that military muscularity. "Something's going on, and you might as well tell me the truth. I'll figure it out, anyway. If you're not seeing someone else, and I don't think you are, then what is it?" His eyes searched her face with a new lack of passion. "Are you MI5 or something? You're just their type."

"Don't be ridiculous. If I were MI5, I'd tell you." That lie made Emma's heart hurt. Rob had known her before the Agency. He knew her real name. He understood her. She couldn't do this. "Please . . . I don't want to fight."

"I don't either. But I also don't want to date someone who isn't honest with me," he said simply. He paused, holding her gaze for a long moment, before saying, "I think we should end this."

Emma's breath caught. "Rob . . ."

"I like you," he said, before she could say more. "I think I might more than like you. But something's going on in your life. I don't know what it is, but I know you're not telling me the truth. I can't accept that. It's an awful feeling not to be trusted."

"I trust you," Emma insisted. "I swear I'm just working—"

He cut her off. "Don't lie anymore. Give me that much."

They held each other's gaze. The words "You were right: I'm a spy" were at the back of Emma's throat, ready to come out. If she told him the truth, he might forgive her. He might stay.

And she might lose the job she loved.

"This isn't what I want," Emma protested, tears prickling the backs of her eyes.

Gently, Rob reached up and brushed her hair back from her face.

"Me neither. But this isn't going to work," he said softly. "It's better if we do this now."

That breakup had really hurt. It had taken her months to get over it. Maybe longer than that. And somewhere along the way, she'd decided never to put herself through that again.

In the two years since then, she'd seen less of her old friends, and she dated rarely, never letting any relationship get serious. In the last six months she hadn't dated anyone at all.

She was busy, she told herself, and she didn't need the distraction.

Her job was all about illusion. But lies—even noble lies—are poison in the well. Everything suffers when you can never tell the truth.

"The problem," Ripley told her once, when she brought it up, "is that you're an honest person at heart. And that's a disaster for a spy. You have to learn to live with the lies."

Of course, Ripley wasn't married. He had no children. He lived for his job. And in the rare moments she was completely honest with herself, Emma wondered if she'd end up exactly the same.

The sky was slate gray and a steady rain had just begun to fall when Emma and Jon emerged from a taxi on a quiet street in west London. Emma wore ill-fitting yoga pants and an oversized top with a pair of men's trainers laced tight to keep them on her feet. It had been thirty-six hours since Jon appeared over the cliffside in a helicopter. For Emma those hours had been a blur of pain, French doctors, false passports, borrowed clothes, and hurried travel.

The helicopter had taken them to a small airport outside Nice. From there, she'd been driven to a safe house in the French countryside by a team of French security officers where she was examined by a doctor and debriefed by MI6 agents with Ripley on a secure comms link.

Now, Emma gazed at the red-brick houses around her with real affection. There'd been moments on the *Eden* when she wasn't certain she'd live to see London again. She didn't think it had ever looked more beautiful. She even felt fondly for the damp English weather.

Jon gave her a quick sideways smile, as if he knew what she was thinking. He had been a rock through all of this. Tracking down clothes and painkillers, backing her up in the long debrief, insisting that she rest. He'd passionately defended Ripley's decision to tell no one she was going to the W Hotel.

"It was the right thing to do," he'd insisted when anyone questioned it. "Her life was on the line."

The one thing no one had discussed with her was the third man. The one she'd heard speaking in the W Hotel. That was far too sensitive an issue to discuss on foreign soil.

The trip back to London had been made in absolute secrecy. She was forbidden to let anyone know that she had returned. She could not, under any circumstances, go to the Vernon Institute or to any MI6 building. She traveled under a false name. For all intents and purposes, she wasn't here at all.

She and Jon turned a corner, pausing to make sure they weren't being followed before climbing the front steps of a narrow Victorian terraced house.

Number 21 Bailey Street was ordinary in every way, with windowsills that needed painting and a bicycle leaning against the rail out front. Nothing about it said "MI6 safe house." Which was the whole point.

"You made good time," Andrew Field said, meeting them in the doorway. The expression on his cherubic face was deadly serious, but as Emma passed him, he eyed her bruises, and murmured with dry understatement, "Nice to see you in one piece, Makepeace."

"Nice to *be* in one piece," she replied.

The house had once been grand—stained glass in vivid carnelian and lemon still brightened the windows at the front, and the stairs were wide, with ornate newel posts. But the carpet was worn thin, and it smelled of damp as they headed down the short hallway to a spacious sitting room, where the high ceilings and ancient wallpaper overlooked a scattering of mismatched furniture.

Ripley was waiting for her there. His cool gray eyes took in the bandage on her temple, and her stiff gait.

"Good to have you back," he told Emma, shaking her hand with rare warmth. "We have much to discuss."

He motioned for the two of them to take a seat.

Emma perched on the edge of an ancient leather sofa. "Any news on Volkov?"

"All we know is he didn't go to France as he promised," Ripley said. "The *Eden* sailed to Monaco, and it's still there. No one has seen Volkov himself since the yacht arrived."

"Cal Grogan is still in intensive care," said Field, taking the chair next to Ripley. "But he's responding to treatment. We should be able to interview him in a day or two. We might learn more then."

Emma doubted they'd learn anything, but she didn't say that.

Jon leaned against the wall near the windows. "Has anyone come off the *Eden* at all?"

"There has been some activity," Field said. "The *Eden*'s captain contacted the harbor master and told him the powerboat was damaged and they needed a replacement. They were put in touch with a local company, and a new boat was purchased in Volkov's name, via a payment from one of his companies. It was delivered a few hours ago. After that, Jason Donnelly was taken to shore by one of the crew, and has not returned to the *Eden*, as far as we know. He appears to have checked in to a hotel in Monte Carlo."

"So Volkov threw Jason out, but hasn't reached out to MI6 for protection?" Emma's eyebrows drew together. "That doesn't make sense. Volkov despises Federov. And he knows how much danger he's in if we don't . . ."

Her voice trailed off, as something occurred to her. That afternoon in Saint-Tropez, which felt like a hundred years ago. And the glimpse she'd caught of Volkov's family.

She turned to Ripley. "There's not much Volkov cares about, but I think he loves his son. He went to a lot of trouble to hide his wife and child in that house in Saint-Tropez. Do you think Federov could have found them there? Threatened them?"

Field and Jon exchanged a look.

"I could go to Saint-Tropez," Jon said, in response to Field's unasked question. "I've got good connections. I can find out if Federov's people have been spotted in town."

"You just got back," Field said. "Let me ask some of our friends in France if they're monitoring the family. I'll come back to you."

Jon inclined his head, but Emma saw his jaw tighten slightly. He wanted to handle it himself. France was his territory.

She would have been exactly the same in his shoes. In the last few days, they had formed a real connection, one that went beyond work. They just got each other. Jon was so easy to talk to, so thoughtful and sharp, it felt as though she'd always known him. She hadn't felt that way about anyone in a while.

She wrenched her attention back to the conversation.

"What happens now?" she asked. "I know we've got Cal Grogan, but if Volkov doesn't come in voluntarily, how do we bring down the rest of Gold Dust? I could go to Monaco and talk to Volkov. He does seem to trust me in a strange way."

The pause that followed her question was ominous.

It was Ripley who told her the truth. "It can't be you, Emma. You're out of the operation. It's over."

28

mma stared at Ripley. "What? *Why?*"

"You've been burned," he said. "And Oleg Federov is too good an opponent. We can't use you anymore. Too dangerous."

"Oleg Federov has never seen me!" Emma's voice rose. "Surely you don't think he could recognize me without ever meeting me?"

"'Surely' isn't a principle on which we operate," Ripley reminded her crisply. "We operate on facts. And the fact is, Federov is ruthless. He might have seen a picture of you—Cal Grogan could have shared one. But he is not the only danger to you. There are others. Too many others."

When she opened her mouth to argue, he shut her down. "Don't question me on this, Emma. The decision is made. *Accept it.*"

There was frost in his voice. Still, Emma seethed. This was *her* operation. She'd been part of it every step of the way. And now she was out. Just like that.

"Is this because you still think I screwed up on the *Eden*?" she demanded, squaring up to Ripley. "Because I'm telling you it wasn't me. They found out about me somewhere else. Volkov told me I was betrayed. I know you don't believe me—"

Field cleared his throat and leaned forward, catching her eye. "We believe you, Emma. We're running two operations now. We're continuing to investigate Volkov, Federov, and their weapons operation, and, at the same time, we're working to identify the person who exposed your identity to Volkov when you were in Spain."

Emma stared at him. Everyone had doubted her for so long she'd begun to wonder if it wasn't all in her head. But she couldn't enjoy the vindication. She wouldn't be part of the team tracking down the traitor.

"Do you know who did it?" she asked, looking from Field to Ripley.

"Not yet," Field said. "It could be the man you saw in the W Hotel, or it could be someone else. We're working on it."

"Either way, until we know more, you must lie low," Ripley interjected. "Remember, it's not only Volkov who knows your identity, but also the mole who's working against us. Either one of them could target you."

For some reason, she hadn't thought about this possibility before. Once she was off the *Eden*, she'd felt safe. But of course she wasn't.

Her personal information—her home address, her mother's address—were buried so deep inside the security department's systems nobody should ever be able to find them. But if the mole working with Federov knew who she was, they might find that information. And more.

"Is my mother safe?" Her voice sharpened. "Are you protecting her?"

"I've removed any information about her from our system," Ripley told her. "We've got a team outside her house. She's constantly watched. We'll keep her safe." When her expression didn't change, he leaned toward her. "I promise, Emma. She's safe."

"Jesus." She let out a long breath. The Agency relied on absolute anonymity. Complete secrecy. Now someone was lifting the curtain and letting in light. And that would destroy everything.

"How will this work?" she asked. "How can you investigate this if someone inside can't be trusted? Everyone's family could be at risk."

Ripley picked up his black cigarette case. "We'll operate in isolation, off the books. A small team of trusted people. Andrew and I will lead. We'll tell no one else at the Agency what we're doing unless we require their help, and even then I will handpick them."

Jon was watching Ripley closely. "It sounds like we're looking for someone highly placed, with influence. A government minister, maybe? Or someone senior inside MI6."

Emma's heart sank. "That's a lot of people, all of them with the power and political access to stop us exposing them."

"We're not starting with nothing." Ripley glanced at Emma. "Your work on the *Eden* helped a great deal. One thing is clear: the person we're looking for has top-secret security clearance. That's the only way they could possibly know about the operation. Odds are it's someone we've met. Someone we know."

Emma listened, a picture forming in her mind of the one person who fit this description perfectly.

"What about Ed Masterson?" she asked.

The temperature in the room seemed to drop by several degrees.

Ripley fixed her with a level look. "Emma. Don't."

But she wasn't about to stop. The whole time she'd been in France, being questioned, being studied, she'd thought about Masterson. He was the only person at the Agency she didn't trust completely. The one who had already proven he was capable of betrayal.

"Ed has access to everything," she reminded him. "He has influence. He's top-secret cleared. And the man I saw in Barcelona could easily have been him."

"It's *not* Ed." Ripley's tone was implacable. "Let it go."

His loyalty was infuriating. Somehow, she had to make him see reason.

"Will you at least investigate him?" she demanded. "He matches the description of the person we're looking for precisely."

Ripley shook his head. "I'm telling you, it's not him. He wasn't in Barcelona."

Emma wasn't ready to let it go. "Are you sure? He could have traveled on a false passport, the same as I did. Ripley, you know what—"

"Emma, *stop*." For the second time that day Ripley gave her a look of real disapproval. "I know it's not him because I've had Ed under surveillance since October. We've monitored his behavior, his bank accounts, his phone usage. If he were in bed with the Russians I would know. If he went to Barcelona I would know. It *isn't him*."

Emma fell silent. All this time she'd wondered how Ed had got away with what he'd done, but of course he hadn't. Ripley was too smart for that. He had quietly and constantly had his deputy monitored while giving every appearance of trusting him. Ripley wasn't blindly loyal. He was *careful*.

The moment felt weighted. Jon avoided her eyes. Field looked down at his folded hands.

"I . . . I didn't know," Emma stammered.

Ripley regarded her coldly. "There's a great deal you don't know. You'd be wise to remember that. Especially now."

He pulled a cigarette from the case and lit it, snapping the lighter shut emphatically.

An uncomfortable silence fell.

"I presume you have a list of names?" Jon said, after a beat.

"Actually, we've been working on this, and so far there are two primary possibilities." Field spoke as if nothing at all had just happened. "Both match the description, and both could have been at the W Hotel in Barcelona that day." He pulled a photo from a file at his feet and handed it across. "There was a delegation in Spain from the Department for Business. The adjunct minister for trade is a man named Brian Jeffers."

Jon tilted the image so Emma could see a blond man who looked to be in his late twenties. He had pale blue eyes and an arrogant mouth.

"Why him?" Jon asked.

"Mostly his background. He's dabbled with extreme politics," Field explained. "He has connections to far-right groups in Europe. We've had him on our radar for a while. We're digging into his bank accounts and internet history right now. The only problem is his clearance is not top secret. So if it was him, then he wasn't working alone. Which is a complication we don't need."

He pulled out another photo. "However, there was another group in Spain at the same time. A team from the Foreign Office was in Madrid for a counterterrorism meeting with Spanish officials."

Emma saw Jon's expression sharpen. The Foreign Office overlapped with MI6 in many areas. They worked closely together. Their budgets were intertwined.

"Who was in that group?" Jon asked.

"The delegation was headed by a junior minister—Martin Dowell." Field handed them a second image. "He was there with a team of civil servants involved in counterterrorism work. The civil servants are not above suspicion, but it's Dowell who interests us the most."

The photo showed a man with hair somewhere between brown and blond, combed back. He had a high forehead and a weak jaw. He was older than Jeffers—early forties, Emma thought.

Dowell, she thought. *How do I know that name?*

"Why does Dowell interest you?" she asked.

"He meddles a fair bit," Field said. "I've had him in my office looking for information more than once. That's not unusual for an ambitious MP, of course. All the same, I find him interesting."

Ripley blew out a stream of smoke. "Dowell was in my office after Stephen Garrick died, demanding to know what we were going to do."

Emma drew in a breath. "That's where I heard his name," she said. "I came to talk to you the day I left for France, but he was there."

Her boss gave her a piercing glance. "Did he see you? Did he know who you were?"

"No . . ." she said. "I don't think so. Masterson saw me standing on the landing and told me to go down and see Martha. Your door was cracked open, but I don't think he could have seen me. Could he?" Even as she said it, though, it occurred to her that if he'd turned at the right moment and looked he might have seen her talking to Masterson.

She wasn't the only one who seemed to be having that thought. The air in the room felt suddenly thicker.

"Did he know we were placing someone on the *Eden?*" Field asked Ripley.

"I didn't tell him any details, only that we were running a full investigation to find who was behind the killing. I kept it vague." Ripley tapped the cigarette in the ash tray. "I do remember that he pressed hard. He said Garrick's father had spoken to the Prime Minister, and the PM wanted details about what we were doing. I thought it was a bit over the top, so I told him that we'd find who did it, no matter what it took."

He paused and said quietly, almost to himself, "If it's him, he's very, very clever. He's not put a foot wrong."

"If it's him, he'll have made sure we can't prove it," Field added. "The Foreign Office will never believe one of theirs is capable of this."

"Would Dowell have access to operational data on Gold Dust?" Jon asked.

"It's not impossible." Field glanced at Emma. "If only you'd got a better look at him in Barcelona."

"What about CCTV from the hotel?" suggested Jon.

"Cameras were in place, but not operational," Field revealed. "Technical problem, apparently."

"Right." Jon's cynical tone said what they were all thinking. It was rather convenient for a hotel popular with Russian billionaires to have an unreliable camera system.

"I'll get started looking into his travel," Field said. "We'll see how the dates match up with Emma's work on the *Eden*. And we'll run a check on his finances."

"I'll see if we can find anything in Stephen Garrick's work that ties directly to Dowell," Ripley said. "Zach can handle that without knowing why he's doing it. I can find an excuse."

Jon's brow furrowed. "What about Emma? If there's the slightest chance the person we're looking for knows her real identity, she's in huge danger. She can't go home, surely."

"Yes. We've been discussing that." Field glanced at Emma. "We think you should stay here for a while."

Emma blinked. "Here . . . as in, in this house?"

"Yes. That's the idea," said Field. "It's off the books. Nobody would know to look here. We've had it for years. For emergencies, you see. Rarely used. Mothballs."

Again, that uncomfortably easy tone she was starting to see as a warning sign.

"What about work?" she asked.

"Why don't you focus on Federov?" Ripley suggested. "If, as you believe, he's the brains behind the operation, we need to find a way to get closer to him. Go through his files again. Figure out what we're missing."

Emma didn't hide her dismay. "So I'm just going to stay here and reread old files? That's my part in all of this?"

It was Field who replied. "The problem, you see," he said in that pleasant voice, "is that you're the one person who can find the third man, and bring him down. You got close to Volkov. You arrested Cal Grogan. Odds are, you've met the mole at some point and didn't realize it. So they know you better than you know them. As far as they're concerned, as long as you're alive, you're a threat. Killing you would solve a lot of their problems."

29

The three men departed an hour later. Emma stood at the front windows watching as they paused on the pavement. Jon said something and Ripley laughed, patting his shoulder before they all walked in separate directions, leaving Emma alone in the safe house.

In the quiet that followed, she didn't know what to do with herself. She turned the TV on and off, and roamed the empty hallways, looking into the bedrooms. Finally, she sat on the leather sofa, staring at the walls.

This wasn't how missions were supposed to end. Normally she'd be at home, rediscovering her life. Reminding herself who she really was. Instead, it felt as if she'd gone undercover all over again, only this time she wasn't sure what mission she was on.

There was always a kind of hangover after an operation ended, but this wasn't a hangover. This was a crash. She'd failed to bring Volkov in. She'd been burned. And, no matter what anyone told her, this felt like punishment.

Ripley hadn't even given her back her personal phone. Instead, he'd given her an Agency phone to use "until things calm down."

"Call your mother," he'd told her, just before he'd left. "She's called you twice. Tell her you've lost it and this is your new phone. That will explain why you didn't phone sooner."

But she couldn't seem to do that. She was too shattered to summon the lies she'd need to tell right now.

In the quiet she heard a car roll down the street and disappear. The sound of voices as someone walked by. Everything felt too sharp; too near. Even the patter of rain against the windows sounded too loud.

She kept finding herself thinking about the *Eden*. The extraordinary blue of the water and sky. The way the morning sun fell on the sea like liquid gold. The pull of the engine that she could feel through the soles of her feet. Sara laughing at her own jokes; Madison demanding another cosmo "for my nerves"; Volkov pleading with her in the corridor to help him . . .

When she closed her eyes she could feel the soft sway of the deck beneath her feet; the rise and fall of the swells.

She was so lost in thought, when someone knocked on the front door she almost jumped out of her skin.

She raced to the CCTV monitor near the front door. Jon's face was on the screen.

When she opened the door, she found him standing on the top step with a suitcase, a laptop bag over his shoulder, and several bags of groceries at his feet.

Seeing her expression, he laughed. "Well, I wasn't going to leave you alone without food or clothes, was I? What kind of homecoming would that be?"

His face was flushed from the effort of carrying so much, and his dark blue eyes smiled down at her.

Some of the loneliness that had threatened to subsume her moments ago dissipated.

"I guess you'd better come in and have a cup of tea," she said, opening the door wider. "As long as you brought tea, that is. And milk. And a spoon."

The two of them lugged in the supplies, and Jon put the kettle on while she went to one of the bedrooms to change.

"You're a bloody hero for doing this," she called as she kicked off the borrowed shoes and dug out her own.

"Don't give me too much credit," he said. "Martha had already gone to your house and packed a bag. She had it ready when I got to the Agency. I did get the food though. So I suppose I *am* a bit heroic."

Emma put on black jeans and a soft pullover and instantly felt better. Wearing her own clothing again was like rediscovering an old friend.

When she walked back to the kitchen, a mug of tea was steaming on the counter and Jon was making toast.

"After a mission I always have tea and toast to settle my nerves," he told her as he searched through the cupboards for plates. "It's a tradition."

Emma leaned against the cupboard and watched with amusement. "I never thought of you as a homebody."

"Oh, don't get me wrong, I fancy myself a sophisticate," he said, spreading butter on a slice of toast. "But everyone needs to have a cup of tea sometimes." He handed her a plate. "Now get that inside you."

But as Emma took the plate, her appetite faded.

"Ripley thinks I failed," she said. "Doesn't he?"

Jon gave her a surprised look. "Quite the opposite. You brought in Cal Grogan. You also uncovered a huge amount of information the analysts are still going through." His eyes searched her face. "I know you feel crap, but this is the normal down after the operation high. Don't believe it. You didn't fail."

"I had Volkov." She stretched out her arm, opening her palm. "He was in my hand. If Grogan hadn't knocked him out . . ."

Jon faced her directly. "Volkov is a criminal. If bringing in criminals was easy, none of us would have a job. You cut a path to him that we can walk down. Ripley's working on a plan to approach him and offer to protect his family. We've got people in Saint-Tropez outside his wife's house." He reached for her hand. "Hey. We'll get there."

Emma looked down to where her fingers were encased inside his.

For the last two days she'd been so numb from failure and exhaustion and doubt she'd wondered if she'd ever feel normal again. But his hand felt real and solid. His skin was warm.

Jon had been the one constant through all of this. Even when she'd hidden things from him. He'd had her back the entire time. Right now, it felt as if he was the only one who had.

His gaze locked on hers. The air between them became electric.

Hesitantly, she reached up and brushed his hair back from his forehead, losing her fingers in the softness. She didn't let herself think about how they worked together, and how merging the lines of the personal and the professional was always a mistake. She didn't want to think at all. She was tired of thinking. And something told her that he felt the same.

"Is this a bad idea?" she whispered.

"Oh, absolutely," he said, with a smile that made something inside her melt, and lowered his lips to hers.

The passion of the kiss took her off guard. His mouth was warm, curious, demanding. His chest pressed hard against her, and she liked the solidity of him. She slid her hands up his shoulders until her arms wrapped around his neck, pulling him closer, leaning against him, opening her lips to his, tasting him against her tongue—the salt and sweetness of him.

His breath hitched in his throat, a slight gasp she felt in her chest.

Emma tugged his jacket back and he straightened his arms and let it slip to the floor, before pulling off the top she'd only just put on.

He leaned forward to trace kisses along her right shoulder as he slowly tugged her bra strap down, and then did the same thing on the left side. His lips and hands seemed to burn her skin like fire and she quivered with urgency. But when she reached back to unhook the bra, he captured her hands with his, stopping her.

"Good things come to those who wait," he whispered.

He turned her around so she faced the cupboard, and pressed her forward with his body so she bent at a slight angle as his hands traced heat down her spine from the neck to the curves of her hips and back up again.

Her breath came in short gasps now. She didn't want him anymore. She *needed* him. She needed to forget about what was ahead, to forget her job, to forget what a terrible idea it was to have sex with someone she worked with — all of it. She needed to forget everything.

As if he knew this and was determined to frustrate her, he unhooked her bra with languorous slowness, but by then she'd had enough of waiting.

Spinning around, she pushed him against the counter, pressing her lips against his neck, and then, as she unbuttoned his shirt, the taut skin of his shoulder and chest. She could feel his heart racing beneath her lips as she kissed a line down across his torso. He watched her as her fingers reached the buttons of his trousers. She gave him a look — a question. And felt the muscles of his stomach tighten with anticipation when he nodded his assent.

She removed his trousers slowly, and when she straightened again, his face was fierce with desire. He removed the rest of her clothes in a rush and lifted her onto the countertop.

After that there was no slowing down. No restraint.

And Emma could forget everything for a while.

30

Emma woke the next morning in an unfamiliar bed with Jon's arms warm around her.

As always, she was instantly alert, but she lay still, her mind rushing through yesterday's events.

After she and Jon had made love more than once, they'd realized they were famished. They'd cooked supper from the supplies he'd brought, and talked for hours over glasses of wine. Emma felt far from the *Eden* now, her feet firmly on solid ground.

There was no rule against intelligence officers having relationships with each other; in fact, it was encouraged. Spy couples were useful. They could be placed easily into new locations. And of course there was no risk, in a relationship where everyone had top-secret security clearance, of a leak. But Emma had never done it before. The Agency was small, and it would be weird to have a romantic relationship with anyone there and then see them in the office.

With Jon, though, everything felt possible. She liked him. She didn't have to lie to him—he already knew everything.

There was something almost dizzyingly freeing about realizing she could be her true self with him.

It was as if the curtains of her life had been drawn back, and everything was suddenly *real*.

So she stayed still, relishing the sensation of his body against hers. The warmth of him was wonderful. Until she sensed his breathing change and the looseness of sleep leaving him, replaced by an alertness she could feel.

He pressed his lips against her shoulder, just above the scar the bullet had left the year before.

"You slept," he said.

"So did you."

She could feel his smile against her skin. "Well, I didn't just come off an undercover assignment that could have killed me," he reminded her. "So it's not as miraculous that I could lie unconscious for hours."

He ran his hand lightly down her body and Emma's skin responded instantly, sending a shiver along her spine.

"I need a shower." She kissed the inside of Jon's lean wrist, and gently disentangled herself from his arms before heading down the hall.

The bathroom was as unreconstructed as the rest of the house, but there were clean towels in the cupboard and plenty of hot water.

In the mirror above the sink she examined the bruises on her face and body. She was still sore but she was already healing.

She'd decided something during the night. Maybe she couldn't go undercover again on this operation, but she'd stay part of it. She'd help bring Federov and whoever he was working with to justice, whether it was Dowell or someone else, even if she had to do it from here.

As she dressed later, the image of Cal Grogan flashed through her mind, as he'd looked in Nice being taken away in a wheelchair. Hunched over, his head loose, he'd seemed weak. Defeated.

His doctors wouldn't allow anyone to question him as long as he was in intensive care. But somehow they *had* to get permission to speak with him soon. He knew more than anyone what Oleg Federov was up to, and whom he worked with. They could make him a deal. Anything to get the truth.

Downstairs, she dug through the supplies Jon had put in the cupboard last night, discovering a bag of freshly ground coffee from the Monmouth Coffee Company—the best coffee in London.

She held the bag to her nose and breathed in the rich scent before turning the kettle on and tracking down a French press and two clean mugs, her mind still puzzling over how to bring down Federov.

I should ask Ripley to let me contact Volkov, she thought. *I could convince him to trust us.*

"Excellent. The coffee's on." Jon walked in carrying a laptop just as she was adding milk. "I think Andrew's sent some files. I asked for more information about Jeffers and Dowell. We need to know who we're up against."

They sat next to each other at the kitchen table, bare feet touching, as they shared Emma's secure laptop to read the intelligence files.

"Jeffers is a piece of work," Emma observed. "Links to Hungarian extremist groups. Big fan of Russia."

"It's almost performative though, isn't it?" Jon mused. "Like he's trying to impress his dodgy mates."

Emma liked the way his uncombed hair fell into his eyes, and the way his foot felt against hers. It meant a lot to her that he'd stayed this morning. That he was including her in the case.

But all she said was, "Yes, if he was the real thing, he wouldn't do any of that. He wouldn't want anyone to notice him."

"But that could be deliberate. He'd know we'd think exactly that," Jon pointed out.

"Anyway, Dowell looks so clean by comparison." Emma got up to refill her cup. "Ambitious. Clever. All the right schools. Cambridge. Good family."

"He's the one who interests me," Jon said. "Kim Philby matched that description exactly. Look how he turned out."

The reference to MI6's most notorious traitor was sobering. Philby had betrayed his country and his friends, handing valuable information to Russia over many years.

Emma reached for the milk and said, "What makes someone do that? I can't understand hating your own country that much."

"Can't you?" He looked up at her. "Isn't your father an example of that?"

Emma's hand jerked, spilling milk onto the countertop.

"Damn," she said. Adding unnecessarily, "Sorry," she hurried to the sink for a sponge.

How could Jon know about that?

"Emma?" Jon sounded concerned. "Everything OK?"

She turned to face him. "I guess I never really thought of my father that way. He was helping us. He was trying to stop a nuclear holocaust. He was on our side."

"And we're the good guys." Jon's voice was calm.

She gave him a puzzled look. "Well, yes. Last time I checked, anyway."

Jon must have heard the anger in her tone because his face clouded. "I'm sorry." When she didn't reply, he stood up and walked toward her. "I didn't mean to upset you. I shouldn't have brought it up."

"It's fine," she said, forcing herself to meet his gaze. "I didn't realize you knew about my dad."

"Andrew sent your files to me the day the operation began," he explained. "That's standard. I have to know everything in your past to know what weaknesses you might have."

He untangled her fingers from the coffee mug and took her hands in his. "What's wrong?"

Emma swallowed hard. "My father wasn't a traitor. He was a hero."

"Yes, he was." Jon's voice was steady. "And I don't mean to equate what he did with the man we're searching for now. I don't think this man is a hero to anyone. I don't think the two compare. I believe our guy is in it for the money."

Emma was relieved to return to the issue that mattered right now.

"But neither Jeffers nor Dowell shows any signs of being obsessed with money," she said.

"That's what's bothering me, too," Jon agreed. "All the money in Dowell's accounts is legitimate. He has a modest house, reasonable car. He doesn't actually appear all that ambitious."

"And Jeffers has a one-bedroom flat in Essex. He's not exactly rolling in cash," Emma pointed out. "If he had access to millions, you'd think he'd pay off some of his debt."

"Which leaves us where?" Jon asked.

"Nowhere." Emma sipped her coffee.

What they really needed was Oleg Federov. He was the spider in the middle of the web. The only person who knew everything.

"Somehow, we need to get closer to Federov," she said thoughtfully.

"It's not possible," Jon said. "He's too careful."

"We could still get to him," Emma insisted. "Everyone's got a weakness. We just have to find his."

Jon selected a clementine from the bowl on the table and tossed it in the air, catching it smoothly and then throwing it up again, his brow furrowed with thought.

"Maybe we could work on someone near him," he suggested, throwing the clementine again. "He's got multiple offices."

Emma shook her head. "We looked at that idea but his offices are too big, and he's never in them. He only comes to London for brief periods. And he'll come less now that Grogan's been arrested."

"You're right. That won't work." Jon stopped throwing the fruit and began to peel it.

Emma watched the short curls of vivid orange falling onto the table but she wasn't really seeing them. In her mind she went through Federov's file again. He was unmarried. No children. His endless array of businesses was his family.

Suddenly, she remembered Kira Zakharova, the Russian defense secretary's daughter, and how easily she'd connected with her. And poor Madison, alone and bored on the *Eden*.

"Does Federov have a girlfriend?" she asked.

"Yeah, of course. They all do." He popped a segment of clementine into his mouth. "Why? What are you thinking?"

"Is she Russian?" Emma asked, ignoring the question.

"I think so."

"Tell me about her," Emma said.

Jon wiped his fingertips on a cloth and then pulled the laptop closer. The deep blue-and-white MI6 logo glowed in one corner as he began typing.

"Right. Let's see." His eyebrows drew together as he read aloud. "Her name is Natalya Kuzmina. She's twenty-five. Swimsuit model and aspiring singer." He glanced up at her. "That's unusual. Usually they want to be actresses."

He turned the computer around so she could see the screen.

Emma angled forward, taking in the photo of a tall, slim young woman with high cheekbones and a mane of blond hair. She was in a bikini, her body turned to show off her figure. Her eyes were a pure, arresting blue.

She looked so like Madison, Emma's breath caught.

It was extraordinary, really, these young, beautiful women walking into relationships with men they couldn't begin to understand. Dazzled by the money, the drugs, and the glitz, the women thought they were so sophisticated, but they were victims waiting to happen. So easily manipulated. So easily discarded.

She stared at the image for a long moment, and then said, "Is she in London?"

"I can double-check but, as far as I know, she hasn't left England in six months." Jon gave her a puzzled look. "Why? What are you thinking?"

Emma raised her eyes to his.

"I think I know how to get closer to Oleg Federov." Emma tapped the picture of Natalya with her fingertip. "If you let me work on her, she'll walk me right through his door."

31

"That is absolutely out of the question." Jon's voice hardened. "There's no way we'll let you go undercover again on this operation. You heard Ripley. You're out."

His mood had changed almost instantly. An icy disapproval hung in the air between them.

"The only way to get proof of the third man's identity is to get close to Federov," Emma reminded him. "I can work Natalya the way I worked Kira and Madison. I know these women. They're young and far from home, living with dull old men. It's fine as long as the drugs and champagne are flowing, but the rest of the time they're incredibly lonely. They're vulnerable. I can *use that*."

Jon looked at her as if she'd suddenly lost her reason. "It's not a bad idea," he said. "But you can't do it. You're burned, Emma. Volkov knows who you are. Federov might know, too. Whatever happens next, it can't be you."

"Federov knows that Jessica Marshall was a British intelligence officer," Emma corrected him. "He hasn't got a clue who Emma Makepeace is."

Even before she stopped speaking, Jon was already shaking his head. "You can't know that for certain. Someone is feeding Federov information. That's why we're here." He swung out his arm, taking in the cheap countertops and faded linoleum floor. "Even if they don't have that much access, we have to assume Volkov told Federov about you. He may have described you." He paused. "Listen to me, Emma. It can't be you. It's not safe."

But Emma could already see this operation in her mind. How it would work. Who she'd need to become to win over Natalya.

"I think Volkov would have told Federov very little about me," she argued. "If Federov ever believed Volkov let a British intelligence agent gather useful information on the *Eden*, he'd kill him. Volkov would have claimed he spotted me from the start, that I was only after Cal, and that he kept me well away from their operation."

"You're guessing," Jon said flatly.

"So are you," Emma shot back. "You forget, I know Volkov. He's arrogant and untrustworthy but most of all he's frightened. He's afraid of the people he's working with. He knows what they're capable of."

"What about Federov?" Jon leaned back, watching her closely. "He might have seen your face that day in Barcelona."

"He didn't see me," Emma said. "I'm certain."

Jon threw up his hands. "I don't understand you. Why would you risk your life like this? I'm telling you it's too dangerous, and you know I'm right but you don't care. It's almost like you enjoy the danger."

Emma flinched. "Oh come on. You'd never say that to a man. Stop treating me differently than anyone else you work with."

"Don't be ridiculous," he snapped.

"It's not ridiculous," she told him. "You'd never tell a man that he enjoys danger. Not like that." Jon tried to argue but she spoke over him. "You wouldn't. Not if his idea was good. Not if you thought he could handle it. This isn't about me being burned. This is about you wanting to protect me. We should never have had sex. It messes everything up."

Emma instantly wished she could take it back. A stony silence descended.

When Jon spoke again, his voice was measured. "It's not about ability and it's not about protecting you. It's about the fact that you should only go into an undercover operation if it's the best option available."

"This *is* the best option." Emma leaned forward, willing him to understand. "This could work, Jon. We are *this close* to breaking this case. There are chemical weapons at stake here. Weapons that can kill thousands of people."

Jon looked away, his expression unyielding. When he didn't respond, she tried again.

"If it helps us find the mole inside our government, surely it's worth any price."

"No. Not any price." He pressed his fingertips against his forehead. "Can you hear what you're saying, Emma? It's like you're trying to get yourself killed."

A sliver of ice slid into her heart but all she said was, "That's absurd."

"Maybe," he said. "Maybe you really want to do this because you're *that* good. Or maybe there's another reason you want to go back into that world. Either way, I can't support you on this. Find another way."

Before she could reply, he stood up and walked upstairs. Emma could hear the floors creak as he gathered his things. She wanted to follow him, to make him change his mind, to make him listen. But she knew it was futile.

When he returned a few minutes later, Jon's shirt was buttoned and his expression was devoid of emotion. He stood in the doorway to the kitchen, the June sun through the dusty windows lighting up his face, but failing to bring warmth to his cold blue eyes.

"You need to know I'm going to make sure you don't go anywhere near Federov," he said flatly. "I can't let you do this. It's an act of self-harm."

"Jon . . ." Emma began, but he didn't wait to hear what she had to say. He simply walked away.

After he left, Emma sat for a long time with her phone in her hand, but she didn't dial. She didn't think there was a single thing she could say that would change Jon's mind right now. She was too angry anyway. Angry that she'd mixed her personal life with work. Angry that she'd given him the power to hurt her.

In the few hours she'd been back in England she'd messed everything up. And now, somehow, she had to fix it.

There had been some truth in what Jon had said. The risks she took often worried her. But they got the job done, and the job was everything. After all, she wasn't doing this for thrills. She was an intelligence officer. She worked for the country. And the country needed to know the truth about who inside the government was conspiring with Oleg Federov to sell weapons to rogue nations. Maybe she was arrogant to think she should be the one to do this. Or maybe she really *was* the one person who could do it.

Putting Jon deliberately from her mind, she spent the rest of the day researching Natalya. It wasn't hard work: the model and aspiring singer had few secrets from the Russian media, for whom she was a favorite interview subject. What she didn't tell the newspapers and interview shows, she shared on Instagram.

It took only a few hours to pull together a profile of Oleg Federov's mistress. And minutes for Emma to figure out how best to approach her.

Still, only when she knew precisely what she wanted to do and how it would work did she dial the number Ripley kept just for her.

"Can we meet? There's something I want to discuss."

Late that night, she made her pitch to Ripley in a quiet corner of the shadowy, elegant bar at the Savoy Hotel.

As a location, it seemed appropriate, given that Stephen Garrick had sealed his own fate when he followed Volkov and Federov here weeks ago. Besides, the dark painted walls and carpet, the low lighting, the quiet corners that promised complete privacy seemed to invite conspiracies of the kind she was proposing.

Ripley ordered a single malt, and Emma a vodka on the rocks, an homage to the absent Andrei Volkov. When the waiter melted back into the darkness and they were alone, she told Ripley what she wanted to do.

Her voice was steady. She felt oddly separate from her plan. Emotionally divorced from whatever decision her boss might make. When she was honest with herself, she expected him to react as Jon had, with fury and flat refusals.

Instead, he listened intently, occasionally picking up that cigarette case with its hidden razor blade, but never opening it. As she talked, his long, complex face remained impassive, his eyes fixed on a point somewhere in the shadowy distance over her shoulder.

It was after one in the morning, and the bar wasn't crowded. There was nobody who could hear her above the jazz music that flowed from hidden speakers as she sketched out a new operation—one that would bring her within touching distance of Oleg Federov.

When she finished, Ripley said nothing for a long moment.

When he finally did speak, he began mid-sentence, in that way he had of skipping the opening gambit of any conversation.

"We can't be certain Federov doesn't know what you look like."

"We don't have any idea how much he knows," Emma conceded, with reluctant honesty. "But there's no reason that he should know."

"You've only just come back from an undercover operation. And the dangers on this one are very high." Ripley lowered his gaze to meet hers. "Are you sure you're ready? You could have been killed on the *Eden*."

"I agree I should have a break, but time matters on this. I think Federov will shut down his UK operation and go somewhere he sees as safer. If we wait too long he'll be gone. I'm aware there's a risk and I'm willing to accept it." Emma's voice was calm.

"You're not the only person who could do this," Ripley pointed out.

"I'm the only agent we have who speaks Russian with believable fluency and who is also female, and the right age. If you don't use me, you have to try a honeytrap with a male agent, and those are notoriously unpredictable. Or a financial trap, and then Natalya will be reluctant to cooperate." She took a sip of her drink. "Befriending her and getting the information voluntarily would be much easier. And faster."

"Yes, agreed." Ripley turned the cigarette case over and over between his fingers. "It would have to be fast. We could give the operation no more than a week, I think."

"I could make that work," Emma said.

Ripley stared into the distance, his eyes hooded. The cigarette case stilled.

"You won't be able to wear a wire," he said.

And with that, it was decided. They were going to do it.

A shiver of apprehension ran down Emma's spine but she kept her expression smooth, straightening the coaster under her drink until it was aligned perfectly with the edge of the mahogany table. "There's one more thing. I would like this operation to be Agency only."

Ripley met her gaze with disconcerting directness.

"Yes. I agree with that," he said. "We can handle this on our own. Andrew has other operations that need his attention right now. And this calls for a small team. I'll need to bring Zach in on it. And Martha. But I trust them implicitly."

His ready agreement was the last thing Emma expected. She'd been braced for an argument. Ripley and Andrew Field had worked together for decades. If he cut Field out, then that could only mean he thought the third man might genuinely be inside MI6. Maybe he even suspected Field himself.

The floor beneath her felt suddenly unsteady, and she thought about what Ripley had said in the safe house the other day.

"Odds are it's someone we've met. Someone we know."

Could Ripley genuinely suspect one of his oldest friends?

"We should keep the actual work out of the Vernon Institute," Ripley continued. "The Neighbors are there too often. Word would spread."

Emma cleared her throat. "Is it safe to continue to use the number?" she asked, referring to the phone number she'd used to call him that day.

He nodded. "Yes, use that only. No other form of messaging. We'll meet in person for most conversations. Open air is safest."

Emma hesitated and then asked, "Ripley, is someone watching the safe house?"

He frowned. "No. Why?"

Emma couldn't explain her suspicions. She'd had a bad feeling since Jon left, but had dismissed it. Now, though, as the secrets piled up around them like barricades, she felt she couldn't ignore the sensation of eyes on her back.

"It feels watched," she said. "I don't know why."

Ripley thought for a long moment. "It's probably nerves, but I trust your instincts."

He pulled a pen from his pocket and scrawled on a cocktail napkin. "Tonight, when you get home, pack your things and take a black cab to this address. Don't go straight there. Use the usual methods. There's a key safe on the side of the house. Here's the code. Don't tell anyone where you are. Even people you trust."

He slid the napkin to Emma. She took it with numb fingers.

She wanted this operation—she believed it could work. But there was no pleasure in this for either her or Ripley. They were trying to trap one of their own. The person they hunted would kill both of them if he could.

And the circle of people she could trust kept shrinking.

32

Three days later, Emma walked through the doors of a pristine white Georgian building on a leafy street in Kensington. Her high heels tapped against the marble floor as she approached the front desk. She wore a fur gilet and designer trousers buttoned low on her hips. Her hair was dyed pale blond and hung straight. Her makeup, designed by Martha, gave her high Slavic cheekbones and glacial blue eyes. The combination rendered her virtually unrecognizable.

The clothes were designed to look like outfits from young designers most favored by wealthy Russian expats—Gazinskaya, Céline, Marni.

"Now, I've been researching what they wear at that posh gym and it's *ridiculous*," Martha had told her excitedly. "You have to go dressed to the teeth or no one will believe you're Russian. Those women dress like they're on a catwalk just to take a yoga class."

A girl wearing a snug black T-shirt, with the word "RETREAT" written on it in white, scanned Emma's outfit before saying, "How can I help you?"

"My name is Anna Petrova." Emma spoke with a slight Russian accent and a brittle smile. "I'm a new member. My card should be waiting here."

As the girl opened a drawer and flipped through the envelopes inside, Emma held her breath. Zach had hacked into the Retreat's systems and created a new membership account for her, marked as pre-paid for a year. If it had all worked it would be here.

"I hope their sauna's better than their firewall," had been his only assessment of the place.

"Here it is!" The girl picked up an envelope and looked through it. "Everything's here: your new membership card, a list of all our classes, and information about the spa. Would you like a tour?"

Emma, who had memorized blueprints of the club until she knew the building better than her own flat, waved the offer away. "It is not necessary. I have been here many times as a guest." She opened the envelope and pulled out the card. "This is fine."

Emma scanned the card on a reader and the security gates slid open silently.

A membership at the Retreat cost many thousands, and there was a waiting list of more than a year to even apply. In return for all that money, the spa promised luxury, privacy, and, most of all, the guarantee that all the other members were just as rich as you.

Oleg Federov had bought Natalya a lifetime membership two years ago, and she came here nearly every day.

The only problem with the plan was that Emma's disguise could not be complete. Wigs and prosthetics were out—they'd be too obvious up close. Just as she had on the *Eden*, Emma had to go into this as a version of herself. This was the part Ripley had openly worried about.

"To get that close to someone like Federov, we should make sure he could pass you on the street two weeks from now and not know it was the same person," he'd told her that night at the Savoy.

"If this goes well, I might not need to meet him at all," Emma had countered. "I might get everything I need from Natalya."

"*Might*." Ripley said the word with contempt. "'Might' is a dangerous word. Like 'almost' and 'maybe' and 'hopefully.' Those are words that get you killed."

Despite his doubts, the one condition Ripley had placed on the operation was a time limit. In seven days, whether or not she had the evidence they needed, he would pull Emma out.

The changing room was a tastefully decorated space arranged around a series of cubbyholes, each lined with glossy walnut lockers with gleaming brass locks. The steamy air smelled of essential oils and a pleasant blend of perfumes and shampoos.

When Emma walked in, a tall brunette stood naked in front of a mirror drying her hair—every inch of her body so toned she might have been carved from the same marble as the floors.

Emma strolled past her and through the rows of lockers until she spotted a familiar blonde in the back corner changing into a leotard.

Staying within view, but far enough away to be discreet, she placed her bag on the padded bench next to her and began to change.

As she dressed, she made sure Natalya saw her face. But when the Russian girl walked by a few minutes later, clad in a skin-tight pink exercise top, Emma didn't look up.

She waited until Natalya was out of sight before hurriedly shoving the bag in the locker. She followed at a distance as Natalya walked up the sweeping staircase to a spacious exercise studio where a wall of tall windows overlooked the trees of Grosvenor Square.

Without glancing at Natalya, Emma chose a mat from the selection hanging on the wall, and placed it within her sightline.

The class was much more intense than she'd expected, and she was sweating by the time she picked up the mat and hung it back up. Again, Natalya walked by her, and again, Emma made sure not to meet her gaze.

Emma knew Natalya always went straight to the spa after a workout, but she lingered in the hallway for a few minutes before following her to the changing room. By the time she walked in, Natalya was already in her swimsuit. The two exchanged polite smiles as Emma walked to her locker to change.

When she walked into the spa five minutes later, though, there was no sign of Natalya.

The space had a peaceful sanctum sanctorum feel. Soothing music played softly through hidden speakers, echoing off the warm tile walls and floors. Arranged in an octagonal pattern around a central ice fountain, a series of chambers were hidden behind opaque glass doors. There were hot saunas and warm saunas, steam rooms of different temperatures and "moods," and something called a "salt room." Emma tried three saunas before locating Natalya in a steam room. The space had low magenta lighting and a crystal ball on a plinth at the center that turned slowly and seemed to serve no purpose. Steam hung so heavily in the air it was hard to see the faces around her as she padded across the room, until she tripped over a pair of outstretched bare feet.

"Прости," Emma said automatically. Her hand flew up to her mouth and she repeated the phrase in English. "Pardon me."

"No need to apologize." Natalya Kuzmina had a surprisingly husky voice. "It's like a cave in here."

"It really is." Emma sat down a short distance away, wincing slightly as the hot tiled bench pressed against the backs of her thighs. She closed her eyes and breathed in the steam.

After a moment, Natalya spoke again. "You were in my yoga class."

Emma's eyes flew open. "Were you in there too? I didn't see you. It was very intense."

Natalya nodded. "T.J. is a brutal teacher. I love her. She makes you do very hard things and then she's like, 'Are you having a good time?'" She gave a wry smile. "She reminds me of some of my teachers back home."

"In Moscow the teachers are worse than here." Emma chuckled. "Where are you from?"

"Irkutsk," Natalya said wryly. "Not so glamorous as Moscow."

"Irkutsk!" Emma marveled. "That's real Russia."

Natalya's laugh sounded as if it should have come from an older body. "Real Russia is one way to put it. Hell would be another."

"London is better?" Emma suggested.

"London will do," Natalya corrected her. "Until we can go back to Monaco."

"Oh, I adore Monaco!" Emma exclaimed. "Why have we not met there?"

"I don't know." Natalya's eyes searched her face. "We're there more than in London these days. I'm Natalya, by the way." She held out her hand.

"Anna," Emma said, reaching out across the steamy air. "Anna Petrova."

Natalya's fingers were warm and damp as their hands gripped briefly.

"I'm new here," Emma confessed. "I've been on the waiting list for *ages*."

"You'll like it," Natalya said eagerly. "And the restaurant is very good." As she launched into a litany of the Retreat's charms, Emma smiled and nodded.

She was in.

33

"Do you want dessert?" Natalya picked up the menu and looked at it longingly. "I don't dare. Oleg thinks I'm getting fat."

"Oleg must be insane," Emma said. Natalya was a perfect size eight, as lithe as a dancer.

"Russian men like thin women. Especially men like Oleg." With a regretful sigh, Natalya set the menu down and pushed it away. "Dieting is my job now."

It was early afternoon in a trendy restaurant called Core near Kensington Palace. It had been three days since Emma first struck up a friendship with Natalya. Slipping into her life had been as easy as she'd hoped.

Natalya believed Emma was the only daughter of a Russian multi-millionaire who owned houses in London as well as places in Monaco and Moscow. Emma made it clear she was a bit lonely after a recent breakup, and Natalya had quickly taken her under her wing.

She was chatty but Emma hadn't pressed for information; instead she let the conversation flow naturally. Natalya talked a lot about her singing and the jazz band she fronted, as well as her flat and her family. But she said almost nothing about Oleg Federov. It was as if he didn't interest her enough to make him worth mentioning.

They had exercised together every day that week, and chatted in the sauna, and in the spa's lounge over coffee.

This morning, Natalya had phoned early and suggested they take a day off from exercise and go to lunch instead.

"We'll be naughty," she'd said impishly.

When the waiter approached, they both ordered black coffees. The second he walked away, Emma spoke casually in Russian. "You know, you never talk much about your Oleg. Who is he?"

Natalya gave a shrug. "Oleg is a businessman. Oil and gas. Big deals." She made a vague gesture that sent the diamonds in her bracelet sparking. "He's very successful."

Her disinterested tone spoke volumes.

"Did he buy you that beautiful thing?" Emma pointed at the bracelet.

"Yes, last Christmas. He is generous." Natalya tilted her hand languidly so the diamonds, pristine in their platinum settings, caught the light and glittered. "He loves giving presents."

Watching her, Emma was reminded again of Madison. It was striking what similar young women these powerful men sought, and the predictable methods they used when cultivating them. It was as if they were following a formula.

"Is he in the country?" Emma asked, although she already knew the answer. Federov was at his mansion outside Cannes, in the south of France, where his every move was watched by French intelligence agents.

Natalya shook her head. "No, he's in Europe on business. He's coming in this weekend." She toyed with her teaspoon, drawing lines in the white linen tablecloth. "Anna, I have news.

Bad news." She glanced around the room, filled with people talking and laughing. "We are moving, Oleg and me. To France. Oleg is putting my flat on the market. And the house in the country, too. He told me yesterday." Her tone was mournful.

Emma's nerves sharpened but she made herself nod with half-interest. "Oh, really? Why does he want to move?"

"I don't know really," Natalya said. "He always liked it here but now he wants very much to get back to Europe. London is not friendly to Russians right now, he says. All our friends are leaving."

"You don't want to go?" Emma asked.

Natalya shook her head. "My band is here. I like London. I love my flat. I don't care about politics, but . . ." She held up one hand in a helpless gesture. "I don't own the flat. Oleg does. He wants to move soon. Next week."

Emma's heart stuttered but her expression didn't change.

"I hope you don't go." She reached out spontaneously and touched Natalya's arm. "We've just become friends."

"But we will see each other in France. You must come visit. You will love our house there. It has beautiful views." Natalya squeezed her hand. "Oh. I almost forgot!" she said, brightening. "We're having a party on Saturday. It's a kind of . . . what do they say in English? A farewell party. It's mostly Oleg's business friends. You should come. Please tell me you are free." Her eyes searched Emma's face hopefully.

Emma smiled. "For you? I will cancel everything."

Natalya clapped her hands together. "Oh, this is going to be wonderful! I usually hate Oleg's parties, but if you're there it will be fun, truly. My band is playing, so you can see me sing." She blushed.

"It sounds fabulous," Emma said. "Is it going to be at your flat?"

"It's at the Shard. You know the Shard?" Natalya said. "Of course you do, it's famous."

The Shard was London's best-known skyscraper. A jagged dagger of glass, thrust into the sky, visible from miles away, dominating the city's southeastern skyline.

"Oleg has rented out the whole bar," Natalya continued. "It starts at six. I'll put your name on the list."

As the waiters appeared with the coffees, Emma laughed and chattered, but her thoughts were on how this would go down with Ripley. He would not be happy about her going to a party hosted by Oleg Federov. It was everything he'd wanted her not to do. But Volkov was still locked away on his boat, and Federov was about to leave the country for good.

This party might be the last chance they had.

A few hours later she walked around the lake in St. James's Park with Ripley. She'd changed into anonymous black trousers, washed off the makeup, and tucked her dyed hair back under her collar. It was a warm afternoon, and tourists walked by them in clusters, oblivious to their presence. Ducks and swans paddled serenely on the glassy water.

While he listened, Ripley drew on his cigarette and blew out a stream of smoke. "So it's just what we expected. They're getting out."

"I'm willing to bet Andrei Volkov's properties are up for sale as well," Emma said. "Have the Neighbors been able to find out about Volkov's family?"

"They haven't left that house. They've been seen through the gates, so they're still inside," Ripley said. "A French agent went in to try and speak with them, but a security guard threw him out."

"Volkov's guard?" Emma asked. "Or Federov's?"

"We're still trying to ascertain that," he said. "Personally, I suspect that security guard is the reason Volkov hasn't left the *Eden.*"

"So Federov's holding Olga and the child hostage, to keep Volkov from working with us," Emma said.

"And now Federov's holding a party in one of the city's most obvious landmarks." Ripley walked up to the iron fence around the pond and turned to look at her. "Why on earth would he do that? He's been lying low for days."

Emma had been wondering the same thing. She thought about the cold Russian oligarch she'd seen at the W Hotel in Barcelona. The cleverness of choosing that hotel, and that specific private room for the meeting when he knew intelligence officers were so close to his operation.

"I don't think it has anything to do with saying goodbye to his friends. Federov doesn't really like anybody." She leaned back against the railing, her heels sinking in the soft earth, and watched a family walk by, the children racing ahead of the parents. "I think it's got to be something else. A distraction. But from what?" She paused. "Natalya told me most of the people coming were Federov's business associates."

"You think the third man will be there." Ripley sounded skeptical. "On what evidence?"

"It's a guess," she admitted. "But an educated one. We've tapped Federov's phone and we're watching his internet usage, yes?"

Ripley drew on his cigarette and inclined his head.

"I think he's been quiet because he knows we're listening." Emma turned to face Ripley and lowered her voice, although nobody was near. "If I were him, and I knew we were watching and listening to everything, I'd throw a party and invite a lot of people to a busy public spot, and I'd hide anyone I wanted to meet secretly in that crowd."

Ripley considered this. "He could have done that in France," he said. "Why come here?"

"Perhaps the third man can't leave the country for some reason," Emma said. "If he works for us, it might be because we're watching everyone right now and he's afraid of drawing attention."

"A meeting in plain view," Ripley mused. "That isn't a bad theory."

"If I'm there, I can melt into the crowd and see if I can spot him," Emma said. "Natalya will help me fit in."

Ripley dropped the cigarette, crushing it under his foot. "I still think it's too dangerous. There may be people there you've met on the *Eden*." He gestured at her hair. "Your disguise isn't thorough enough for them not to recognize you."

"I can make it work," Emma insisted, increasingly impatient with his caution. "Besides, if I don't go to this party, the operation's over. Natalya's leaving the country. Nobody else has got this close to Federov, have they? Phone-tapping him isn't going to get us the information we need. We have to do it the hard way. We have to take chances."

Ripley looked out across the park to where the gilded gates of Buckingham Palace glimmered in the cold afternoon light. The long, straight lines of his face shifted as he thought it through.

Emma could sense how conflicted he was. Running an operation completely off the books like this was dangerous. Getting that close to a man as unpredictable as Oleg Federov without backup would be hard to explain if it all went wrong. And she knew better than anyone that it could go wrong very quickly.

"I don't want to ask you to do this, but I fear you're right, and it is the only way," Ripley said at last. "If we don't identify the traitor inside our organization soon an internal investigation will be launched and the person we're looking for will go to ground. Months—maybe years—will pass before we identify them, if we ever get that lucky. Until then we'll be side by side with him, sharing our most secret information. Our work will be eviscerated. More lives could be lost." A muscle twitched in the tight line of his jaw as he turned his gaze back to her. "But you need to understand the seriousness of this. You won't be able to bring a weapon; you'll have to go through a metal detector to get into the Shard. We can't put this operation on the books without revealing it to the person we're looking for, and that means no backup inside the building to help you. Federov will bring his own guards, and they will not follow any of these rules. If anyone recognizes you, a skyscraper is a hard place to escape from. You'll be outnumbered, and help will be far away." He paused. "Knowing that, are you still willing to go in there on Saturday? Do you want to do this?"

Emma's mouth went dry. She knew what was at stake. Ripley's job. Her job. Maybe even her life. Jon was right to forbid her to do this. It was far too risky. She shouldn't go anywhere near Federov.

And yet. Somewhere in that vast building, she'd find the truth.

The job is everything.

"Yes. I'll do it," she said.

34

On Saturday afternoon, Emma took a taxi to an unmarked MI5 address in east London. At first sight, the place didn't look promising. The battered metal fence bore a rusted sign reading "HALF MOON MOTORS" but from the street it appeared abandoned. There was no visible activity and an overgrown laurel hedge hid the property from the street. The only indication that it wasn't all it seemed was the state-of-the-art electronic lock into which Emma entered the code she'd been given. Instantly, the gate swung open on oiled hinges.

On the other side, a row of modern cars gleamed. There were about forty in all, everything from a Mini Cooper that would blend in on any London street to a scarlet Lamborghini that stood out like a lipstick stain.

"Bet you hope they're giving you that one." Zach stepped out from a metal building at the back of the lot and walked toward her, pausing near the sports car.

Beneath a loose blazer, he wore a David Bowie T-shirt with "MODERN LOVE" written on the front. If she hadn't known better, Emma would have taken him for a grad student pausing on his way to class.

"I'd have no idea how to drive it," she replied.

"Me neither. But I'm willing to learn." He held up his hand. "Hey. Welcome home. What a bastard of a job."

Emma gave a wry smile. "You could say that."

"Who would have thought pizza and a bit of CCTV would have brought us to this, huh?" His voice was sober.

"Yeah." Emma glanced around at the rows of vehicles. "Why do I need a car? The Shard's in central London."

"It's not where it is that matters," he said. "With this crowd, you can't just rock up from the Tube like a normal person. They'll notice how you arrive. Anna Petrova needs to fit in."

"So which one's mine?" she asked.

"This one." The voice was Ripley's.

Turning, she saw him standing next to a low silver Porsche Boxster convertible that gleamed in the summer sunshine.

"It has speeds up to one hundred and eighty miles per hour, although we're hoping you don't need that." Ripley motioned at the tech expert. "Zach, tell her what we've done."

Zach opened the passenger door. "We think the Russians might check underneath so I've hidden a tracker inside the paneling here." He tapped the paneling near the door handle. "We'll be able to follow you wherever you go. Also there's a microphone here." He touched the dashboard. "Anytime you speak in the car I'll be able to hear you. There's no need to call us. Just get in the car and talk. If you need to get out of there in a hurry, just tell me. I'll hear you." He straightened. "But this is mostly if the unexpected happens. Odds are, nothing bad will happen while you're in the car."

Emma didn't miss the caveat at the end. The bad things wouldn't happen in the car. If anything went wrong, it would happen inside the tallest skyscraper in London.

But all she said was, "Got it."

"The phone," Ripley ordered Zach brusquely.

"Oh yeah." Zach held out his hand. "Give me your phone. I'm going to put a thing on it."

When Emma handed him the device, he lifted it up to his own mobile, pressing buttons and watching the screens closely.

Emma turned to her boss. "How's it all looking?"

"Everything's in place," Ripley told her. "Martha's waiting for you now. Zach and I will be in a room on the thirty-fourth floor of the Shard. Adam will be with us, in case of trouble."

Emma was quietly relieved to know Adam would be there. Like her, he had been a soldier. He was completely reliable, and a vicious fighter.

"You're to take no chances," Ripley reminded her. "If I tell you at any point to abort this mission, you do it. Am I understood? No games this time."

His demeanor was unusually stiff, his tone distant. His mind seemed to be already in the Shard, searching for the unanticipated traps that could upend their plans.

They both knew a small team couldn't fully cover a seventy-two-story skyscraper, especially one with multiple restaurants and bars, as well as offices, a five-star hotel, and a public viewing gallery on the top floor. It was like a vertical city. She had to be ready for almost anything to happen.

So all Emma said was, "Understood."

The door to a metal building behind them swung open and Martha appeared, looking subdued in a black dress, with her hair pulled back. Only her vivid red lipstick betrayed her usual boisterous nature.

"It's time, Emma."

"I'm coming," Emma called. Still, she hesitated. She'd rarely seen Ripley this stressed. It worried her.

"Is everything OK?" she asked quietly.

He looked at her, and for a second she thought there was

something he wanted to tell her. But then he seemed to change his mind. "Operation nerves. Go get ready."

There wasn't time to press him. They didn't want to be here long enough for anyone to question what they were up to.

The metal building was an office of sorts, with a desk in a corner and a rack of keys. Martha had set up a makeshift makeup table and hung a clothing bag from a curtain rod.

As soon as Emma walked in, Martha handed her a dress. "Try this on. Let's see how it fits."

The tension had affected everyone. Emma and Martha talked little as she pulled the dress over her head and studied herself in the mirror. It was a good choice, a black, one-shoulder design, ending just below the knees with a bit of flow that would allow her to run.

"What shoes am I wearing?" Emma asked.

Martha grimaced. "Heels unfortunately. Anything else would stand out."

She handed her a pair of stilettos.

"It's fine. I'll kick them off if I have to." Emma slid them on and glanced at Martha, who was notoriously protective of her supplies. "If I lose the shoes, will you kill me?"

Martha gave her a fierce look. "Fuck the shoes. All I want is for you to find what you need and get out of there in one piece." She took a deep breath and smoothed her expression. "Now. Sit down, and let me do your makeup."

Without a word, Emma sat and let Martha get to work, but as she brushed powder on her face, Emma met her eyes in the mirror.

"Talk," she ordered.

Martha put down the brush and reached for another so her face was turned away when she said, "You should know, he's risking his job on this. If it goes wrong, they'll bring him down. And all of Ed Masterson's dreams will come true."

Emma's chest tightened. She was aware of the danger they all faced, but the fact that Martha felt the need to say it aloud made it somehow worse.

There was nobody she admired more than Ripley. He'd seen the spy in her when she was twenty-four years old. He'd always believed in her ability. She owed him everything.

She would not be the reason his career ended.

"I won't let that happen," she told Martha. "You have to believe—"

The door behind them flew open and they both jumped.

"Ripley says to hurry," Zach announced. Glancing at Emma's dress he asked Martha, "Haven't you given her the kit yet? We need to test it."

"I was just about to." Reaching into a bag, Martha pulled out a necklace with a silver pendant.

Zach took it from her, holding it carefully. "This is a camera," he told Emma, turning the pendant around in his fingers. It looked perfectly ordinary, a chunky piece of carved silver. "It will record everything you see. Keep this side facing out." He tapped the design on the pendant, which looked like nothing but a few carved lines.

Emma slipped it over her head.

"And you'll need these." Martha handed Emma a pair of small disk-shaped earrings.

"One is a microphone that will let us hear what's happening around you. The other will transmit our voice to you," Zach explained. "We don't want to risk an earpiece. They might spot it." He handed her back her phone. "I put some software on your phone to connect it all together."

Emma walked across the room to test how the necklace felt. "How fragile is it?"

"It's a little delicate," he conceded. "It can handle normal life but don't bash it into anything."

"I'll do my best," she said.

"One more thing." He handed her a gold lipstick. When she looked at it blankly, he said, "Open it."

Emma slid the lid off and saw nothing inside but red lipstick. "It's not really my color."

Zach grinned. "Open the other side."

Emma did as she was told and a short, sharp blade emerged, glittering in the light. It was no more than three inches long.

"It's not much," Zach said, "But it could do some damage."

He was right, it wasn't much, but Emma knew just how to use it. And she'd hated the idea of going into this unarmed.

"Cool," she said, sliding the knife back into its case.

"Drop it in here." Martha handed her a small glittering bag, just big enough to hold her phone and lipstick. "They'll search you, so we give them nothing to look through and they won't find anything. That's my theory."

When she finished, Emma looked at her reflection in the mirror Martha had set against the wall. In heels, with her long blond hair, she looked every inch the wealthy Russian woman out on the town.

Zach ran over to a makeshift work station he'd set up on a rough wood trestle table, and checked the sound and images.

When Ripley walked over a few minutes later, Zach glanced up at him.

"We're golden," he said. "Everything's working."

"Right, then." Ripley handed Emma a set of keys. "The car's ready. It's nearly six. You should get going."

Nerves swirled in Emma's stomach. Now that it was happening, this seemed like a terrible plan. They were risking everything. She had to do this right. She had to.

She would.

She turned to Ripley. "I just want you to know, I'm not going to let you down."

He gave her a long look. For an instant, Emma saw something she didn't recognize in those gray eyes. Something like regret. But all he said was, "I know you won't. Now go get our traitor."

The drive was short. As Emma navigated London traffic in the powerful Porsche, the Shard was always visible—a long slice of glass dominating every view until she fell into its shadow and could no longer see its distinctive outline against the sky.

The huge structure had multiple entrances, but Natalya's invitation had instructed her to come in through the entrance used by the Shangri-La Hotel.

One lane of the entrance had a sign reading simply "PARTY." Emma pulled up to it. She'd barely stopped the car when a heavily muscled man in a bulletproof vest appeared next to her door.

"Turn off the engine," he ordered through the glass.

Emma didn't like the look of him, or the others currently searching the Lexus ahead of her. When one guard bent over, she saw the bulge of a handgun in the back of his trousers.

These were, she suspected, all British mercenaries. The most unpredictable, expensive, and ruthless security option anyone could go for.

She watched with what she hoped looked like lazy irritation as the men swarmed around the Boxster. One held a metal pole which he shoved under the car and swung from side to side.

As Zach had suspected, they were looking for trackers. She hoped his devices were hidden as well as he'd promised.

After a second, the man searching under the car stepped back and nodded at the one by her door.

"You can go," he told her gruffly, and pointed at a valet standing nearby, watching the men nervously.

Emma walked over and handed the keys to the valet.

"Sorry about . . ." He waved a hand in the direction of the men.

Emma shrugged and said in a Russian accent, "Is not a problem." And walked away.

Inside, the subtly lighted hallway in neutral colors reminded her queasily of the *Eden* as she headed to where a woman stood behind a table, smiling at her brightly.

"Here for the party?" the woman asked.

Emma nodded.

"Your name?"

"Anna Petrova," Emma said.

The woman typed something on the laptop in front of her, and paused to read what it said before smiling brightly. "Perfect! We just need to search your bag and you can go up." She winced apologetically. "Rules, you see."

Emma handed her the small clutch. "So cute!" the woman exclaimed as she opened it. Seeing only a phone and a lipstick, she closed it instantly. "Wonderful. Take the lift to the fifty-second floor. Enjoy the party."

Emma walked past her to where an elevator stood open.

When the doors closed behind her, she spoke quickly, knowing Zach would hear. "Armed security guards on the door. Ex-military. No metal detector, just a bag search."

"Copy that." Zach's voice came through the earpiece, clear and close.

"They have weapons and you don't," Ripley's voice came through. "Let that influence how you handle this."

"Understood." Emma shook her shoulders, releasing the tension there.

She was ready. All she had to do was watch people. Speak believably in Russian. Find a bad guy. And go home.

The elevator reached the fifty-second floor and stopped. The doors slid open. Music and laughter flowed around her.

Emma took a breath.

"I'm going in," she said.

35

Emma stepped out of the elevator and into a long, artfully lit hallway. She followed the sound of voices to the end of the corridor, where the hallway opened out into a sophisticated cocktail bar.

A waitress in a black apron with a tray of champagne flutes stood at the entrance, a smile fixed in place. Emma took a glass and walked into the crowd.

The silver pendant swung on its chain as she turned a slow circle as if looking for someone, ensuring that every face would be captured by the camera. The images would be analyzed by the Agency's software later, until every person was identified.

The room had an elegant pan-Asian design, with polished mahogany and bamboo wood, and chairs upholstered in vivid Chinese red with touches of gold. At the center was a long bar where four bartenders shook silver cocktail shakers and poured champagne. Most of the tables had been removed to make more space for the guests and the staff circulating with trays of canapés and drinks.

A five-piece band was set up at one end of the room, playing jazz.

As she finished her first casual circuit of the room the tension in Emma's chest eased. There was no sign of Federov. Nobody she recognized from the *Eden*. But also, no Brian Jeffers, or Martin Dowell. No familiar faces at all.

"Anna!" Hearing the name, she turned to see Natalya running up to her. "I'm so glad you came."

Natalya wore a form-fitting dress with heels. Her silvery blond hair swung over her shoulders in cultivated waves. Even dressed up, she looked younger than her years.

"Your dress is *stunning*," Emma exclaimed as they kissed each other's cheeks.

"Yours too!" Natalya beamed. "Now, come see the view." Taking her hand, she pulled Emma to one of the floor-to-ceiling windows.

At this time of year, the sun wouldn't go down until after nine o'clock, but the early evening light was velvety. The long windows captured London in spectacular fashion, like something from a film. Emma took in a breath when she saw the distinctive spires of Tower Bridge, which seemed to glow gold in the sun.

"Wow," she said. "That's really something."

"It's so beautiful," Natalya agreed. "A perfect place to say goodbye to my London."

"I can't believe you're really going to leave." Emma squeezed her hand.

Natalya gave an unhappy smile. "We're actually leaving on Wednesday. I don't want to go so soon, but Oleg wants to spend the summer there because of work and . . ."

She chattered excitedly and Emma half listened, nodding and occasionally making appropriate comments while angling her body so the camera could catch images of the people around her.

A black-clad security guard bumped into her hard enough to

make her wine slosh over the lip of the glass. She could feel the Kevlar of his vest beneath his shirt.

When she turned, the insolent look he gave her reminded her so much of Cal Grogan she suppressed a shudder.

Frowning, Natalya pulled Emma away. "The security are everywhere today," she confided, lowering her voice. "I don't like them. Oleg says they must be here. I don't know why. We never have so many at parties normally."

Emma counted three guards in the bar. They seemed to be roaming the room, as if they were looking for someone. She kept her face tilted away from them, just in case. As Ripley said, Grogan or Volkov might have shared an image of Jessica at some point. She didn't want a guard with a sharp eye to put the pieces together.

Hooking her arm through Natalya's, she said, "Why don't we walk around and you can tell me who everyone is. I want to know who all the famous people are."

The two walked through the crowd, with Natalya obligingly identifying all the "interesting" people, in a quiet, constant stream of information. When she was sharing gossip she would whisper into Emma's ear, which was very convenient for the microphone there.

Natalya's back was to the door when Emma noticed Oleg Federov walk in. He spoke to a security guard, who pointed to Natalya.

Federov headed straight toward them with that distinctive limp. Emma let her gaze stray past him, as if she'd never seen him before in her life. But her heart beat faster.

"There you are," Federov said in Russian, resting his hand on Natalya's arm before turning his attention to Emma. "Who is your friend?"

His voice held no warmth at all.

"This is my friend Anna," Natalya said. "I told you she was coming. We met at the gym."

Emma smiled innocently and spoke in Russian. "It's nice to meet you. Thank you for inviting me to your beautiful party."

He studied her with uncomfortable interest. "Natalya talks about you all the time. Of course I had to meet the famous Anna." His voice was polite but behind the thick glasses his small eyes were hooded.

"And I must meet the famous Oleg," Emma said brightly. "Natalya has said wonderful things about you."

"How kind. But I fear you've distracted my Natalya from her obligations." He gave Natalya a look. "It's nearly seven o'clock."

Natalya's eyes widened. "I'm late!" Turning to Emma, she explained in a rush, "I'm supposed to sing with the band. Please, have more champagne. I'll find you afterward."

Oleg watched with what looked like benign affection as she dashed across the room to join the band, which stopped playing and gathered around her.

"I've never heard her sing," Emma said, still speaking Russian. "I'm so glad I'll have the chance."

"I suppose there's no opportunity for singing at the gym." As Federov turned to her she saw a faint flicker of curiosity in his expression. He looked at her more closely. "We have not met before, have we?"

Emma's stomach dropped.

"No, I don't believe we have," she said. "Although you perhaps know my father? Uri Petrov? He is a property investor in Moscow."

There was a real Uri Petrov; it was one reason they'd chosen this name.

Federov considered this for a long moment, as if flipping through a mental list of enemies.

"No, I do not know him." His answer was decisive.

Emma could sense that he was still trying to place her. She kept her expression interested but incurious. She was just Natalya's friend. Why would she care what Oleg thought?

"Sometimes he is in London. I should introduce you," she said, before reminding herself, "But you are going away. I'm sad you are leaving. I hate to lose Natalya. She has become a good friend."

"Well, it is because of business." He was still watching her too closely. "I could swear we have met before."

Before he could ask more questions, a security guard walked up and whispered in his ear.

Emma heard the man say, "He's arrived."

Distracted, Federov turned back to her. "If you'll forgive me. I must speak with someone."

"Of course."

As he strode away across the bar, Emma exhaled slowly. That had been too close for comfort.

Ripley must have come to the same conclusion because Zach spoke quietly in her ear. "Emma, Ripley says get out of there as soon as you can."

Dismayed, Emma swore under her breath. She couldn't go now. They'd worked so hard to get here. But she knew Ripley wasn't wrong. The risk level had just ratcheted up.

Still. Before she left, she had to find out who Federov was meeting. Something had made him leave abruptly. Whoever would cause that had to be important.

"Give me one minute," she said quietly. "Then I'll go."

Across the room, Natalya approached the microphone.

"Hi, everyone," she said, and her voice rang out from the speakers.

The crowd burst into applause. "Sing, Natalya!" several people called.

She laughed. "I will, don't worry. And you must dance. This is a celebration, not a funeral."

The band broke into a light, fast version of "Blue Skies" and Natalya began to sing.

Her voice was a rich alto. She had a powerful stage presence, light and electric. She really was, Emma realized with surprise, quite talented.

Emma strolled to the bar and paused as if watching the performance, but her attention was on Federov. He wasn't staying to watch his girlfriend sing. Nor had he stopped to talk to his other guests. Instead, he was walking through a swinging door, with two security guards on his heels.

For a long moment Emma considered her options. Then she set down her glass and followed them.

She pushed open the swinging doors to find herself in a kind of service area with stainless-steel counters. Waiters and kitchen staff in black aprons loading trays and washing dishes glanced at her with mild curiosity. There was no sign of Federov.

The necklace moved as she turned, and she knew Zach and Ripley could see what she was seeing, and yet her earpiece was silent. She was surprised Ripley wasn't shouting at her to get out of here.

They wanted to know who Federov was meeting, too.

There was a single door at the other end of the room. Emma walked up to it and paused to listen, but the industrial dishwashers and the noise from the party made it impossible to hear anything.

Emma caught a waiter's eye and pointed at the door, her expression a question.

He nodded.

She put her finger in front of her lips. The waiter turned away, quickly busying himself with the dishes. Whatever the champagne-drinking people at this party were up to, he wasn't about to get involved.

Carefully, she opened the door and peered into a service hallway—industrial flooring, scuffed walls.

The security guards stood in the middle of it staring at her.

Fixing a smile on her face, Emma stepped out, closing the door behind her. As she walked, she reached into her bag and pulled out the lipstick.

"I'm so sorry," she said, holding the gold tube so they could see it. "I'm just looking for the ladies' room."

"It isn't here, luv," one of them said.

"Isn't it?"

She launched a wheeling kick at him, planting her stiletto directly in the middle of his chin. He never stood a chance. His head snapped back against the wall, and he slid down, slowly, eyes glazed.

Emma turned to the other, who was reaching into his waistband where she knew he'd have a gun.

"I wouldn't if I were you." She kept her voice low. "I need you to turn around and walk out of here, fast."

"Who the fuck are you? The police?" he demanded, his hand pausing.

"There's no easy answer to that question." She loosened the blade from the lipstick, keeping it hidden inside the palm of her hand. "But trust me. You need to go now."

"Can't do that." He pulled out the gun.

Emma kicked his wrist before he could even get a good grip on the weapon, and the pistol flew down the corridor. He lunged for it, but she got to him first, wrapping her arm around his neck from behind, gripping her hand to pull her forearm tighter against his trachea.

"I just don't understand," she whispered in his ear, "why men never bloody *listen* to me."

He writhed in her grip, reaching back to grab a handful of her hair, yanking it until sharp pain sent tears to her eyes. Blond strands fluttered from his fingers as his breath grew labored.

His strength waning, he struggled in her grip. And then, after a while, he stopped. She held him until his body was limp. At last, breathless and sweating, she let him fall to the floor, unconscious. She could see his chest moving; he wasn't dead. But he'd be out for a while.

"You ruined my hair," she told him.

Sliding the blade back into the lipstick, she stepped over his body toward the first closed door, where she paused to listen. Hearing nothing, she opened it to find a stairwell twisting and turning, up twenty flights, and down fifty-two.

Emma's heart sank. If Federov had gone that way, he could be anywhere in this building. She'd never find him.

But she had a feeling he hadn't. After all, the guards had been waiting here.

She ran to the last door. She was greeted by the faint, acrid smell of cigar smoke.

The voices on the other side of the door were speaking Russian. Beneath the music she could hear only snippets.

"What are you saying? I'm doing everything you asked." That was Federov. He seemed to be standing nearest the door.

The second voice was too low for her to make out. But she sensed the person was angry. He was speaking Russian but with a British accent. It was the same voice she'd heard in Barcelona. The only words she could make out were, "Investigation . . . Prison . . ."

Emma held her breath, struggling to hear. Federov was furious, that much she was sure of.

"I can't help what your people are doing. That is not my problem. You knew the risks when you came to me. It's too late now. We shouldn't meet again. I'm being watched."

The other voice rose and at last she could hear it properly. "You can't just walk away from me. They know. And I'm not going down alone."

The door flew open so abruptly she nearly tumbled inside.

Two faces turned to her with identical expressions of shock. One was Oleg Federov. The other was Jon.

36

Time stopped. Emma looked at Jon in complete confusion. This didn't make any sense. What was he doing here? Was he running some sort of operation for MI6 that Ripley hadn't been told about? That would be funny, in a way.

"Jon?" she asked.

He didn't reply. He just stared at her, the color draining from his face. His silence didn't make any sense.

"What the hell do you want?" Federov demanded in Russian, waving a cigar like a weapon. "What is going on here?"

Emma spoke, but not to him, her voice clear and strong.

"Jon Frazer's here. How is he here?"

Federov looked from her to Jon, his brow creasing. "What is she talking about? How does she know your name?"

"Emma, Adam is headed to you now." It was Ripley's voice in her ear, dangerously calm.

And suddenly Emma understood.

In that moment, she could see every part of it. How Volkov knew who she was after going into Barcelona. Cal Grogan running into the Blue Room minutes after she'd spoken to Jon on the phone. Jon in the helicopter coming to save her—from France, she'd thought. But no. He'd been in Spain. Meeting with Federov. Each piece slotted into its place until she could see the entire picture of his betrayal.

She wouldn't let herself think about the safe house. Or how she'd believed in him. And all along he'd been looking for information. Trying to stop her from coming here today.

She felt sick.

"How could you do this?" Her voice sounded small and bewildered, and she hated that. She wasn't a child. She knew how he'd done it, and why. After all, he'd told her that day in the safe house. *I believe our guy is in it for the money.*

Jon seemed to gather himself physically. His shoulders squared and he met her gaze.

"Christ, Emma. Thank God you're here."

He took a step toward her. She backed away.

She saw him notice this.

"Federov here has been chatty as hell," he continued. "We should take him in. I think I have enough information to bring him down."

Still standing in the doorway, Federov looked from Jon to her, and then out to the bodies in the corridor. Turning on his heel, he ran, limping more with each step but not slowing, his heavy arms swinging as he fled back to the bar.

Still Jon didn't move. His eyes were fixed on her.

Emma thought quickly—Adam had started from the thirty-fourth floor. It was eighteen flights to get to her. It would take him ten minutes from the moment Ripley contacted him.

She didn't have anything like that kind of time.

Jon took another step.

"Don't come near me." Emma reached into her bag. Her fingers felt cold. Every movement seemed strangely unreal, as if someone else were doing it. Someone else slid the hidden blade out of its holder. Someone else gripped it tightly, and braced herself.

"Come on, Emma." Jon held out his hands. His mouth twisted into an awful smile. "Don't be ridiculous. I'm on your side."

Then he threw himself at her.

Emma twisted away at the last second so his hand caught only her dress, yanking it from her shoulder.

She kicked at his wrist, but he held tight to the fabric. She could hear it rip as he pulled her closer.

Her breath came in short sobs now. He still smelled like Jon — that clean, safe smell. But he wasn't Jon. He wasn't anyone she knew.

"You should have run," he told her, his smile evaporating. His eyes were chips of blue ice.

Emma gave him a regretful look.

"So should you," she said, and swung the blade into the side of his neck.

Jon reeled back, reaching up to his throat, his fingers finding Zach's knife, and pulling it out. He stared at the small gold blade with disbelief as blood streamed down to his shoulder, and gave a broken laugh.

"Fucking toy," he said thickly.

Throwing it to the floor, he turned and ran.

The knife had clearly missed his artery. The blood loss was heavy but not enough to stop him.

"I'm in pursuit," Emma said, racing after him. Pausing only to pick up the gun the guard had dropped in their fight, she hurtled into the stairwell.

Jon moved fast even when injured, but he'd left a trail of blood drops that would have been easy to follow even if she hadn't seen where he was going.

"He's on the stairs," she said, running after him. "Going up. Tell Adam."

"Copy that." It was Zach this time. Deadly serious.

Emma knew Ripley would be on his way to her now. Because that was what he did.

Emma flew up the stairs following the scattering of crimson drops. There was a lot of it. Jon was still moving, but he had to be weakened.

The droplets stopped outside a door four flights up. Emma threw it open to find a hotel corridor, lined with doors.

It was under construction—the carpet had been taken up, and wires were exposed in the ripped-out ceiling. "Fifty-sixth floor," she told Zach breathlessly. "He's gone in. I haven't got eyes."

"Understood," he said. "Adam is on the fiftieth. Coming up to you now."

All the doors stood open and pools of evening light formed on the cement floor, but there were no overhead lights, which made it much harder to follow the blood drops.

Emma slowed, crouching down. Her breath sounded loud and harsh in her ears.

The workers had gone for the day, leaving their tools and ladders behind. She seemed to be completely alone.

A crash split the silence. It sounded as though someone was pounding on a wall.

Pressing her back to the wall, she walked slowly toward the noise, holding the gun in her hand. A smear of blood on the wall told her she was heading in the right direction.

She whispered to Zach. "Room 5609."

"Copy." His voice came back instantly. "Adam is close."

Cautiously, Emma stepped into the room, her back to the wall, the gun in her hands.

Like the hallway, the room was being renovated. All the furniture had been removed and the floors stripped. Workers' tools lay scattered around; a stepladder was open at one end.

Jon stood by the window, a sledgehammer in his hands. He'd

been pounding it against the glass, which was chipped and cracked.

Outside, the sun had begun to drop, filling the room with lemony light. Even from where she stood, Emma could see London, glowing with life and beauty far below.

"Jon, put it down," she ordered.

He froze with the sledgehammer in mid-air, and slowly turned around. The twisted expression was gone, replaced by a look of almost heartbreaking sadness.

Emma pointed the gun at his head. The barrel was steady.

"Put it down," she said again.

"Emma, I'm sorry," he said, and she thought she heard genuine regret in his voice. "I don't care about anything else. I don't care about this government or this country or my job. None of it means anything to me. But I betrayed you. And that will haunt me."

Emma held the Sig Sauer firmly, the palm of her left hand supporting the base of her right. She didn't feel anything. She wondered where her emotions had gone.

"Just step away from the window."

"I can't do that." He looked from the gun to her face, and gave a slight smile. "The things we do for money, huh?"

In a whip-fast move, he spun around and crashed the sledgehammer against the window. The glass bowed but held.

Emma kept the gun pointed at him. "Stop!" she ordered.

But he raised it again and slammed it again. This time the glass, damaged by the previous blows, finally shattered.

"Jon, what are you doing?" Emma lowered the gun, bewildered. "This is madness."

Ignoring her, he hit the glass again and again, clearing the last pieces. Warm summer air rushed in, filling the room as he looked at her over his shoulder. They were too high to hear the traffic down below. Far too high.

Jon's shirt was soaked in blood. His freckles stood out against his pale skin like wounds as he looked back at her.

"I'm not going to prison. You have to understand. I can't do that."

Dropping the hammer, he leaped onto the windowsill.

"No!" The gun slipped from Emma's fingers and thudded on the floor.

She could feel herself running without being fully aware she was doing it. She reached for him just as he jumped. Her fingers caught his sleeve and she gripped his arm with all her might as he fell. His weight and gravity dragged her with him. Her feet left the floor, and she felt herself tumbling into the nothing on the other side. She saw the buildings below—the bright glorious sun.

And then someone grabbed her by the waist in a powerful grip.

"Hang on!" She heard Ripley's breathless voice, his arms like iron around her. And then, to someone else, "Get him."

Adam jumped onto the windowsill and reached down through the broken window gripping Jon's arm below the point where Emma's own hands still clung to him.

Together, they heaved him back through the broken glass until he collapsed, bloody and unconscious on the floor at Emma's feet.

She turned to Ripley and drew in a sharp, devastated breath.

He put his hand on her shoulder.

"It's over," he said.

SIX WEEKS LATER

"Are they still in there?" Emma asked as she walked into Ripley's office. Zach and Martha were already inside.

Zach glanced up at her. "No change."

"Why is it taking so long? It's been five hours." Emma perched on the arm of Martha's chair. "What could they be doing?"

"Providing incontrovertible evidence that Jon Frazer is a Russian asset," Martha said, "is time-consuming."

Ripley and Andrew Field had gone into a meeting in a secure, soundproof room inside MI6 at two o'clock that afternoon. They were meeting the Prime Minister, the heads of MI5 and MI6, as well as the Home Secretary.

This was a very rare Star Chamber, where the most senior members of the government would decide how to handle an act of treachery.

Emma, who'd had weeks to process Jon's betrayal, felt oddly disconnected from her emotions. A kind of numbness protected her from a pain that had been, in the first hours after she'd seen him in that room with Federov, excruciating.

After Jon had been dragged back into the building, Emma had tried to stop the bleeding from the wound in his neck while Ripley contacted Special Branch and requested assistance. Adam went down to meet the paramedics and police officers, who'd arrived in minutes.

While the medics worked on Jon and the police searched the building for Federov, Ripley led Emma out of the room. She moved stiffly, her hands curled into fists. The second they were alone, she turned on him, a fury she didn't fully understand rising inside her like flames.

"You knew it was him, and you didn't tell me. *Say it.* You let me walk into this nightmare and you fucking *knew* what would happen." Her voice rose.

By then, she'd had time to figure it out. To remember how strange Ripley had seemed when they'd been planning the operation. His uncharacteristic willingness to cut Jon and Andrew Field out of the operation. Nothing else made sense, except that he'd already known what she had just discovered.

"You knew at the Savoy. You knew every day since. Why didn't you tell me?" Her face felt hot with betrayal and humiliation.

Ripley let her finish and then answered with unbearable calmness. "I didn't know. I wasn't certain. But yes. I suspected it was Jon." Emma tried to speak but he talked over her. "I couldn't tell you. I couldn't tell anyone. You know why." He put his hands on her shoulders and said, with infinite sorrow, "And I am so very sorry that I was right."

"You should have told *me*." Tears of frustration burned her eyes but she wouldn't let them fall. "You shouldn't have let me find out this way."

"There's no good way to learn you've been betrayed," Ripley told her gravely.

Emma kept finding it hard to breathe, as if the last hour

pressed on her chest, suffocating her. "I trusted him," she said, her voice shallow and torn. "I trusted him completely."

She thought she saw understanding dawn in Ripley's face, and that made it worse.

"No one could blame you for trusting Jon," he said. "Andrew saw him almost as a son. I couldn't tell him my suspicions for that reason. I knew he wouldn't want to believe."

Emma stayed silent, trying to breathe, but her lungs felt heavy.

When she didn't speak, Ripley put his hand on her shoulder. "A wise man once said, 'Love is whatever you can still betray.' In our own way, we loved Jon. He betrayed all of us." He met her eyes, and she saw the pain carved into his face. "You are not alone with this, Emma. We were all deceived."

There'd been little opportunity to talk further that day, as all hell was breaking loose about Federov. The Russian had disappeared while Emma chased Jon through the building, and a nationwide manhunt was soon underway.

Jon had been treated in hospital for several days, and then placed in a high-security prison on holding charges of fraud, while the government decided what to do with him. His arrest was not announced.

Behind the scenes, a contingent of French and British security agents had contacted Andrei Volkov on the *Eden* to offer him a deal. He'd been promised British citizenship in return for his cooperation with the investigation into Oleg Federov and Jon. He would not be charged with Stephen Garrick's murder.

Volkov got everything he wanted, and in return he agreed to provide enough evidence to charge Federov with illegal weapons dealing, Cal Grogan with murder, and Jon with treason. All would have been right in the world, had Federov not managed to elude arrest. Despite a manhunt that stretched from the Isle of Skye to Land's End, the ex-spy had slipped out of the country, probably by private boat. Although the Russian government strenuously denied it, he was believed to be back in Moscow.

He hadn't taken Natalya with him. She'd been arrested at the party and questioned for twenty-four hours, until it became clear she knew virtually nothing about Federov's businesses.

Emma had lobbied hard for her to be allowed to remain in the UK. She knew it was irrational but she wanted Natalya to have the chances Madison and Kira never had. She wanted her to live in the city she loved, and to discover that she didn't need a rich man to pay her way. She only needed to discover the strength of her own voice.

So Jon and Cal Grogan were likely to be the only ones to face true justice. But punishing Jon wouldn't be easy.

The meeting today was to decide whether to admit publicly that an MI6 agent had betrayed his country in exchange for money and try him in a British court. That process would humiliate MI6 and the government and reveal secrets the intelligence service would rather keep hidden.

The alternative was to trade Jon to the Russians in exchange for Russian citizens who'd spied for Britain and were currently moldering in prisons there. The exchange would never be publicly revealed. Jon would simply disappear, taking the political consequences of his actions with him.

Ripley and Field were making the case for a trial. But it was not up to them. The more senior officials would decide whether a trial was worth the damage to the government's reputation.

Through all of this, Jon had said nothing. He'd not spoken in any interview. His court-appointed lawyers said he refused to speak even to them. He'd been completely silent since his arrest.

But other people were talking. Stephen Garrick, for instance, was speaking from the grave.

His files, when finally translated by a team inside MI6, showed that more than fifty million pounds had been paid by Volkov and Federov through a series of shell companies to an offshore account believed to be held by Jon. In return, he'd stopped investigations into the two men, and prevented the truth being found. He was the one who'd suggested to Field that Garrick's original investigation should be dropped. He'd told his boss Garrick wasn't getting anywhere with the work. In fact, Garrick had been very close to identifying Jon as the third member of Gold Dust.

Field believed it was Jon who revealed Garrick's identity to Volkov. Thus setting up the murder that triggered Emma's undercover role on the *Eden*.

Volkov told French security investigators that Jon had first begun working with Federov four years ago, after discovering their operation in the south of France. At multiple meetings at Federov's mansions in Cannes and Monaco, they'd formulated a lucrative plan. Jon would help the two Russian men fly under the radar, putting MI6 and French Intelligence off the track, ensuring they could base their operation in London and Europe, and sell weapons and drugs with impunity.

But then Stephen Garrick had begun looking into the numbers. And it had all fallen apart.

Emma wondered what Jon must be thinking. He'd traded his soul for money, and ended up with nothing.

She kept thinking of that moment in the Shard, when Jon had told her he didn't care about his country or his government, he only cared about her. She didn't for one moment think this was true. She believed he was sociopathic and manipulative, that he'd done it all to prove to himself that he was smarter than everyone else. That he could beat the system. Instead, the system had beaten him.

All the same, she felt certain that memory would leave scars which might never heal.

The thing she couldn't understand—the part that haunted her—was that she'd missed it. He'd been *right there* the entire time, and never once had she considered that he might be the one. She'd blamed Masterson, Dowell, Field. Anyone except Jon.

She hated him for deceiving her. That day in the safe house, there'd been a moment when she'd imagined the two of them as a real couple. Now, the very thought of his hands touching her made her skin crawl.

She'd thought, more than once, about quitting. What was the point of continuing when she couldn't see a traitor standing right in front of her? But Ripley had convinced her to stay.

"It won't be the last time you're wrong about something," he'd told her simply. "Every human being makes mistakes. But always remember how you feel right now. That pain will remind you to be careful who you trust."

"I wish they'd just *decide*," Martha said, with sudden anger, drawing Emma's attention back into the room.

Someone tapped on the door, and Ed Masterson walked in. "It's done. Ripley's on his way back."

"What did they decide?" Zach asked.

Masterson shook his head. "He wants to tell us in person. He said to get everyone together."

He stepped inside and Emma saw that Adam was behind him, his expression dark, followed by Esther, who handled the front desk, as well as two analysts from downstairs, and other staff. They all crowded around Ripley's empty desk.

A hum of tense conversation rose. Everyone talked about anything except the reason they were here. It was too serious for gossip.

Only a few minutes passed before the door swung open and Ripley walked in.

The last few weeks had aged him. He looked thinner, and the circles under his eyes seemed to be permanent now. The deeper lines made it even harder to read his always enigmatic expression as he stood by the door, cigarette case in hand.

The group hushed as everyone turned to look at him. He didn't make them wait.

"Jon Frazer is going to be traded to Russia for two assets who risked their lives for this country." Ripley's voice was impassive. "Two patriots in exchange for a traitor. The decision was unanimous."

A murmur of disapproval swept the room, but Emma said nothing. She felt utterly drained.

Jon would not serve time in prison. Despite breaking every code she believed in, he'd keep his freedom.

That wasn't justice.

And yet, he would lose everything—his job, his home, his life, his country, his family.

Actually, perhaps it was justice, after all.

It wouldn't undo the damage. But it was close to what he deserved.

Ripley walked through the crowd to his desk and stood looking back at the Agency's small team. His expression was deadly serious.

"I know this has been a blow, but we will come through it. We've had traitors before and we'll have them again. Their existence doesn't make what we do less important. It makes it *more* important. It doesn't diminish us. It makes us work even harder. We will come back from this more determined to do our jobs. More willing to serve the people who rely on us. The work doesn't stop because of one man."

For a long moment, nobody spoke. Then Emma broke the silence, her voice quiet but steady.

"We're with you, Ripley."

He met her gaze and the corners of his mouth lifted, just a little.

He turned to the group. "Now. There's a jet due in at Farnborough in two hours. On it is Daniel Alekseev, a sharpshooter

316 | AVA GLASS

connected with the GRU. I want to know what he's doing here, who he's visiting, and where he's staying. If he meets with someone, I want to hear every word he says. We'll need to stay on him constantly. I intend to know everything he does while he's in this country."

He opened the cigarette case with a click.

"Right. Let's get to work."

Acknowledgments

No book is possible without a wonderful team, and *The Traitor* is blessed with the absolute best team in the business. Huge thanks to everyone at Century in the UK and Ballantine in the US who worked so hard to make this series a success. I'm especially grateful to my wonderful editors Selina Walker and Anne Speyer, who offer so much wisdom and guidance at every step of the way. There are so many people who contributed to this book, and I owe them so much, especially Emma Thomasch, Sarah Breivogel, Najma Finlay, Allison Schuster, Meredith Benson, Joanna Taylor, Jesse Shuman, Charlotte Osment, and Katie Horn, but I know there were many more people behind the scenes who worked hard to make this series a success.

As always, huge thanks to Madeleine Milburn, Hannah Ladds, Liv Maidment, and everyone at the Madeleine Milburn Literary Agency who keep everything running so smoothly and make it possible for me to keep writing.

I owe a huge debt to that powerhouse human Tory Lyne-

Pirkis, who makes sure everyone finds out about Emma Makepeace, and who personally puts my books into more hands than I can count.

I'm so lucky to work with Emma Waring, who is one of the first and most astute readers of my books, and who also makes sure I show up for interviews on the right days. Without her there is chaos.

I owe too much to more friends and fellow authors than there is space for me to say, but you all know I love you and I am grateful to you, and also I owe you lunch. Lexi Casale and Holly Bourne, thank you for keeping me sane for another year.

Finally to Jack, my husband and best friend in the world, without you this book wouldn't have been written. This one is for you. Always and forever.

PHOTO © JACK JEWERS

AVA GLASS is a pseudonym for a former crime re-
porter and civil servant. Her time working for the
government introduced her to the world of spies,
and she's been fascinated by them ever since. She
lives and writes in the south of England.

Avaglass.uk
Twitter: @AvaGlassBooks

ABOUT THE TYPE

This book was set in Electra, a typeface designed for Linotype by W. A. Dwiggins, the renowned type designer (1880–1956). Electra is a fluid typeface, avoiding the contrasts of thick and thin strokes that are prevalent in most modern typefaces.